DANGEROUS
HARDBOILED
MAGICIANS

Borgo Press Books by MEL GILDEN

Dangerous Hardboiled Magicians: A Fantasy Mystery (Cronyn
    & Justice, Book One)
The Planetoid of Amazement: A Science Fiction Novel
The Return of Captain Conquer: A Science Fiction Novel

DANGEROUS HARDBOILED MAGICIANS

A FANTASY MYSTERY: CRONYN & JUSTICE, BOOK ONE

MEL GILDEN

THE BORGO PRESS

MMXII

DANGEROUS HARDBOILED MAGICIANS

FIRST EDITION

Published by Wildside Press LLC

www.wildsidebooks.com

DEDICATION

For Gar and Judy,

An Inspiration to Us All

CONTENTS

CHAPTER ONE: From the Sublime to the Ridiculous . . . 11

CHAPTER TWO: Easy Come, Easy Go. 15

CHAPTER THREE: Cronyn Returns 24

CHAPTER FOUR: Three Pack Rats. 28

CHAPTER FIVE: Puppy Love. 35

CHAPTER SIX: A Funny Shade of Pale Green 43

CHAPTER SEVEN: Back on the Bicycle 47

CHAPTER EIGHT: The Closest Thing to a Witness 55

CHAPTER NINE: "No Wizard in His Right Mind". 61

CHAPTER TEN: The Broken Wand. 68

CHAPTER ELEVEN: An Insulting Idea. 76

CHAPTER TWELVE: Enough Rope 81

CHAPTER THIRTEEN: Justice 86

CHAPTER FOURTEEN: A Broken Chair. 93

CHAPTER FIFTEEN: *The Rack of Time* 100

CHAPTER SIXTEEN: Meeting the New Tolstoy 109

CHAPTER SEVENTEEN: Dialog Over a PJ & J

Sandwich 114

CHAPTER EIGHTEEN: An Entertaining Evening 117

CHAPTER NINETEEN: Make the Call 127

CHAPTER TWENTY: That Old Black Magic 135

CHAPTER TWENTY-ONE: Busy Morning 142

CHAPTER TWENTY-TWO: Trapped 149

CHAPTER TWENTY-THREE: Dirty Little Secrets . . . 157

CHAPTER TWENTY-FOUR: Pucker Up 163

CHAPTER TWENTY-FIVE: Hounds of Hell 173

CHAPTER TWENTY-SIX: The Blue Diamond 179

CHAPTER TWENTY-SEVEN: The Magic Vault 188

CHAPTER TWENTY-EIGHT: A Delicate Constitution . . 195

CHAPTER TWENTY-NINE: A Nice Hovel 201

CHAPTER THIRTY: A Very Special Individual 210

CHAPTER THIRTY-ONE: Curiosity 214

CHAPTER THIRTY-TWO: Old Home Week 221

CHAPTER THIRTY-THREE: Justice Happens 228

CHAPTER THIRTY-FOUR: Freak Accident 234

CHAPTER THIRTY-FIVE: Two Propositions 238

ABOUT THE AUTHOR 244

"With gods like these, who needs enemies?"

Turner Cronyn
Through A Keyhole, Darkly

CHAPTER ONE
FROM THE SUBLIME TO THE RIDICULOUS

The Pico and La Cienega branch of a chain store called Spell-Mart had hired me to find out who was stealing packets of domestic magic: Clean-Up (a dust collector), Flying Saucers (the dishpan miracle), and Pretty Face, which was exactly what it sounded like. The case was not the sort that makes headlines, but the Spell-Mart people offered to pay me so I took the gig anyway.

The store was a block square, modern as next year's automobile, and full of light. The whole operation had as much warmth as a phlogiston station restroom.

After two weeks of tedium I had narrowed my search to one of the clerks. He was a head taller than I was, twice as wide, and had a constant leer on his face that made him look as if he were always thinking about girls, but not in any way a girl would want to be thought about. The largest red and blue Spell-Mart vest was too small for him, making him look like an organ grinder's monkey despite his size. For reasons known only to him he liked to be called Chick. I was about to start a casual conversation with him when somebody called my name.

"Mr. Cronyn!"

I turned and was surprised to see Lord Zorn Slex standing in the headache and cold remedy aisle as if he'd grown there from an acorn. He was built like a snowman, with a round pink head atop a round body that showed even under his robes of office.

Strings of dishwater-blond hair hung from the back of his head like a beaded curtain. Unlike me, he had gotten older in the past twenty years.

I glanced back at Chick and saw that he was not even aware of my existence. Working at his usual lethargic pace, he would be stacking loaves of fairy soap for a while. I smiled and hurried toward Lord Slex with my hand out. He shook it as if he were trying to pump water out of me.

"Mr. Cronyn," he said, "how nice to see you again."

"Me too," I said with more feeling than grammar.

He lowered his voice. "Uh, you work here?"

"You've discovered my terrible secret," I said.

He smiled as if he had a pain somewhere. "Maybe you can help me," he said.

"I'll try."

"I'm looking for a spell that will stop some itching."

"Itching?"

"Some rather private itching." On hearing exactly where this itching was located, I learned a lot more than I wanted to know about his personal life. But a lot of guys itched, even there. What surprised me about his request was that he was in here looking for a commercial medical spell at all. I'd have thought that a board member of Stilthins Mort could whip up one of his own spells without much trouble.

Still, I wasn't so ill-mannered that I asked. Being curious didn't make it my business. I just took him to the right section, where he eagerly picked up a couple of packets. He stood there for a moment weighing the packets in the palm of his hand. He was obviously making up his mind about something.

"I heard that after you left Stilthins Mort you became a private detective," he said, his voice low again.

"That's right," I said. "From the sublime to the ridiculous."

"It guess it didn't work out." He looked around him meaningfully.

"I guess," I said and tried to sound sorry.

"Would you take an investigative job if it were offered to

you?"

I didn't answer immediately. After all, I supposedly had a steady job here at Spell-Mart. When would I have time to go off poking my nose into the affairs of other people? "I'd like to get back into the business," I answered as if admitting a perversion.

"Fine, fine," he replied as if everything was all settled. "Come to the school on Monday at about three p.m. and we can talk further about what I want done."

"Yes, sir. Monday at three."

We shook hands again and he headed for the cash registers. I didn't have time to wonder what Lord Slex had in mind because when I looked at the end of the aisle it was empty. Chick had finished with the soap and moved on.

I ran to where he had been. The woman behind the nearby small appliances counter was staring into space.

"Where did Chick go?" I asked.

She pointed toward the warehouse area at the back of the store. I ran in the direction she pointed, hoping she was right.

The loading dock was empty—no deliveries at this hour, nobody sitting on the far edge smoking—only the residual shimmer of unused moving spells falling like golden dust through the hazy afternoon sunlight. Imps floating near the ceiling lazily waved rattan fans, making a breeze no stronger than the breath of a sleeping baby. In the large cool space beneath the imps the stacks of crates made mazes in whose turns and dead ends many forbidden activities took place.

I didn't see Chick. He could be anywhere in the maze, but on a hunch I went to the place where I knew the Clean-up was stored. None of it had been stolen for a few days. If I had figured the rotation right, it was time.

I made no sound as I walked between stacks of crates higher than my head. I rounded a square corner and confronted Chick with his hands in a busted crate, digging out packets of Clean-up and shoving them into the pockets of his pants.

"Hello, Chick," I said, calm as if I'd found him smoothing the Velcro on his shoes.

He froze and then turned his head slowly to look at me with a face out of a horror comic book. "Just getting some new stock," he grumbled.

"Like hell," I said.

Suddenly he ran. I ran after him. I could corner him if there was no way out of the maze on that side, but if he found an exit—well, he moved pretty fast for a man his size. In a moment or two I was out of the maze and looking across an open space at Chick's retreating back. I could never catch him.

But a push broom stood next to me. I grabbed it and broke the handle across my knee, creating about a foot and a half of club. I flung the club spinning across the floor and it caught his feet like a snare. He fell flat on his face and stayed on the floor without moving.

I approached him carefully. Guys had been known to fake how badly they were injured. I picked up the club where it had bounced off a pallet of tooth-whitening spell and stood over him with it while I watched him drool onto the floor. He didn't fight me as I put handcuffs on behind his back. He didn't fight me when I turned him over and sat him up against the wall. He was still sitting there with a vague expression on his face when I came back from calling the police.

The manager of the Spell-Mart store promised that I would have my check by the end of the week. I wasn't surprised when I still didn't have it by the following Monday, the day I was supposed to visit Lord Slex.

The usual detective's deal.

CHAPTER TWO
EASY COME, EASY GO

One-horse-open sleighs were popular that year, though without the horse, of course. Roman chariots, Conestoga wagons, and even bathtubs were also on the road. The definition of what was street legal was broad, and with magic you could get almost anything up to freeway speeds.

A teenaged girl on a broom almost cut me off when I attempted to turn left into a phlogiston station. "Cover me," I yelled to the dust monkey as he trotted out of the tiny office eager as a puppy.

"Sure thing, mister," he said. He gestured magically at my five-year-old Puck in a confident way, but he was obviously new at the job because he had to read that week's proprietary fuel spell from a sheet of paper. The spell fell over my car like a gossamer blanket, briefly making it glow.

I waited for a barbershop chair to pass, then drove out of the station and down to Canal Street, where I was supposed to have lunch with Harold Silverwhite. He was an expert on magic who lived in one of the cottages that lined what remained of the Venice canals.

The city had cleaned up the canals, and gentrification had set in. Like most of the other houses in the area it was small and neat and painted in bright candy colors. Silverwhite's cottage was different from the others in that it had a brown shingled roof that was oddly peaked and raked; an enthusiastic pink trumpet vine covered the walls. The day was unseasonably warm for

Venice, but wisps of white smoke drifted from the chimney of Silverwhite's cottage.

A hundred feet away a man leaned against the railing of one of the old bridges that arched picturesquely over the canal, smoking and contemplating the ducks circling in the placid water.

I pulled into the driveway next to Silverwhite's van—white, and with his name on the side in a circus font—and went to knock on the door of the house. "Come in," the door said as it opened. For some reason, no matter how many times it happened I was tickled by the fact the door recognized me—it was like being loved by a dog everyone else thought was vicious.

The house was much larger inside than it seemed outside. You could put the entire outside into the living room, a cozy nook that looked like the reading room in an old-fashioned men's club, all dark wood and soft studded leather. Floor to ceiling book cases lined the walls, with books showing behind the glass windows in the doors, each one now carefully closed. A big fireplace took up one wall, but nothing in it was burning so the smoke had to be coming from someplace else. Clever deduction. Me and Sherlock Holmes. The suggestion of a really terrible smell fought its way into my nose.

"In here, old chum," Silverwhite called out.

I followed the sound of his voice to a room that was even larger than the living room. It seemed part kitchen and part laboratory. Vials, retorts, and flasks were everywhere. Books, like heavy prehistoric butterflies, were open on a lab bench. In the fireplace a fire burned under a pot like the ones in cannibal cartoons—it was big enough to boil at least two men whole. The smoke was rising from there, and the smell was much worse. It scoured the inside of my nose like a pad of metal wool.

"Can't you open a window?" I asked.

"No can do, old chum. I'm afraid the smell is part of the whole experimental experience."

"I'm a little surprised you're not stinking up the whole neighborhood."

He shook his head. "It doesn't have to smell after it leaves here, so it doesn't."

I stared at him for a moment as if he were a wonder I'd paid to see. "I'm sure I ought to understand that."

"No need, old chum. No need."

I grumbled and tried to ignore the smell as I crossed the room to where Silverwhite was sitting on a stool before a skrying ball the size of a beach ball studying thaumaturgical formulae. He was a thin gentleman wearing a long lab coat buttoned almost to his chin. Beneath it I could see the beautifully tied knot of a dark tie. He had delicate features and tightly packed curls of a brown so light in color it was almost blond. I always got the impression that he was just visiting from an earlier, more decorous and genteel age. He waved his hands through the air, making the formulae in the skrying ball change.

"Very nice," I said. "No keyboard."

"Nothing to it really," he said.

"What is it?" I asked, using my chin to point at the formula in the ball.

"Programming to stop the Meltdown virus. Heard of it?"

"Everybody who owns a skrying ball has heard of it," I said. If the virus infected your skrying ball, it melted into a steamy and evil-smelling mass. So far I'd been lucky. "How are you coming?"

"Close now," Silverwhite said. "Shall we eat?"

He knew that I didn't like to eat in his laboratory, but he usually forgot. When I asked him if we could eat in some other room he chuckled. "I've been eating in here for years, old chum. So far I remain untroubled by curses, hexes, germs, or poisons." He got up and strolled to a bench across the room. It was piled high with white paper bags.

"Except for that time you had snakes instead of hair for three days," I reminded him as I strolled over to join him.

"That had nothing to do with me, old chum. Anyone can be infested by imps."

"Last time you said it was demons."

He made an equivocating motion with one hand. "Six of one," he said.

I knew better than to continue the argument, particularly because Silverwhite was buying.

"But I will shut off the smell while we eat," he said, and over his shoulder gestured with one hand at the fireplace. The fire and smoke froze as if for them time had stopped, and a few seconds later the smell was gone.

"Show off," I said, and reached for a bag. When I opened it, a wonderful smell of fish and rare spices escaped and floated upward. "Atlantean food from Oricalcum?" I asked hopefully.

"Mostly marax and praxa sushi," Silverwhite said as he took the bag away from me and lifted out trays of rolled-up raw fish. He began to arrange the sushi on the serving plate in an artistic design. "Beer?" he asked.

"Root beer, if you have it. I need to be at the top of my game this afternoon."

"I have ginger ale," he said, and took a small green bottle from a refrigerator that was otherwise filled with chemicals, leaves, stems, seeds, and other magical supplies that needed to be kept cold. "What's happening this afternoon?" he asked.

I told him about my time at Spell-Mart and my meeting with Lord Slex.

"It is odd, isn't it?" he agreed. "But perhaps someone at his level can't be bothered reproducing spells that can be purchased over-the-counter."

"Perhaps," I said, unconvinced.

"What has that to do with this afternoon?"

"I have a meeting with him up at the school. He wants me to do some detecting for him."

"What? Stilthins Mort?" he asked, smiling around his food. "I haven't been up there in ages. What does the old boy want?"

"He didn't say. I got the idea that he was a little embarrassed about his problem, whatever it is."

"He must have decided you were all right, after all."

"Hmm?" I asked, my mouth full of marax and cabbage.

"Sorry to break it to you, old chum, but he always thought you were kind of a doofus."

"That's not exactly news." I thought while I chewed. "But you're right. It does seem odd," I told him.

"You probably owe him a term paper."

"If I do, I'll hire you to write it for me."

We both enjoyed that. In the old days we had been students together, he the star and I the goat. I don't know why we got along, but we did. Chemistry, maybe. Whatever that means.

"You always wrote your own papers," Silverwhite said.

"That's me," I replied. "Honest to a fault—and I do mean a fault."

"Speaking of academia," Silverwhite said, "In my copious spare time I've been writing spells for this year's Spelling Bee."

"You don't have any spare time," I remarked. "From Spelling Bees you make a living?"

"Mostly, old chum, I do it for the honor of the thing."

"I wish I could afford to be so magnanimous."

"You don't do so badly."

"No. Not if I'm careful to eat only every other day."

"Have some more sushi," Silverwhite said and put a few more rolls onto my plate.

The air behind Silverwhite wavered, as if somebody had lit a fire on the floor near him. Suddenly a short man appeared. He had a large square face, lumpy with ugly features that at the moment were snarling. He wore a red satin jacket and spikes of black hair stuck up from his head at odd angles.

Silverwhite must have seen the surprised expression on my face because he turned suddenly and looked at this apparition. The short man pointed at me. "Stay outta my way," he cried angrily and came at me with his hands outstretched, as if he were going to strangle me.

I leaped backward, knocking over the stool I'd been sitting on. Silverwhite leaped to one side and gestured at the man while speaking a formula. The spell had no effect whatsoever on the man. He kept coming.

"Who are you?" I asked.

"Your worst nightmare," the man said.

"About average, I'd say," I said as I continued to back away. I knew I would run out of room eventually, but I didn't know exactly when. "If you want something, spill it. Threats tell me nothing."

"If you make trouble for me, you're in big trouble—that's all."

Silverwhite was still flinging spells into the air, trying to get one to take. He was looking chagrined and desperate now. I knocked over some glassware, and it crunched beneath my shoes as I continued backing. I was probably looking a little desperate, myself.

"Look, mister—" I said, but was interrupted when he lunged at me. I ducked out of his way and pushed open a pair of French doors. I was now outside on Silverwhite's back lawn, where I hoped I would have more room to maneuver. Silverwhite followed, watching us closely but keeping his distance, like the referee in a prize fight.

We danced like that while I wondered how to escape this guy. He seemed awfully determined, but a little unsure about what. The ducks had flown away at the first sign of trouble, but the man on the bridge seemed fascinated by the show.

I growled and rushed the guy hoping he would back up, and to my surprise, he did. He was now at the edge of the canal. "Smart boy," he said as if it were an insult. "Smart boy with big plans."

"You're not making any sense," I said.

He laughed with disgust. "You're a fine one to talk." He saw Silverwhite coming closer. "And tell your pet magician to stay away from me."

"Anything you say," I said and rushed him again.

He took a step back and windmilling his arms, fell into the water. He thrashed around as anybody would, and while he was busy I jumped in after him.

The water was cold and about four feet deep, coming up just

to my armpits. He bobbed to the surface sputtering, but before he could catch too much breath I grabbed him by the shoulders and pushed him back under. I didn't want to drown him, just slow him down a little. Maybe we could still talk things over.

Suddenly my hands were empty. He hadn't twisted out of my grasp or gone limp, he just wasn't there any more. I looked around in the murky water and saw nothing but murk.

"Need some help?" the guy on the bridge called—a little late, I thought.

"No, thanks," I said.

I walked carefully to the bank on the slippery bottom and Silverwhite put out his hand to pull me onto the grass. I turned to look back out at the water and saw that nothing had came up. The ducks returned, though. I suppose that was something.

"Where did he go?" Silverwhite asked.

"I thought maybe you would know," I said.

"No."

"Modesty?"

"No, not really, old chum. I don't know why or how that gentleman disappeared. I had nothing to do with it."

"Unless he turned into a fish and swam away."

"If he did, he didn't do it with magic. I would have noticed. Did you ever find out what he wanted?"

"He just warned me away. He seemed a little unclear about why." I looked down at myself. "The water seems to have made me wet."

"Tsk, tsk, old chum," Silverwhite said. "Lord Slex won't like that. Come in and put on a robe while I do a little domestic magic."

Like many people, I knew a little domestic magic too, and I could have taken care of myself. But having someone else do it was pleasant, and Silverwhite would have been insulted if I hadn't let him help, so I let him. Besides, I was still shaking a little, charged up by fear and exertion.

He dried my clothing and pressed what needed pressing, all with magic. He could have been a pretty good valet if he'd been better at taking orders. Meanwhile, I dried myself the old-fashioned way with a fluffy towel and thought about who my attacker was and what he wanted. I went over the whole incident again and couldn't make it make any more sense than a single piece of a jigsaw puzzle. I wanted to know more, but that didn't mean I wanted the guy to come back.

"Assuming he wasn't crazy," I said, "he knew something about my future that I don't know." I shook my head. "Time travel?"

While Silverwhite watched with pleasure, my shirt folded itself neatly. My pants, already dry, creased in exactly the right place.

"The formulas necessary for time travel require a small book to record them," he said, "and a lot of equipment not even I possess. Still, old chum, if he came prepared...." He shrugged and handed me my pants.

"And where did he go?" I asked.

"Perhaps he dissolved," Silverwhite suggested. "It's been known to happen."

"What? When?"

He told me a long involved story about a sheik and a camel and a dram of rancid coconut milk. I think he got it from the *Arabian Nights*. By the time he finished I had all my clothes on and I was once again fit for my meeting with Lord Slex. That had probably been his intention all along, to give me a chance to calm down. I had stopped shaking, but I was still worried. Nobody enjoys being attacked, especially by someone as unpredictable as my attacker.

"We do not know who the guy was or what he wanted or how he got here—do we know how we got here?" I asked as I tied my tie.

"No," Silverwhite said. "It wasn't even magic. I checked."

"Figures," I said. "So we don't know any of those things or where he went or how."

"Finding out should keep you occupied for a while."

"Sure. Between that crazy guy and Lord Slex I guess I'm set

for life. How about one of those beers you offered me earlier?"

"Coming right up, old chum."

CHAPTER THREE
CRONYN RETURNS

For the first time in many years I was driving up Western Avenue to Stilthins Mort, the wizard college that crouched at the top of the boulevard like a gargoyle. A newspaper hack once said the college looked as if it were guarding the fairy kingdom of Griffith Park, the huge hilly green acreage that lay just beyond.

The last time I had visited Stilthins Mort was as a failed undergraduate with no more talent for wizardry than a baked potato, hold the sour cream. After I'd gotten used to the idea, washing out had actually been a relief.

I made my left turn off Western and into the college parking lot, where a curtain of gossamer that was almost invisible in the daylight prevented me from passing the yellow guard shack. A uniformed guard stepped out of the shack to ask me what I wanted.

"Turner Cronyn to see Lord Zorn Slex," I said, trying to sound as if I dropped in on one of the board members every day.

The guard referred to something in his shack and nodded. He wiggled his fingers, doing a little security magic, and the gossamer curtain faded to nothing. I waved at him jauntily as I drove on.

The car's engine labored as I drove up the hill to the first building, which was Administration. Like the other buildings farther up, it was a big gothic pile designed to look like a medieval church. Students and faculty strolled along the paths and sidewalks, everybody on important business.

I found a place to park and was about to walk inside under a stained glass window depicting a bearded old gentleman wearing a conical hat and a long robe covered in stars and quarter moons. He was waving his hands over a smoking cauldron. Though the smoke rising from the cauldron looked as if it might be trying to solidify into a beautiful woman, at the moment the smoke was still just smoke.

But I didn't go inside right away. Students jostled around me while I remained an annoying obstruction in the doorway, looking at a short gnarled man who watched me from behind a bush. He was dressed in a fire-engine red suit and tie. His shoes were shiny black, which made the suit look even redder. When he saw me glance in his direction, he turned his back to me and made a big production about tying his shoe—but not before I saw that he had a cauliflower nose, a rounded pebbly object in the middle of his face. A lot of dark coarse hair stuck out at odd angles from the top of his head, and from inside his ears, giving him a disturbing family resemblance to the customer I'd met in Silverwhite's lab. That in itself was no crime, so I tried to keep my paranoia under control. He didn't look like a student to me, but you never know. I looked like a student when I was here, but few scholars had been less scholarly. The little guy didn't do anything startling, and I had business, so I went inside.

Inside, the medieval theme continued. The cool dim hallway was lined with doors, each of which was made of rough-hewn wood inset in its own archway. The door handles looked like big bald brass heads, and the keyholes were big enough to put your fist into. The keyholes were fakes, of course. You wouldn't need a key to get into any of those rooms, just the right spell.

Though I hadn't ever been really happy at Stilthins Mort it was good to be back. I felt a certain satisfaction in walking casually over the closely laid stones of these crowded hallways, relaxed in the knowledge that all my homework assignments had been turned in years ago.

At the end of the hallway was a large mirror in a frame that looked as if it had been constructed of tarnished armor, mostly helmets and breastplates. I squinted at myself, trying to make myself look more handsome by force of will alone. But no. I still had the big mouth and the little piggy eyes. I sighed and went on.

Just around the corner I found Lord Slex's office, its door ajar. I had my hand on the doorknob when a woman's voice called out from inside. "Oh, please," she said with some disgust. I didn't think she was talking to me.

"Do I need to prove myself to you?" a male voice asked. It was Lord Slex, but without the confident air I recalled. "Should I impress you with simple tricks like some first-year student?" Though a few people looked in the direction of the door and giggled, none of them stopped to pick up the thread of conversation.

"That would be an improvement," the woman said, "but you would still bore me. I'm tired of giving you chances to pick up the pace. Besides," she went on as smoothly as a snake flicking its tongue, "first-year sleight of hand is a little beyond you, isn't it, darling?" I never heard anyone say "darling" with less sincerity.

"That was uncalled for," Lord Slex said.

"The truth is always called for, darling." Her voice was a lot closer to the door now. I backed away and listened from the next archway down the hall.

"Please don't go," Lord Slex said.

"Good-bye, darling," the woman said. "And the next time you try to pull a rabbit from a hat, make sure you have a rabbit." She chuckled musically. "And a hat, too."

The door opened wide then. The woman was a little taller than I was, perhaps because of her lime-green high heels, and dressed in a skirt and blouse ensemble designed to show off her figure, which would have been evident if she'd been wearing a gunny sack. A purse that matched her shoes exactly hung over one shoulder. Instead of hair atop her head she had what looked like a single red flame, but it gave off no heat and I smelled nothing burning. I had never seen anything like it before. The astonishing things they did with glamour spells these days.

Her face was beautiful, with good bones giving it a solid structure. It was a placid face despite the scene she'd played out in the office. As she pulled the door shut she gave me a smile that made me feel as if I'd won the big award. I turned and watched her part the crowds. She was a one-woman parade.

It was none of my business, of course, but I wondered who she was. And what she was doing tonight. And whether she liked middle-aged detectives with big mouths and squinty eyes. "Get a grip, Cronyn," I ordered myself, and knocked on Lord Slex's door.

CHAPTER FOUR
THREE PACK RATS

During the short silence that followed I imagined Lord Slex wondering whether the woman had returned. "Come in," he invited after a while. So I went in.

Lord Slex was standing in the middle of his office with his hands behind his back. He stared hard at the floor as if some important message were written there.

At last he looked over at me. "How are you, Mr. Cronyn?" he asked and shook my hand. His hand was warm and dry.

"Fine, sir. And you?" I wasn't just being polite. He probably needed to tell somebody about what had just happened, and I was ready to be that person, but I didn't want to drag the story out of him.

"Fine," he replied as if he was thinking about something besides his condition. Using his entire body, he shook off his pensive mood and went to sit behind his desk. It was covered with papers and books except for an area right in front of him, on which a skrying ball stood.

On one corner, angled so visitors could see it, was a framed photograph of a young Lord Slex and two other men. The Lord Slex in the photograph was many pounds thinner than the man who sat before me. The three men were standing in front of a Duesenberg Suzerain, a very fancy automobile that had been new about fifteen years before. With its two-tone paint job, chocolate with accents of a warmer light caramel color, it looked good enough to eat.

Bookshelves along three walls of the office carried everything from paperbacks to enormous tomes that were bound in ancient leather and clasped shut with golden hardware. An orrery stood in one corner of the room and a world globe in another. Dust floated in the columns of light that slanted in through high windows and fell noiselessly to the floor.

"It's been a long time," Lord Slex said once he'd gotten comfortable.

"Almost twenty years," I said. If the talk got any smaller, I'd need a microscope to see it.

"Too bad you left. I still believe we might have made a wizard out of you eventually."

"That's nice of you to say, sir, but I don't think so. I'd reached my ceiling of abstraction. The spells, formulae, and philosophy became too difficult. Besides, if I'd gotten my degree I would have lost everything during Prohibition. As it was, I almost had my private investigator's license revoked."

Lord Slex nodded gravely. "Not that it matters if you are working at Spell-Mart."

"That was just a cover. I'm a full-time private investigator. And I still have all my textbooks. I can't seem to make myself throw them away."

"Really? Impressive."

We both shook our heads over the general strangeness of life. From the looks of his office, he was something of a pack rat himself. He smiled at me across the desk and I suddenly felt responsible for getting the show on the road. "So," I said, "what can I do for you? You certainly didn't invite me here just to find out if I wanted to re-enroll."

"No." He seemed reluctant to continue. I waited. He'd go on. They always do.

"We have a graduate student here by the name of Misty Morning," he explained when he began to speak again. "She is quite brilliant, actually, and not a little eccentric. She has already registered some important patents: the industrial gravity shunt and the car-of-a-different-color, to name just two."

I'd actually heard of the car-of-a-different-color, but it was a little out of my price range. My Puck was blue when I bought it, and it would stay that way. "And I come into this where?"

Lord Slex rubbed the baggy skin beneath an eye with one finger, then set his hand back onto his desk exactly where it had been. "Ms. Morning is working on a new project," he said, "something very important that could not only make her a lot of money but add infinite prestige to the reputation of this college."

"Infinite prestige," I remarked. "That's quite a bit. Must be some project. What is it?"

He opened his hands as if to prove they were empty. "Ms. Morning is keeping the exact nature of the project to herself. The truth is, not even the board knows what it is. But we do know this, Mr. Cronyn: We don't want her project to fall into the wrong hands. That's where you come in. We want to hire you as her bodyguard."

"Whose hands exactly are you worried about?" I asked.

"Oh, the usual," Lord Slex said, affecting a casual air. "Other colleges, industrial spies—that sort of thing."

"Given adversaries like those, my professional opinion is that Ms. Morning wouldn't be in much physical danger. Would I be protecting Ms. Morning or her project?"

"That's needlessly cynical," Lord Slex said. "You would be protecting both, of course. And let me assure you that colleges and industrial spies sometimes play rougher than you imagine. What are your fees?"

My fees? I didn't know whether I should charge him at all. Lord Slex had been my advisor when I was in school here, and he'd always been straight with me, if not always sympathetic. On the other hand, I was in business and he was obviously speaking to me as a professional. Plus the fact that Stilthins Mort was hardly a broken member. I wasn't greedy, but at last practicality won out. "I normally get a hundred a day plus expenses."

He slid a check across the desk. I picked it up and saw it was already made out to me for $700. "Here's a week's retainer," he said. "I hope that's satisfactory."

I knew better than to ask how he'd happened to have that check prepared. "You're good," I admitted.

"There is one more thing," Lord Slex said while I folded the check and put it into my wallet.

I looked at him expectantly.

"I want to put a spell on your face to improve your appearance."

I continued looking at him, but my expression was now more surprised than expectant. "And why would that be?" I asked. I was pleased to see that my question made him a little uncomfortable.

"When you meet Ms. Morning, you will see that she is exceptionally beautiful. I've heard some of her students refer to her as a babe."

He waited for me to say something, but I refused to cooperate. This was his party.

"The truth is, Mr. Cronyn, I don't believe you are handsome enough to be a convincing escort for Ms. Morning."

I studied his expression for signs of gaiety, but he seemed quite serious. "Maybe what you really want is an actor to play a bodyguard," I said. "I understand that some of them can be pretty convincing." I wanted to throw his check at him but controlled myself. There is always time to lose an assignment.

"Now, now, Mr. Cronyn. Let's not get testy. I don't intend to change your appearance entirely, merely to widen your eyes a little, tighten your lips, and square off your chin. You'll still recognize yourself in the mirror. Probably." A momentary smile slipped across his face and slinked away.

"Anything else?" I asked tightly.

"Just one more thing," Lord Slex said. "And you may appreciate this reason more than the other: I don't want casual observers to know Ms. Morning is being guarded. I want your appearance changed so there will be no chance of a Stilthins Mort old-timer recognizing you."

"What difference would it make? Not many of them would know I was a private detective."

"It takes only one," Lord Slex suggested.

I drummed my fingers on the arm of my chair while I weighed his insulting suggestion against my ability to pay the rent next month.

"All right," I said. "But you better get to it before I change my mind."

"Very good," Lord Slex said, and took a packet from a drawer in his desk.

"Commercial magic?" I asked. This was the second time I knew of that he used a packaged spell instead of mixing up his own from scratch. Despite Silverwhite's theories, I still didn't believe Lord Slex used instant spells because he was too good to mix up his own.

"Oh, Nu-face is quite safe," he said as he studied the instructions. He tore open the packet, pronounced the spell, and threw the powder over me.

I sat unmoving, waiting to feel some change. Then I chuckled to myself. Whatever was going to happen had happened already. The spell hadn't actually altered anything about me of course, only what people saw. Applying the spell was like putting on a mask.

"Look here, Mr. Cronyn," Lord Slex said as he rose and took a few steps to a cabinet, which he opened, revealing a mirror hanging inside the door.

I joined him at the cabinet and looked at myself. Though I knew I would look different, actually seeing the changes the spell had wrought was kind of a shock. But it was a good shock. I looked like my handsome brother. "One hot dude," I remarked.

"Indeed. Come along, Mr. Cronyn. I want to introduce you to the other two members of the board. I don't believe you met them when you were a student here."

When we left his office, the hallway was empty, which was just as well because I was self-conscious about my new appearance. Would anybody notice? Would women sigh and fall at my feet, instantly my love slaves? Intellectually I knew neither of these things would happen, but I still felt as if I were wearing a neon sign for a hat.

Our footsteps echoed as I followed Lord Slex diagonally across the hall to another office. Without knocking he pulled the door open, then stood aside to let me enter first.

In details, this office was different from Lord Slex's, but generally it was much the same hodgepodge of books, papers, and magical paraphernalia I had seen earlier. It seemed that being a pack rat was a prerequisite for being a wizard; maybe I should have stuck around after all.

There were two men in the office. Sitting behind the desk was one of the thinnest, pruniest men I had ever seen. His shoulders were barely wide enough to support his robe of office, and every line in his face—and there were many—was vertical, making him look even thinner. He wore a monocle and a tiny mustache. Leaning over the desk, pointing to something in a book that covered most of the desktop, was a very handsome man—noble, wise, and sympathetic. He was that rare thing, a man who looked enough like what he was to play one in a movie. He might have posed for the stained glass fantasy over the front door of the building.

They were the same two men who had been with Lord Slex in the photograph of the fancy chocolate car, now fifteen or so years older.

They froze in place as if they'd been caught doing something naughty, turning only their heads to look at us.

Lord Slex introduced us. "Mr. Cronyn, the seated gentleman is Lord Trask. His learned colleague with the accusatory digit is Lord Philpot. Gentlemen," he went on, indicating me as if I were a sideshow attraction, "this is Turner Cronyn. I have just engaged him to protect Misty Morning."

Lord Trask nodded.

"Delighted, I'm sure," Lord Philpot said as if it might even be true, and shook my hand.

Without much trouble Lord Slex ushered me out of the office. We left the Administration building and walked up the hill in the bright sunshine to one of the classroom buildings. It looked much the same as the Admin building, lacking only the stained glass window over the main entrance.

Most of the classroom doors were closed, but through them I could hear the rumble in the time-honored cadence of instructors attempting to impart knowledge. We went up to the second floor and once again Lord Slex held a door open for me.

We stood together in the back of the room watching as a big soft bear of a boy wearing glasses fiddled with a long sheaf of colorful ribbons. He looked as if he'd slept in his mismatched sweater and corduroy pants, a costume whose patterns seemed determined to fight each other to the death. The boy never took his eyes off the instructor as she moved gracefully up and down the room lecturing, and he maintained a dopey sort of smile the whole time. If I had to guess, I'd say he was in love with her. Most of the other male students and a few of the females seemed similarly entranced. I was a little entranced myself. It was difficult not to be.

CHAPTER FIVE
PUPPY LOVE

The instructor, whom I assumed was Misty Morning, was a slim, twentyish woman who looked very appealing in a crisp man's shirt and tight jeans. Her blonde hair was short and artfully mussed, as if she kept it trimmed and clean but otherwise wanted to give the impression she didn't pay much attention to it. She had an easy, friendly smile and a voice one might spread on one's morning toast.

"If you read last night's assignment," she said, "you know there are two basic laws of magic." She nodded, inviting the class to join in. "The Law of Similarity and the Law of Contagion," they all said together. "Give me the test ribbons, Mr. Hillyer," she said alone, and held out one hand to the fat kid. He trotted forward and laid the sheaf gently across her hand as if he were laying a wreath at a monument. "Thank you, Mr. Hillyer," she said. Then she mumbled a few magic words and threw half the ribbons into the air. The other half she waved around as if she were leading a cheer. The ribbons she'd thrown away danced in the air, following the pattern she made with the ribbons in her hand. Basic as pulling iron filings with a magnet, but a demonstration like that never ceased to fascinate me and make me smile.

"You see," Ms. Morning said, "once magically connected, the first set of ribbons continues to influence the other set, even at a distance. All magic, no matter how complex and impressive, springs from the principles demonstrated here." She glanced at the clock. "That's all for today," she said. "See you in lab tomorrow." She caught the flying ribbons and put the two sets on a table, where they lay motionless as if she'd killed them, though I knew that was silly.

Members of the class gathered their school supplies and drifted out of the room. Mr. Hillyer collected his stuff and then spent a lot of time making sure that Ms. Morning didn't want him for anything. I got the impression that jumping off a building would not have been too much to ask.

"No, thank you, Mr. Hillyer. That will be all. See you in lab tomorrow." Her voice had firmed up some, and the temperature had dropped, but she still had to repeat herself a few times before Hillyer took the hint. He backed out of the holy presence smiling and shuffling. If he'd had a forelock, he would have tugged it. It was a shameless display of puppy love. Had I ever been that young?

Lord Slex made introductions all around. Electricity went up my arm when Ms. Morning and I shook hands. I'm afraid I stood there a little longer than I should have, dazed by her high-voltage smile. Hah! If this was puppy love, so be it! I was glad to be hiding behind my masking spell, though I had no idea how Ms. Morning would have reacted had I been my normal self. At the worst of times no woman had ever run screaming when she saw me.

"The college has hired Mr. Cronyn to protect you," Lord Slex said.

She seemed surprised. "From what?" she asked.

"Industrial spies, I am told," I said.

Ms. Morning laughed. She had a beautiful laugh. "I'm more likely to be done in by jealous colleagues," she said.

"The board takes your welfare very seriously, my dear," Lord Slex said.

"Your welfare and the security of your big project," I added, always trying to be helpful. Lord Slex shot me an irritated glance.

"I see. Very well, then—Mr. Cronyn, is it?—you may guard

my body."

That was the best offer I'd had in a long time, but I didn't do more than smile and thank her. I was, after all, a professional on assignment. Getting mixed up with a client in a romantic way could only lead to difficulties.

Ms. Morning picked up her briefcase, and I followed her and Lord Slex down the stairs while they spoke about her dissertation in terms I remembered only dimly from my time at Stilthins Mort. At the foot of the stairs we met a well-buffed male who was nearly as old as Ms. Morning. "Ready to go?" he asked her.

"You go on ahead, Rodney," she said. "Mr. Cronyn will drive me home."

Rodney appraised me as if I were a beaten-up pair of shoes. "If you're sure," he said without certainty. I guess I failed to come up to his standards, even with my new face.

"I'm sure. We'll talk later on the phone."

Rodney nodded and stood aside to let us pass. Getting back to the Administration building took a long time because Misty Morning seemed to have a lot of friends and they all wanted to speak with her. Once or twice someone even spoke to Lord Slex.

We got to the Administration building at last and stood for a moment under the stained-glass wizard while Lord Slex assured Misty Morning that everything would be fine now that Turner Cronyn was on the job. To seal the bargain she threw me another one of her dazzling smiles, nearly knocking me over.

Though my legs were wobbly, I managed to stay upright all the way to my car, opened the passenger door for her, then went around to slide in behind the wheel. She told me she lived in an apartment up Benedict Canyon and directed me how to get there.

I turned right onto Western and rode my brakes down to the meat grinder that is rush-hour Sunset Boulevard and turned west, fighting traffic all the way. Traffic would not have been a problem if the municipal magic bond issue had passed. Trust the voters.

Hollywood traffic was always a trifle more ostentatious than it is in other parts of the city, excepting perhaps Beverly Hills. A number of vehicles, like my Puck, looked like the automobiles of old. But there was also an assortment of Hansom cabs, row boats, and stage coaches.

The variety of magically motivated vehicles didn't lighten the traffic on Sunset Boulevard any. It took us across town with all the grace and élan of mud being forced through a pipe, while all around us capered what the travel folders are pleased to call "the heart of Hollywood," a city that actually has as much to do with the movies as Pittsburgh. Most of the studios are in the valley or on the west side of town. Hollywood is, however, a great place to purchase a T-shirt, a postcard, or a case of syphilis.

During our time together, Misty—she asked me to call her Misty—and I got to know each other. Which somehow made the whole Hollywood experience worthwhile. She told me she was left-handed, which I already knew, having seen her write on the board in her classroom.

"Me and Leonardo da Vinci," she said, enjoying the idea.

"How's that?" I asked.

"He was left-handed, too. I always admired him, the archetypical Renaissance Man. We lefties have to stick together." She went on, explaining at length how she fancied herself a Renaissance Person like Leonardo. She made being a Renaissance Person sound like fun.

She was describing her parents, a couple of straitlaced customers from Chicago, when I noticed a small burgundy car that seemed to have been trailing us for some time. It was missing most of the paint on its front bumper.

"You know anybody who owns a burgundy car?" I asked.

"Huh? What?"

Just beyond a shoddy court full of offices tricked up in art deco architecture and called with wild optimism "The Crossroads of the World," I made a sudden turn up Orange Drive, trying not to hit any valuable tourists, and rolled along slowly as if I were looking for an address. What I was actually doing was watching my rearview mirror. The burgundy car had turned behind us and was now sniffing at our tail pipe even though there was plenty of room to go around. I was close enough to see that the driver was all alone—no passengers.

Next to the Roosevelt Hotel at the end of the block was the hotel's new parking structure. Making an instant enemy, I suddenly turned in front of a one-man riverboat that had been coming the other way. The sound of its steam whistle faded as I took a ticket from the entry machine and rolled into the dimness of the structure.

"He's coming in here," Misty said as she watched out my rear window.

"I thought he might," I said. I drove up the lane between parked cars as quickly as I dared, turned and started up the incline. After a moment I saw what I was looking for—not a parking space, but a car just pulling out. I hurried so I would be beyond him when he momentarily blocked the open lane. He had to stop with a jolt to avoid hitting me. I was making enemies left and right today.

I rounded the corner at the top of the incline and followed the arrows to the exit. "Do you see him?" I asked.

"No."

I stopped behind the gossamer barrier at the bottom of the structure where the guy at the little booth glanced at the time on my ticket. I hadn't been inside the structure more than five minutes.

"You weren't in there long, sir," he said.

"Nope. Forgot all about the young lady's saxophone lesson."

He nodded and made the gossamer barrier go away.

"Thanks," I said and waved to him as I bounced down the driveway. I turned right and soon was back on Sunset heading west. The burgundy car was no longer behind me. If I was lucky, he'd be tangled up inside the parking structure for ten or fifteen minutes.

"Who was it?" Misty asked.

"I thought you might know," I said. "A detective hired by another college? An industrial spy? Maybe somebody you work with at Stilthins Mort? You seem to have a lot of friends, not to mention admirers."

I felt her squirm in her seat. "Do you really think I'm in danger?" She sounded lots more worried now than she had been in her classroom.

I wanted to pat her hand, but that seemed patronizing. "Probably not," I said. "But if you are, I'll do what I can to keep you safe."

"I know you will," she said and patted *my* hand. I liked it, actually, though keeping my mind on driving was briefly a problem. I only hoped that I could keep her safe *enough*.

"You'd make my job easier," I said, "if you'd name a few names. For some reason the board members at Stilthins Mort were kind of secretive on that point."

She smiled. "Bad luck to call on your enemies," she said.

"Worse luck to stumble around blindly."

"All right," she said after a moment. "You probably know about Stilthins Mort's crosstown rival, the California Institute of Thaumaturgy."

"I thought that was just football."

She shook her head. "Football is only the beginning. Both sides compete for big-name lecturers and count the publications of academic papers as if they were dollar bills—which, in a sense, they are."

I nodded. It was all coming back to me now. When I was a student at Stilthins Mort, I'd been too busy failing my classes to get involved with extracurricular activities. "School spirit," I suggested.

"Yes. In the least reputable sense of the word. Cal Thau might hire its own detective to watch over its staff."

"Do you know anybody over there?"

"Just to say hello to. Nobody special."

"What about big business?" I asked as I tried once again to chose a lane that didn't move quite so slowly.

She took a while to answer. I glanced at her quickly and saw her looking out at the tourist traps. We had plenty of time. Traffic was moving hardly at all.

"The most likely candidate," she said, speaking to the window, "is PrestoCorp."

"Why them?"

"I sold them the rights to the car-of-different-color spell." She was suddenly so angry she almost spit. "What a rotten deal."

"They cheated you?"

"Depends on whose lawyers you ask." She shrugged and almost smiled. "Old news. It was a learning experience."

"Life is full of them," I agreed. "And you think they would be interested in your latest project?"

"They already told me so. Dr. Hamish seemed a little miffed that I wouldn't tell her anything about it."

"Dr. Hamish?"

"Heather Hamish. She's the vice-president of PrestoCorp's research and development department."

"Ruthless?" I asked.

"About average for that crowd, I guess," Misty said.

"And your project is?"

"You don't need to know that."

"I suppose not. But you can't blame me for being curious."

"No."

"So you're not going to tell me?"

"No. I don't like to talk about my projects until I finish them."

I broke through a knot of rickshaws and miniature locomotives, and on the other side found no reason for the hold-up. I've been driving for years but I still don't understand why traffic acts the way it does.

She turned toward me. "What will you do now that I've named names?" she asked.

"Check around. With a little luck I might be able to prevent some trouble."

Once again her eyes were wide and full of worry. "You said you didn't think I was in danger."

"There's all kinds of trouble. Not all of them involve physical danger."

She nodded.

Sunset became more hip, advertising the hot rock star and the hot actor and the hot movie with big animated billboards that were nothing but distractions. We passed supper clubs with valet parking, small music clubs without it, all closed and looking much too gaudy this early in the evening.

Suddenly we crossed over into Beverly Hills and the street became awfully residential, lined with miniature mansions and long, low-slung ranch-style houses, each having enough lawn in front to play nine holes. We passed the big pink tit of the Beverly Hills Hotel and turned up into the hills along Benedict Canyon.

The houses were much closer together here, the wall of one on top of the hedge of another. Little cottages sat primly near gigantic estates, each of which had its own sweeping drive and damned near its own weather. The road turned and twisted back on itself, so I was busy steering.

"The next time you can turn right, do so," Misty directed.

I nodded, but almost missed the turn because I thought it was a private driveway. Misty yelped and pointed and I turned onto a narrow lane called Rigby Court, which wound down into a canyon shaded by big pepper trees. There were no sidewalks—the houses on this street bellied right up to the street with sherbet-colored walls, each with a scattering of windows.

"Slow down," Misty said, "we're about there."

I'd probably have spotted it even if I'd been going faster, but at the speed I was maneuvering along Rigby Court I couldn't miss it—the burgundy car that had been following us was now parked facing the way we'd come. It might have been some other burgundy car, but I didn't think so, not with those scrapes on the front bumper. Either the driver was one terrific tail, or he'd guessed where we were going all along. Either way, it was my problem, not Misty's. I said nothing about it to her. There would always be time for that.

CHAPTER SIX
A FUNNY SHADE OF PALE GREEN

At Misty's direction I pulled into a tiny lot that had been carved out of the hillside. My front bumper gently touched a banana tree that looked as if it had been bumped before.

"You go on in," I said. "I have a little professional security stuff to do." I glanced along the street and could see someone sitting in the burgundy car. I was too far away to see who it was.

She followed my eyes. "Burgundy car," she said.

"Yes. Go on inside where you'll be safe. Lord Slex would be very angry if I let you come with me."

She nodded once with fear in her eyes. I hadn't thought she was the type of client who would want to help me play detective, but you never know.

Misty walked up a serpentine cement path that led under a keyhole arch hung with bougainvillaea. I was about to stroll across the street to see what was what when she ran back and pushed a key into my hand. "It's my front door key," she said. "Number six. I give keys to a lot of people I trust. I'm always locking myself out." She ran off again like Alice's White Rabbit.

I slipped her key into my pocket and walked across the street. The little burgundy car was a Honda Augury. And unless two of them had most of the paint on the front bumper scraped off just this way, this was the car that had been following us. The driver was still sitting behind the wheel. I was about halfway to it when I saw something that caused me to rethink my plan. Trying to hide himself behind a bush that was much too small for the purpose was the red-faced man with the cauliflower nose I'd seen watching me up at Stilthins Mort. He was a little conspicuous to be a spy, his red suit not being exactly camouflage, but maybe that was part of his charm.

I kept walking as if I hadn't seen him, but as I passed his bush I grabbed him by the arm and yanked him onto the sidewalk. He howled, wriggled free, and ran along the street. I followed.

The street curved a few times, but not violently. I never lost sight of him until suddenly he was gone. I kept running, thinking he was hidden by a turn or had ducked behind another bush, and shortly came to a dead end—not just a sign announcing it, but a high rock wall spotted with hummocks of grass. I stepped into a zone of fresh sea air, unlike the rest of the thick warm air at the bottom of Rigby Court, but before I had a chance to enjoy it, the breeze whirled it around and it was gone.

The guy would have had to be an orangutan to climb over that wall before I got to the dead end. I was collecting a fine zoo of disappearing guys—first a fish and now an ape. Silverwhite said that the fish guy hadn't used magic to disappear. Maybe the guy with the cauliflower nose hadn't either. The more I knew the less I understood.

I walked slowly back up the street, searching behind trees and under shrubs. I might as well have been searching for the guy in my closet at home for all the good it did me.

I came to the place where the burgundy Honda Augury had been parked. It was gone now. Pretty good, Cronyn, losing two suspects in less than ten minutes. Only a real professional could do that. Don't try it at home.

Still grumbling to myself, I walked along the serpentine path under the bougainvillaea arch and entered the courtyard of Misty's building. The path wound under overhanging trees and past colorful beds of flowers. On either side, curved walls rose to a second floor, and above that were the traditional terracotta pantiles. Open doorways led into small round anterooms. There was not a straight line anywhere. In the center of the courtyard was an open patio paved in flagstone, with Adirondack chairs casually scattered about. The whole courtyard was pleasantly cool. None of it seemed quite real.

I found number six through a two-story atrium and up a couple of narrow steps. I used the lion-head knocker on the door and waited, but all I got for my trouble was silence. She should have opened the door right away, full of concern and curiosity. I grew more uncomfortable and at last used the key Misty had given me.

I unlocked the door and pushed it open with one finger. The door swung open easily, making the soft complaint of an old man settling into a chair.

"Misty?" I called. I don't know why. If she hadn't answered my knock, she probably would not answer my call. Fear entered the apartment with me and climbed onto my back. I carried him with me as I searched the bottom floor. The living room was neat and clean and furnished with a few pieces of dark heavy furniture. A TV stood off to one side, as if she didn't watch it much. Bookcases full of books lined the walls. The tiny kitchen was neat, too, and organized like a ship's galley—crowded with jars, canisters, and appliances. Both rooms were filled with more silence. Fear grew heavier as I carried him up the dark stairs to the second floor. There I found a bedroom, feminine but not fussy, a bathroom, and a large room that looked like Misty's laboratory.

The laboratory had a faint musty chemical smell. A cement table dominated the center of the room, with a battered but serviceable-looking desk pushed against one end of it. Glassware and Bunsen burners lined the middle of the cement table, ready for use. The desk was piled with papers held down by colorful rocks. Standing on one corner of the desk was a big three-way mirror, a main mirror with a smaller mirror on each side that could swing away. It was a false note, given what I had seen of her décor so far. Misty didn't seem like the type who would pluck her eyebrows during business hours.

Golden late-afternoon sunlight poured in through a big window that had a standing electric box fan in front of it. One whole wall was shelves full of reagent bottles, and another was taken up with a blackboard that had been wiped clean with a wet rag. I wondered what had been written there, and whether I would have understood it if I knew. If Misty was as advanced as Lord Slex said she was, maybe I wouldn't have been alone in my ignorance.

"Misty?" I called again, sure it would do no good.

I circled the cement table and found what I had known I would find eventually—Misty's body on the floor. She looked peaceful, like a little girl dreaming about unicorns and fairy princesses, but her skin was a funny shade of pale green. I quickly knelt beside her and tried artificial respiration. I didn't enjoy touching my lips to hers—she was too dead.

I went downstairs and called the police, then went back to the laboratory to sit with the body until they arrived.

CHAPTER SEVEN
BACK ON THE BICYCLE

For a while I sat in the chair at Misty's desk thinking about how badly I had screwed things up. It was no longer just a matter of losing a couple of suspects on a dead-end street. I had broken rule number one of the private eye biz—I had failed to protect the client. My mood got darker as the sun went down, and pretty soon I was good and disgusted with myself. Then I decided that being disgusted wasn't doing either of us any good, not me or Misty.

But as I continued staring into the gathering gloom, I began to notice things. Hanging in the air in three places, each in one corner of the room, were round areas like lenses—space puckers, if you will. Each was about a foot across, maybe less—and it distorted the area behind it a little. I wanted to see them better. I don't know why. It was just something to do.

By all rights I should have just sat there chewing my cud until the official boys arrived because the place might be lousy with clues: fingerprints, cigarette ashes, aura glimmers, hair clippings. Who knew? But instead I got up, used the eraser at the end of a pencil to click on the lights, and nosed around.

I looked closely at one of the space puckers. From one side it distorted space, and from the other it wasn't even there. I wondered whether these puckers had anything to do with Misty's big secret project. I tapped the surface of the pucker with my pencil, encountering no resistance and making no sound. But some force nearly took my arm off as it pulled the pencil into the pucker. I let go just in time and breathed hard as I stood looking at the distortion. It hung there as before. Why didn't it suck up all the air in the world? Maybe Misty could have told me. I sighed. I was just glad the puckers were out of the way in corners, rather than where somebody was likely to walk into one.

I wandered around her apartment trying to see everything, because I didn't know what I was looking for. I checked all the windowsills and door frames and saw no sign of forced entry. There was no back door. Was she murdered by somebody who had a key? A "friend?" Or had the murderer entered and exited through one of the space puckers?

And then there were my two suspects: first, some guy in a burgundy Honda Augury with a scraped front bumper who probably knew where Misty lived and certainly guessed that's where we were going; second, some guy with a cauliflower nose, a guy who could either climb like a monkey or had a lot of wizard training. My murderer could be either of them or some-body else entirely. I rubbed my face with both hands. Motive, means, and opportunity were all mysteries.

I went back up to the laboratory and searched it again. I riffled the papers on her desk, hoping that something she'd written in her small neat handwriting would leap out at me. I recognized some of the symbols in her calculations, and a few of the doodles—she drew a killer Starship *Enterprise*—but that was all. The top drawer contained paper, clips, pens, and pencils of various colors. The center drawer contained nothing but a couple of Milky Ways. The bottom drawer was locked. I shook it because that's what you always do with something that's locked, then studied it. The keyhole looked like a keyhole in a cartoon. How old-fashioned of her. I wondered whether it actually locked the drawer or was just for show.

I tried a couple of unlocking spells Silverwhite had taught me, but I might as well have been reciting dirty limericks, so I took a ring of slim skeleton keys from a pocket. I'd barely touched the lock with the first key when imps leaped up around me. Each one was a black ball about five inches across with a demonic face. The ball had arms and legs that were thin but strong. The hands had long grasping fingers. "Hey, bud. Lay off. That ain't yours," one of them said in an irritating scratchy voice. "Ain't yours," the others echoed. Each voice was different, but all were as irritating as the first—Munchkins who had gone over to the Dark Side.

I ignored them and kept working. No one had ever won an argument with an imp, mainly because there was nothing to argue with. An imp was no more than a single-minded physical manifestation of a spell, designed to do a specific job in a specific way. Silverwhite might have been able to finesse them with magic eventually, but I wasn't that good.

"Ain't yours," the imps said and plucked at me. Others got in my way. I kept trying keys as best I could, but it was like working in a rain of gravel; soon more of the imps popped into existence and they became rougher. Their fingers were like pins. Their voices bored into my ears like the hard harsh whine of a dentist's drill.

"All right!" I cried and leaped back, breathing hard.

"Ain't yours," one of the imps said, and suddenly every one of them was gone.

I contemplated the drawer from a distance. I'd made a few scratches around the keyhole, but that was all. If Misty had put something in there to be safe, it was still safe.

I had more luck with the wastebasket next to the desk. In it were two packets of commercial rat-killing spell, the kind of thing you could purchase at Spell-Mart. I lifted them gently out of the basket and set them on the cement table. Each of them had a corner torn off. After having been emptied, each had been twisted in the middle so it had a girlish figure with a narrow waist—it looked like a party favor. I put one of them into my pocket and dropped the other back into the wastebasket. I would share my clues with the police. I was that kind of guy.

Three loud demanding bangs punctured the silence of the apartment. That would be the police. I went downstairs to let them in.

Two big men entered—football-player types, each a little past his prime. Each wore a business suit and a conservative tie. Three uniformed cops came in behind them. More uniformed cops looked busy outside. The plainclothesman with wavy blond hair introduced himself as Detective Fotheringay. His assistant, a man with dark hair plastered with too much goo, was Siltz. Siltz nodded when Fotheringay introduced him and then took out a pen and spiral-bound notebook, ready for business. Nobody introduced the men in uniform.

"You call it in?" Fotheringay asked.

"Yes."

"Where's the stiff?" Fotheringay asked brusquely as he glanced everywhere but at me.

"Upstairs," I said, and led the way. I didn't like him calling Misty a stiff, not even if she was dead, but I let it alone. Sometimes making an enemy of the police department is unavoidable, but it's never a good idea.

We entered the laboratory, and the uniformed cops spread out to look for clues. Even with all the lights on, the space puckers were almost invisible. I wasn't sure they were important, but that wasn't the reason I didn't feel obligated to point them out. Someone with a more finely tuned conscience than mine, someone who had only one concern and that for justice, might have done all he could to help the police. What did it matter who solved the crime as long as somebody solved it? But I wasn't quite that open-minded. I figured I had done my duty by calling them. I felt responsible for getting Misty killed, so her murder was my problem. I wanted to bring the murderer to justice myself. Besides, I wasn't stopping the police from seeing the puckers.

I led Fotheringay and Siltz to where Misty lay. Siltz rested his notebook on the cement table while Fotheringay got down on one knee and studied the body. He touched her cheek, then picked up her arm and let it fall. We all watched it fall.

"Dead for less than an hour, I'd say," Fotheringay commented.

"I could have told you that," I said, a little irritated that he hadn't asked.

"I guess you could have," Fotheringay admitted. "What's your story?"

I told them who I was, and that I was a private detective hired by the board of Stilthins Mort to protect Misty Morning. Fotheringay commented with a single rude guffaw. Siltz wrote as I spoke. I showed him my license, and he noted the serial number.

"She'd been threatened?" Siltz asked.

"Not that I know of," I said. "The board was just concerned because she was working on an important project. They felt that someone might try to steal it."

"What was the project?" Siltz asked.

"I don't know. The man who hired me claimed not to know either."

Fotheringay nodded. "We'll look around," he said. "Maybe she left notes."

After the experience I'd had with the imps, I wished them luck. "Look," I said, "I had no reason to believe she was in any physical danger. Industrial spies and jealous colleagues aren't usually up for murder. In theory, I was here just to make sure nobody walked off with her project."

"We don't know whether you were successful," Fotheringay said thoughtfully. "I mean, not knowing what the project is, we don't know whether it's missing. Where were you when she got it?" he asked.

I told them about the guy in the burgundy Honda and the guy with the cauliflower nose.

"So you get hired as a bodyguard," Siltz said as if he were trying to work out a problem, "and the first thing you do is abandon the client."

I got a little hot then. "You weren't here," I said, "and you don't know how it was. The guy in the car or the other man could have been the murderer. Maybe they were working together. The point is *nobody* knows. As far as I could tell, when I stayed outside to speak to the guy in the car and to chase the man with the cauliflower nose, I was doing my job. You try being in two places at once."

"Cool off, Cronyn," Fotheringay said. "Nobody's accusing you of anything."

"Does that include Siltz?" I asked.

Gently and with great deliberation, Siltz set down his pen on the cement table, the better to glare at me. "You watch your mouth," he said. "A little police brutality could come in here."

I smiled at him.

Before he had a chance to make another threat, a man carrying a black bag entered the room. "Morton, coroner's office," he announced at the doorway.

"Come join our sewing circle," Fotheringay said. He got to his feet, and Morton took his place at Misty's side.

Using a piece of chalk, Morton drew a pentagram around Misty on the hardwood floor. At each point of the star he set a small metal tray into which he tapped some dried greens from a big plastic bag. He lit the greens, filling the room with a strong acrid odor. Making complicated motions with a big feather, probably from an eagle, he stirred the thready smoke around a little. After a moment of watching what the smoke did, he clambered to his feet and made a note on a form.

One of the uniformed policemen approached Fotheringay and handed him something. Both their backs were to me so I couldn't see what it was, though I could guess.

"I know what killed her," Morton said.

"And that would be?" Siltz said.

"A commercially available poisoning spell, the kind used to kill mice, rats, and other small vermin."

"It take any special skill to use such a spell?" Siltz asked casually, just to pass the time of day.

"Not much," Morton explained. "Anybody with two hands and a voice could have done it."

"Good call, doc," Fotheringay said. "Here's your murder weapon—or what's left of it." He let a small sealed plastic bag fall to the cement table. Inside was the twisted spell packet I'd left in the trash can. We all stared at it as if it were removing its clothes.

Morton picket up the plastic bag, opened it, and sniffed at the contents. He nodded. "That would do the job," he said as he sealed the plastic bag again.

"What do you say, Cronyn?" Fotheringay asked.

I shrugged. "I'm no expert," I said, "but I'd say that unless analysis downtown tells you more, you still have a wide-open case."

"Who asked you?" Siltz asked snidely.

"That's enough," Fotheringay said.

We all watched grimly while more of the coroner's staff came in and took away Misty's body. Maybe Siltz was right to be sarcastic. I'd been hired to do a job and had failed miserably. I owed Misty, if not the Stilthins Mort board. If you fall off a bicycle, you have to get right back on. It was time for me to get back onto the bicycle.

Pretty politely, considering, Fotheringay asked me to join him and Siltz downtown for a look at the mug books. I agreed because no other answer was possible.

We were on our way out of the room when we were stopped by an scratchy irritating voice. "Hey, bud. Lay off. That ain't yours," it said.

"What the hell?" Siltz said.

Two more plainclothesmen were staring at Misty's desk from a few feet away. Imps took a last baleful look at them before they disappeared. "Something in the drawer, sir," the younger of the plainclothesmen said.

"And that would be?" Fotheringay said too politely.

With great interest, I watched the two men hurriedly get back to work. In my business you never know when you're going to need to get past some imps. I might learn something.

The young plainclothesman pulled small plastic bags from an attaché case, each containing a small amount of powder or dry leaves or bark. Soon quite an apothecary lay on Misty's lab table in front of the other cop, a round dark man with hair like a wire brush. The round man pushed his partner aside and impatiently took a mortar and pestle from the attaché case. Without weighing anything, he chose a pinch or two of a few ingredients and used the pestle to grind them together in the mortar.

"What's he using?" I asked the world at large.

Fotheringay shook his head and Siltz smiled using all his teeth. Neither of them said anything, nor looked as if they wanted to. Like any other professionals, the police liked having their little secrets.

After a moment or two the round man nodded and backed away. The other plainclothesman took a pinch of the dry mixture in the mortar and threw it at Misty's desk as he spoke a spell. He spoke quickly and I did not catch the words. Imps rose from the bottom drawer like dirty soap bubbles. Each one burst, leaving behind a shred of ash that was caught by a current of air I could neither see nor feel, and carried it away.

When the show was over, the round man stepped forward and set a black plastic box over the keyhole. A moment later he opened the drawer without trouble. "Empty," he said.

"Do you have any idea what she might have kept in there?" Fotheringay asked me.

I was wondering the same thing. I was also wondering who had it now, whatever it was, and whether it would do him any good. "No," I said.

Siltz chuckled as if I'd said something funny.

"All right," Fotheringay said. "Let's go."

CHAPTER EIGHT
THE CLOSEST THING
TO A WITNESS

I sat in the back of an unmarked car staring through the barrier at the wavy blond hair on the back of Fotheringay's head. Siltz sat behind the wheel, his hair shining in the light from a street lamp. Fotheringay turned down the police radio until the dispatcher whispered at the edge of my consciousness like a bad dream. Siltz started the engine, and we followed a couple of prowl cars out of Rigby Court and down Benedict Canyon. As he drove, Siltz hummed an unrecognizable melody to himself.

Siltz parked the car in the police lot and helped Fotheringay escort me into Parker Center, for Los Angeles a low and rather modern public building. We went upstairs to the police department the tourists never see, if they're lucky, and into the offices where the homicide guys hang out.

Fotheringay led us through the chaos into a smaller room that contained one long wooden table and a few ancient chairs. Siltz pushed the door closed behind us until the latch clicked. In one wall was a bookcase containing huge books, each with a number on its spine. Siltz put his hand on my shoulder and pushed me down into a scuffed chair.

"Thank you," I said. "I will have a seat."

Fotheringay chuckled while he pulled a huge book from the case and carefully set it down on the table in front of me. Siltz took up a position in one corner of the room, leaning across the top of a filing cabinet on one elbow, his face a bored mask.

Fotheringay flipped open the book to the first page. It was empty. "If you see anybody who looks familiar, just point to him and say, 'that one,' and the parade will stop."

I nodded.

Fotheringay made motions over the blank page and a line of men appeared near the top edge, each about six inches high, each with a precise and distinctive face. Each one moved a little—coughing into fists, swaying, scratching an ear—as if alive.

"Any of these guys your man with the cauliflower nose?" Fotheringay asked.

"No."

"Yeah, it's too much to hope for to strike gold right off the bat, but I have to ask. You never know."

The first group of men disappeared and was replaced immediately by a second group, each just as distinctive and lifelike.

"No," I said again.

We ran through the first book and three more. The faces, as distinctive as they were, all began to look the same. I did my best to look for the guy with the cauliflower nose, but by the time we were finished, I don't think I would have recognized my own mother.

Fotheringay closed the fourth book on the last line of men and put it away. Siltz yawned and seemed barely awake. I felt like the bottom of a birdcage. I waited. We all waited.

A woman in uniform came in with a file that she handed to Fotheringay. She left again without looking at me or Siltz.

Fotheringay sat down across from me and tried on an interested expression. Somehow he only succeeded in appearing more tired. "It would have helped if you'd been able to point out the guy," he said.

"I sympathize. Right now I must be your number one suspect."

Siltz was awake enough to laugh sarcastically.

"You would be but we've done some checking." Fotheringay tapped the file. "You never met Misty Morning before today."

"And worse yet," I said, "I had every motive for keeping her alive, and none at all for wanting her dead."

"We'll decide what's worse," Siltz said, making it sound like a threat.

"It so happens you're right," Fotheringay agreed as if what Siltz had said meant no more than the dust in the corners. "But don't leave town. Even though you're not exactly a suspect, you are the closest thing we have to a witness."

"It's nice to be wanted, I guess," I said as I stood up.

"Siltz will drive you back to your car," Fotheringay said, causing his assistant to scowl as if Fotheringay had asked him to make the coffee.

"And me without an anti-rabies spell," I said.

Fotheringay smiled. "Play nice, boys," he said. "Oh, and, Cronyn: if you get any bright ideas, don't keep 'em to yourself."

"You too," I said, and Fotheringay nodded as if his mind were already at home in bed.

With all the grace you might expect, Siltz led me back through the building and down to the parking lot. Most of the way back to Misty's place he weaved in and out of traffic, riding the siren. We did not converse. He stopped at the top of Rigby Court and waited for me to get out.

"Thanks," I said.

He said nothing, but nearly ran over my foot as he zoomed away.

I walked down into Rigby Court and found my car in the little parking lot. It had been leafleted with an advertisement for Chinese health food. Any kind of food sounded pretty good about then, but I balled the paper up, threw it into my back seat, and drove home.

That year I was living in an apartment in the La Brea Towers. I drove along Sixth Street at the edge of the tar pits, then turned left onto Hauser, which took me into the maze of the apartment complex. I maneuvered my car up streets and around traffic circles, past identical white apartment buildings, then parked as close as I could to my building, which wasn't very.

Leaning against the wall, I rode up to my floor in a flat-smelling elevator barely large enough for two people and a bag of groceries.

Once I got into my apartment, I found that I was too wired to go to bed. Dinner was a handful of peanuts and a glass of water, and even that seemed like a lot of trouble to prepare.

After my gourmet meal I sat on the couch for a long time looking out the window at the lights of the city. Far-off red and white navigation lights blinked on broomsticks in the landing pattern miles east of the airport. Much closer, the water floating on the tar in the tar pits shimmered, all that remained of the magic paraphernalia thrown into them during Prohibition. Occasionally, some magical something rose from the pits and attacked an innocent bystander. Usually the thing that triggered the magic was an accident of nature, but I'd heard rumors that the magician who had put the paraphernalia together always maintained a connection with it, and he could still control it to some extent—the law of contagion hard at work. Whatever. Apparitions always caused the local politicians to do a lot of tap-dancing and hand-waving about ecology and public safety, but a week later the incident was forgotten.

The guy in the little burgundy Honda Augury was out there, as was the guy with the cauliflower nose. Were they sleeping, or like me, were they too hyped-up from the day's entertainment to sleep? A locater spell would have been handy about then, but as far as I knew no such thing existed. Too bad Misty had not bent her mighty mind to such a thing when she had a chance.

"Anyone with two hands and a voice could have done it," the coroner's man had said. I put my hand into a pocket and found the empty twisted packet of vermin-killing spell. All it suggested to me was that Misty had been murdered by some-body with two hands and a voice. At this hour, and in my condition, a conclusion any more clever was impossible. When I awoke on the couch the next morning, I still had the packet cupped in my hand. I shuffled to my desk and put the packet into a small drawer with some pencil stubs I hadn't yet found the time to throw away.

When I stumbled into the bathroom and looked into the mirror for the first time that morning, I was shocked to see a face I didn't recognize. It took a moment to remember that Lord Slex had given me the face the day before. His reasons for messing with my appearance now seemed frivolous. Maybe they always had been. I looked pretty good, but somehow that didn't gladden my heart.

Sleeping on the couch in my clothes made me feel like a bum, so I took extra care showering and getting dressed. I had to tie my tie three times before I got it right.

I took a gander into the hall outside my front door and was just in time to see morning papers popping into existence in front of a few doors, including mine.

I made eggs, bacon, and toast for breakfast, and ate them while I found out what everyone else had been doing while I'd been losing a client. Misty's murder got a small amount of space on page one below the fold. Her photo was displayed prominently. According to the story, the crime had been phoned in by an anonymous tipster, and the police had arrived in seconds. Detective Fotheringay was quoted as taking a bold stand against evil-doers. He was assisted by Ormund Siltz. A quick solution to the case was expected.

It being a slow news day, also on page one I read an article about Eulalie Tortuga, estranged wife of Vic Tortuga, famous best-selling novelist. There was no photo, but given what I knew about Vic Tortuga's taste in women, she would not be ugly. Ms. Tortuga had been found wandering through Westwood with a blank expression on her face and a head full of nothing. The police had tried to take her in for her own protection, but she'd managed to elude them. Officer Hodel, the man on the beat, said she'd acted like a zombie—but she may have just been drugged, zombies not being so common. Anybody with information leading to her apprehension is asked to—etc. etc.

After educating myself with the funnies, I folded the paper neatly and stacked the sections on the kitchen table. I washed the dishes and let them dry in the drainer while imagining what my next interview with the board at Stilthins Mort would be like. I couldn't make it pleasant. Still, I would have to go see Lord Slex and his pals sooner or later. Not only would they want to hear my version of what had happened to Misty, but I had a few questions for them.

While putting stuff into my pockets I found the check for 700 bucks Lord Slex had given me an age ago. It would have to go back. The hour Misty had been safe in my care barely counted.

I was just patting my pockets to make sure I had everything I needed when the telephone rang. It could have been somebody asking if I wanted to change my long-distance service. But it wasn't.

"Mr. Cronyn? This is Lord Slex." I guess he'd read the morning paper. His anger was obvious but controlled. "We'd like to see you over here at Stilthins Mort at your earliest convenience. In the boardroom. *Now* would be good. I'm sure you know why."

"Yes, sir. I was just on my way when you called."

He hung up and I did the same. Neither one of us had said good-bye.

CHAPTER NINE
"NO WIZARD IN
HIS RIGHT MIND"

I don't remember how I got to Stilthins Mort. I don't even remember leaving my apartment. Driving was a blur of automatic responses. The last person to ride shotgun in my car had been Misty Morning, and her perfume, a light clean flowery scent, seemed to be riding with me still.

When I arrived, the same bored guard let me in through the same gossamer barrier. This time he had to live without my jaunty wave. I drove up to the administration building and parked. Students milled and lounged upon the grass just as if I wasn't about to have one of the worst hours of my life.

I marched under the stained-glass wizard, who might have been sneering at me while he continued trying to condense a woman out of smoke. I sneered right back, then took the stairs to the third floor of the building, where I walked down a long corridor that had no classrooms to a desk in front of double doors. From behind the desk, a prim woman with white braids pinned across the top of her head watched me approach with disapproval, as if I were delivering the garbage.

"Turner Cronyn to see the board," I announced as if I didn't care whether she liked it or not.

She nodded, a motion so small I wasn't sure she'd made it, and slipped between the double doors in such a way that I couldn't see what was beyond. I waited for what seemed to be a long time, but still not long enough. "Come in, Mr. Cronyn."

Saying it hurt her, and she held the door open barely enough to admit a starving cat.

I opened it a little wider and, stepping inside, found myself at one end of a long room. At the far end was a large wooden block that looked like a judge's bench. On either side of the bench was a cauldron with smoke rising from it—sandalwood, I think. The three board members sat behind the bench, concentrating on me while I crossed the tessellated floor as if they were grading me on my walk. I think there was more stained-glass fantasy on the walls, but I wasn't there to see the sights, so I kept my eyes on Lord Slex, who sat between Lord Trask and Lord Philpot.

I cozied up to the bench, which I believe surprised them a little, and stood on tippy-toe to set the $700 check down in front of Lord Slex, lining up the long edge of the check exactly with the long edge of the bench. I backed off and for a few seconds we stared at each other.

Lord Slex spoke as if he were pronouncing sentence. "Mr. Cronyn, we hired you to protect Misty Morning. Shortly after she entered your care, she was murdered by person or persons unknown. I admit that the return of your retainer shows honesty on your part, but need I point out Ms. Morning is still dead?"

"No need at all," I replied.

Lord Trask dabbed at his rabbity eyes and took a deep breath. When he spoke, he spit out the words. "Tell us how it happened, Mr. Cronyn," he said.

"In your own words," Lord Philpot added.

I wanted to ask him whose words he thought I might use, but I was in enough trouble already. I told them everything: about the guy in the burgundy Augury, about the other guy with the cauliflower nose, about how I'd found Misty dead in her own laboratory. I spoke about the space puckers and about the vermin spell. I didn't mention how the spell packet had been twisted. It didn't seem important. I told them I'd been through the mug books downtown but hadn't found anybody I wanted to get to know better.

While I spoke, they gave me their full attention, but no part of the story got a response—no nods, no frowns, no cries of surprise. Except for the fact that Lord Trask worked hard at picking the skin around his thumbnail, they might as well have been carved from wax. Of course, by that time they had read the story in the paper and probably had gotten a report from the police.

When I finished, the quiet in the room seemed so heavy with meaning you could crack nuts with it.

"Thank you, Mr. Cronyn," Lord Trask said. "That will be all."

"Not quite all," Lord Philpot said in his beautiful voice, surprising Lord Trask. "There is the matter of the—what did you call them? Space puckers?"

"Indeed," Lord Slex said, agreeing.

"I told you everything I know about them. They float a few feet above the floor and suck in pencils but not air. If you're thinking they might have something to do with Ms. Morning's big secret project, you may be right. I have no idea. The police will be going through Misty's stuff. You'll probably hear from them if they find anything they can't handle."

Lord Philpot nodded thoughtfully. The other two just stared at me as if still waiting for me to speak. Then Lord Slex shook his head violently, clearing it. "Thank you, Mr. Cronyn," he said. "You may go now."

"Not just yet," I said.

"What?" Lord Trask asked, astonished again, causing the wrinkles in his thin face to deepen.

"I came here to answer your questions and to give back your money, but those are not the only reasons I came. As Lord Slex pointed out, Misty Morning is dead. His implication is that I had something to do with it, if only because I bungled my assignment to protect her. Maybe he's right. But I'm a detective, and I can't let a situation like that just rest. I have to do some-thing about it—like find the person or persons unknown who murdered Misty Morning."

"You believe that we have useful information?" Lord Philpot

asked.

"You knew the deceased," I pointed out.

Lord Slex sighed. "What do you wish to know?"

"Did she have any enemies that you knew of? Perhaps that short guy with the cauliflower nose?"

Lord Slex shook his head and laughed at my foolishness. "Misty Morning was a lovely young lady with a pleasant personality. To my knowledge, anybody who met her liked her."

I shrugged. "I had to ask," I said. "Even the best people have enemies. Besides, it's pretty obvious that *somebody* didn't like her."

If they were faking, they were good at it. From their response to my statement, it was obvious they had never thought of Misty's murder quite that way.

"Someone may have murdered her because she refused to turn over her project," Lord Philpot suggested after a long moment.

"Exactly," I agreed. "Especially if you're right about Ms. Morning's irresistible charm. What about her family? I hear they're fairly conservative people from the Midwest. Have you heard anything different?"

Lord Slex was shocked. "You don't believe someone in her own family killed her," he exclaimed.

"Probably not," I said. "But they might know things about her background that we never thought of. I figure it's worth a phone call to find out—or will somebody from back home be attending the funeral?"

"No," Lord Slex said. "They're going to have the body shipped to Chicago. I got the idea they didn't quite approve of this place or what she was doing here."

"Which is probably one of the reasons she came."

All three lords nodded. Lord Slex opened a file and squinted at its contents. He made a note on a scrap of paper and shoved it across the top of the high desk at me.

"In any case," Lord Slex said as I folded the telephone number once and slid it into a pocket, "we have no thoughts about either a psychotic killer or a professional killer."

"You must have had some villain in mind when you hired me," I said. "Ms. Morning mentioned a few possibilities: somebody from PrestoCorp, or from one of your cross town rivals."

Lord Slex nodded. "Yes, of course," he said as if the idea had never occurred to him. "There is a lot of jealousy in the academic game, as there is in any other business." He looked sideways first at Lord Trask and then at Lord Philpot, checking on how they were taking all this.

"We know no one at PrestoCorp," Lord Trask said.

"Still," said Lord Philpot, "it is more likely you will find the murderer there than at Cal Thau or Thau Tech. At neither school is murder on the curriculum." Lord Philpot tried on a tiny smile, pleased at his turn of phrase.

"That said," Lord Slex continued for him thoughtfully, "it must be admitted that Lord Meston and Lord Dillon both have a great deal of school spirit. If Ms. Morning refused an offer to join Cal Thau's staff as an instructor or to do research, they would have taken it very badly."

"Badly enough to kill her?"

Lord Slex shrugged.

"We don't like to speak ill of colleagues," Lord Trask said.

"Even if they deserve it," Lord Philpot added.

The three lords allowed themselves a small drawing-room laugh over that. We were all just a bunch of sophisticates.

When they recovered, Lord Slex made piles of the books and papers in front of him as if preparing to leave. "Perhaps somebody at the Broken Wand can help you," he said as he held one volume aloft.

"What's that?"

"It probably opened since your time here," Lord Slex explained as he set the book on his pile. "It is a small bar in Ferndell, a hangout for Stilthins Mort students. Many of them knew Misty. One of them may know things about Misty that she didn't share with her teachers."

I nodded. "Thanks for the lead," I said. "I'll give it a try.

Meanwhile, I understand Ms. Morning gave out copies of her house key like bad advice. Do any of you have one?"

They looked from one to the other. "I believe we all do," Lord Slex admitted. "But as you point out, this was hardly unusual."

Lord Slex's admission didn't seem to buy me anything. "I agree that's quite a pool of suspects," I went on, spinning my web. "But just for fun, let's change the sitch a little. Is it possible that someone, perhaps a wizard, could have gotten in *without* a key? Could the murderer have gotten in through one of those space puckers, for instance?"

This suggestion shocked them even more than the possibility that somebody hadn't liked Misty Morning.

"That's a nasty idea," Lord Philpot said, his handsome face curling with distaste.

"Why? There must be a troubled wizard somewhere."

"Perhaps," Lord Philpot admitted with difficulty.

"Isn't it more likely," Lord Trask asked, "that someone broke in?"

"But no one did," I said. "The police and I seem to agree on that."

"No wizard was involved," Lord Philpot stated firmly.

"I repeat," I said, "there must be a troubled wizard somewhere."

Lord Trask seemed about ready to explode. His deeply furrowed face was red again, and his lips crawled over each other like worms. "Perhaps," he said, his voice shaking, "you are not aware of what Prohibition was like for a wizard. There were literal witch hunts. Anyone who could fan a deck of cards was suspect. No wizard in his right mind would ever give the public or the government an excuse to put the craft through a period like that again."

The other two wizards mumbled agreement.

I could see that the three lords were sincere, and sincerely upset. Still, there was no way to avoid rubbing them the wrong way, not if I was to do my job. "I believe," I said, "the operative phrase here is 'no wizard in his right mind'." I let the prospect of more investigation hang in the air like a line of dirty laundry.

"Apparently," Lord Slex said, "you are no better a detective than you were a wizard." It was not just a statement but an accusation. "This interview is at an end."

The three wizards rose as one and went out a side door, leaving me in the room alone. There seemed to be no point to standing there, so I left.

CHAPTER TEN
THE BROKEN WAND

Getting to rustic Ferndell, I had to make an inconvenient left turn just up the hill from Stilthins Mort, after Western Avenue changed into Los Feliz Boulevard. When I entered Griffith Park, the air became cooler than it had been below, and far away tiny bells seemed to ring constantly. On either side bushes and gnarled trees that looked like Arthur Rackham drawings crowded close to the street, except for the few places where dirt paths wound off into the wilderness.

The Broken Wand had its own parking lot about half a mile up into the park. A dozen or so cars were in the lot, and one of them looked like the burgundy Honda Augury that had followed Misty and me the day before. I walked all around the car, noting the scraped front bumper, but it would take a better man than I to know whether or not that was a clue.

A small finger sign next to a dirt path pointed the way to the bar. I had a pleasant walk of a few hundred feet up to a small house made entirely of smooth egg-shaped stones. Over the door hung a wooden sign with the name of the bar on it, and a crude drawing of a sure-enough broken wand. I had seen no fairies on the way, but people rarely do. Fairies are harder to spot than movie stars, especially in Los Angeles.

When I stepped inside, I stood in the doorway for a moment allowing my eyes to adjust to the low level of light, which was helped very little by will o' the wisps flickering in cages in corners and along the walls. A strong odor of beer and pizza charged at me like a bull elephant. All around me conversation and occasional laughter continued, working against the soft rock 'n' roll that dribbled from a jukebox.

I stepped farther into the room, avoiding tables and chairs and clumps of people, and stood at the bar, which ran the length of one side of the room. Nobody at the tables paid any attention to me or to the bartender. The bartender didn't look old enough to have a driver's license, let alone to dispense alcohol.

"Nice place," I said.

The bartender nodded. "Student?" he asked.

"Once," I admitted.

"What can I get for you?"

"Beer. Whatever's cheap. Want to see some ID?"

He laughed briefly. "Coming up," he said.

All around the walls, wherever there wasn't a light cage, wooden shields hung, each with a device of a sorority or fraternity drawn on it. I had been a member of Abracadabra House, whose device was a hand pulling a rabbit from a hat. One of our rivals was Hey, Presto!, whose device was linking rings. The only other frat I knew was Sim Sala Bim, which used a fanned deck of cards. I didn't recognize any of the others. A lot had changed since I'd attended school at Stilthins Mort.

The bartender set a thick, sweating mug on the bar in front of me. I gave him a bill and began to sip. The beer was as cold as death and bitter as a jealous heart. The bartender took a step or two away from me and began to polish a hole into the bar with a damp rag.

"Too bad about Misty Morning," I said.

"Yeah," he said and shook his head. It was a tough old world.

"Did she come in here much?"

"Sometimes. Not often."

I sipped my beer. "Did she hang out with anybody in particular?"

He shrugged. "Mostly the other grad students."

"No steady boyfriend?"

"Not that I know of."

"You wouldn't tell me if you knew, would you?" I suggested.

He smiled at that and shrugged again. He kept polishing. I drank a little. One of the things that makes a good bartender is a closed yap. This one wouldn't give me the time of day without permission from the guy who owned the clock. I picked up my beer and drifted over to a table to try my luck with some of the customers.

Four people sat at one of the tables, three men and a woman, all about the right age to be students. The men wore the uniform, flannel lumberjack shirts, hair indifferently cut, skin spotted with youth. All three of them peered at me through glasses. The girl was a slim blonde, nicely scrubbed, and almost beautiful. She wore a pink cardigan sweater over a tight t-shirt sprinkled with stars.

"May I sit down?" I asked.

"I hope you're not selling something," one of the boys said, and got a laugh.

"Nothing like that," I said and hooked an empty chair toward me with a toe. "My name is Turner Cronyn."

John introduced me to Fred, Mike, and Marjory.

"I'm a private detective investigating the murder of Misty Morning."

The boys shook their heads in sorrow. The girl sniffled. I was about to speak again when a tall handsome dude exploded from a back room carrying a pizza. He set it down on the table with a flourish, asked if anything else was wanted and, like a bird in a cuckoo clock, went back where he'd come from.

Fred picked up a hot slice, fumbling it so as not to burn his fingers, saw that nobody else had moved, and with embarrassment put it back. For some reason Marjory looked a little worried. Each of them made magic passes through the air over the pizza. The pan rocked, and then triangular slices separated themselves from the pie on the table. Each of the men levitated a slice before him, but Marjory couldn't control her slice any more than she could a paper airplane. We watched with morbid fascination as the slice circled her, tying her in hot mozzarella cheese. She howled with pain, and the three men helped her pull the cheese off, leaving behind angry red lines.

"I can't seem to get that incantation right," Marjory moaned. She stuck two fingers into a glass of water and rubbed them against her face where the hot cheese had been.

"First-year stuff," John said. "I'll help you."

"Thank you, John." Marjory smiled at him.

"Excuse me," a voice behind me said—a little viciously, I thought.

I turned and was looking up at the fat kid with the strangulated fashion sense, Misty's teaching assistant. "Mr. Hillyer, isn't it?" I asked. I stood up and put out my hand.

Hillyer ignored it. "You were hired to protect Misty."

I lowered my hand. "Bad news travels fast I see," I said.

"A funny man," Hillyer said. "Nobody at Stilthins Mort thinks Misty's murder is funny."

Some people make me tired, and Hillyer would be one of them. "Can I help you with something, Mr. Hillyer?" I asked.

"You let Misty get murdered," Hillyer said. "I ought to murder you."

I sighed. "I don't suppose it matters to you," I said, "but the situation is a little more complicated than that. Sit down and we can discuss it."

My suggestion caught him off guard and for a moment his belligerence became confusion. Then he noticed a lot of people watching us, and he was merely embarrassed. He pulled over a chair and sat down at the table with Marjory and me and the others.

"Hey," he said by way of greeting.

"Hey, Herb," the other four said.

"If it makes you feel any better," I went on, "Lord Slex doesn't think much of me either."

"Lord Slex, hah!" Hillyer said with contempt. "He was never half the wizard Misty was, and now that he's getting older, he's losing it entirely."

"He always speaks well of you," I said and took a drink.

Hillyer's eyebrows rose at that. Then he saw he was being kidded. "Yeah, right."

"Do you know what secret project Misty was working on?"

"No. Nobody knew."

"Do you have a key to Misty's apartment?"

Hillyer half-rose from his chair. "What am I, now, a suspect?" he asked.

"Nothing that important," I said. "But I thought you might want to help me find Misty's murderer."

"Are you working with the police?"

"The police and I have agreed to share information." It was almost true. Certainly true enough for Herb Hillyer.

Hillyer sat down again. "Yeah, I had a key. But don't get the wrong idea. A lot of people had a key."

"Too bad, huh?"

The other kids around the table kind of snickered at that.

Hillyer's face went red, and he looked stricken. Perhaps he thought nobody had noticed that he worshiped Misty.

"All right, settle down," I said. "Let's try to focus here. Is that your burgundy Honda Augury out in the lot—the one with the front bumper that looks as if it has the mange?"

"What if it is?"

"Somebody in a car just like it followed us yesterday and then beat us to Misty's apartment. I thought it might have been you. And I thought if it was you, maybe that wasn't the first time you stalked Misty. You might have noticed somebody else with an interest in her."

"*Stalked* is a offensive word," Hillyer said quietly.

"Am I right? Is it your car?"

Hillyer didn't say anything for a long time, but only glared at the pizza as if it had insulted him personally. At last he stood up. "Let's talk over here," he said.

I picked up my beer and followed him to an empty table in a corner of the room under a will o' the wisp. The fairy light made him look smarter and healthier than he was. I wondered what it did to the appearance spell I was wearing.

Hillyer started to speak a few times, but he got no further than a sharp intake of breath. He made a whole catalog of small useless motions with his hands. His eyebrows went up and down. By himself he was a whole circus. I waited. He needed to tell me something, and I was confident he would let fly with it eventually.

"You're right," he said. "That wasn't the first time I followed Misty. But I wasn't stalking her. I never intended to do her any harm. I don't think she even knew I was doing it."

"All right. You weren't stalking her. Bad choice of words. I'll try to get over it if you will."

"Smart mouth," he said.

"It's a curse. Do you want a beer?" I asked and sipped my own.

"No, thanks," he said in a calmer tone. "A few days ago I was hanging out in front of Misty's apartment when I noticed another guy doing the same. He was short and ugly and dressed all in red."

"He had a big nose like a cauliflower?"

"That's him. Who is he?"

"We'll get back to that. Go on."

He glanced at the table where Marjory and her admirers were eating pizza. They weren't paying any attention to us.

"I approached him and ordered him to leave Misty alone. He just laughed at me. He said, 'I might say the same to you, kid. Get a life.'"

"The nerve."

"Yeah. It was the same guy I saw you chasing into the canyon yesterday just before you found Misty dead."

"How do you know I found her dead? The newspaper didn't say who found her."

"Just a guess. It was you, wasn't it?"

He may have been arrogant and lovesick, but he wasn't stupid. I nodded. "Go on."

"While you were chasing that guy, another guy ran from Misty's building. He wore a costume spell that made him look like Brent Martin."

"The Prohibition-era movie actor?"

Hillyer nodded.

"You saw this second guy leaving, but you didn't see him arrive?"

"Maybe he was already inside when all of us got there."

"Or maybe he has nothing to do with Misty at all." I rubbed the back of my neck. There were too many mysterious guys around.

"Who is he?" Hillyer asked. "The little ugly guy."

"I don't know. Down at Stilthins Mort I thought he was watching me. But maybe I was just something to look at while he waited for Misty."

"You were supposed to protect her," Hillyer said, letting his anger and frustration boil over again. He set his fat hands flat on the table as if pushing it against the floor.

"You were there, too," I pointed out. "And you didn't save her either."

His eyes got big and grew shiny with tears. He rubbed one eye with the heel of his hand while he looked anywhere but at me.

"Did you kill her?" I demanded.

"I loved Misty," he said, and put his head down on his folded arms.

I took my time sipping my beer, waiting for him to come up for air. He hadn't looked up again by the time I finished, so I stood to leave. "Hey, Mr. Cronyn," one of the students called as I walked across the room.

I went back to the table where the four students were sitting. "You rang?" I said as I sat down. Most of the pizza was gone and the marks on Marjory's face had faded. Time marches on.

John looked from side to side dramatically, making sure the coast was clear. Then he lowered his head and whispered to the table. "I know some people who didn't like Misty," he confided.

"Oh?"

"A rumor is going around that she was working on something

really big, but that she wasn't going to sell it to PrestoCorp. She felt she could get a better deal elsewhere. If you know what I mean."

"I do," I said, thinking about what Misty had told me. Apparently student rumors flew beneath the board's radar.

"Anything else?"

"Somebody hired by PrestoCorp did it," Fred said. "That's what we think."

We nodded at each other, all very secret agent. I saluted the table and continued to the door. I stopped briefly at a pay phone and spent a few minutes with the phone book. I found what I wanted and went outside. Factoids in my head rattled against each other as I drove back down the hill.

CHAPTER ELEVEN
AN INSULTING IDEA

Twenty minutes later I made the big left turn on the flying ramp that looked like something from a science-fiction cover painting of a futuristic city, and went south on the San Diego Freeway. As usual, the San Diego was choking on its own traffic, and it took me another half hour to get to the Crenshaw exit.

Driving south on Crenshaw took me past squat raw phlogiston tanks and into something called the South Bay Business Park. The neat two-story office buildings no more made a park than the tanks made a forest, but maybe real estate people have better imaginations than I do. The building I wanted looked just like all the others except that big letters on a wall spelled out PrestoCorp. I parked and went inside.

The lobby was a big air-conditioned room made of chrome and glass. One wall was completely taken up with a photographic montage of all the PrestoCorp products. Somewhat larger than the other photos was one of this year's Nexus that changed colors every now and then as it rolled along an empty but picturesque road. Misty Morning was important to them— oh yes she was.

A dark-haired woman sat behind a desk that was three steps above the floor of the lobby, like the ornament on top of a wedding cake.

I climbed her little staircase and smiled at her. She smiled back, but it was as meaningless as a facial tic. "My name is Turner Cronyn. I'm a private detective here to see Heather

Hamish," I said casually.

"Do you have an appointment?"

"No. But I think she'll want to see me. It concerns Misty Morning."

Her eyebrows went up, and she did calisthenics with her lips. "I'll see if she's in. Please have a seat." With difficulty she recovered her smile.

Sitting across from the photo collage I could not hear what the receptionist said into her telephone, but she was having a serious conversation with somebody.

"Sir?"

A woman with the figure of a hot dog was standing at the foot of a stairway. She wore a gray herringbone suit and pumps the same undistinguished brown as her hair. Glasses with black frames and thick lenses hung from a cord around her neck. She lifted the glasses and peered at me through them.

"I am Mary Reed," the woman said, "Dr. Hamish's assistant. Please step this way."

Mary Reed and I did not speak as I followed her up the stairs to the second floor. She led me along a hallway painted and carpeted in shades of gray to another waiting room, this one somewhat smaller than the one downstairs. Next to a black door tall enough for giraffes was a floor-to-ceiling tank full of darting fish.

"Dr. Hamish will be with you in a moment," Mary Reed said, and walked out without waiting for me to ask her who fed the fish, or even how.

To my surprise Dr. Hamish actually appeared in more or less a moment. She was only slightly older than Misty Morning, and the fact that she would never be beautiful no longer bothered her, if it ever had. Over her dark suit she wore an unbuttoned lab coat so clean it seemed to gleam by its own light. With a benevolent smile she watched two men and two women as they marched from her office carrying clipboards. They looked young enough to have been recruited by PrestoCorp right out of college.

"Mr. Cronyn?" she said as she put out her hand. We shook and she invited me into her office. She indicated a wooden chair that looked as if had been carved from a single redwood burl, and I sat down in it. Her desk was empty but for a skrying ball, a telephone, and a few very clean and flat sheets of paper.

"Mary tells me that you are a private detective who wishes to speak with me about Misty Morning," Dr. Hamish said as she settled behind her desk. She seemed indifferent to the subject. We might have been discussing where to go for lunch. It was just a ploy. If she hadn't been very interested in the subject, I would not now be sitting in front of her.

"I understand that PrestoCorp holds the rights to her spell for the car-of-a-different-color."

Dr. Hamish nodded, her face without expression.

"Would you happen to know what she was working on lately?"

"No." Her answer was as short and abrupt as the slamming of a door. "What exactly is your interest in all this, Mr. Cronyn?" She touched a paper on her desk, letting me know that she was a busy woman with better things to do than talk to idiot detectives.

"You heard that she was dead?" I asked.

"Murdered," Dr. Hamish said, and shuddered. "Terrible."

"More terrible that you think. I was supposed to be protecting her."

"I see," Dr. Hamish replied. "What has that to do with PrestoCorp?"

"Before she died she told me that she would not be selling you whatever she was working on."

"Oh?" She said the word without surprise.

"Yes. She felt that she'd gotten a raw deal on her car-of-another-color."

"I'm sorry she felt that way, but I don't see—"

"I was hired by the members of the board at Stilthins Mort because they thought you might try to find out on your own what she was working on."

"If you are speaking of industrial espionage, I will say only that that's a very insulting idea." Like a soft sea creature, she pulled back into her big leather wing chair and crossed her arms, the picture of affronted virtue.

"Industrial espionage happens," I said, striving to sound reasonable.

"Not at PrestoCorp."

"What about murder?"

Dr. Hamish stood up, the tips of her fingers touching her desk. "That will be quite enough, Mr. Cronyn. I bid you good day."

"I didn't mean to suggest you did it personally," I said without moving.

She picked up her phone and said, "Send security."

"You can throw me out but that won't stop me from discovering the truth!" I cried. I'd always wanted to say that. That fact that I still hadn't moved was making Dr. Hamish crazy.

In a minute or two a uniformed rent-a-cop came in without knocking and stood in the doorway looking a little frightened. He had iron-gray hair and a small pot belly. I don't think he wanted to be there. He poised one hand over his pistol like a frontier gunslinger.

I stood up before shooting began.

"If you come back here, Mr. Cronyn," Dr. Hamish said, "I will have you arrested."

"But I haven't had a chance to ask you how you feed the fish."

"Good day, Mr. Cronyn." She nodded at the security guy, and he grabbed me by the arm using a grip that was much stronger than I'd expected. I didn't fight him. He walked me through the waiting room and into the hallway, where he let go. He pointed meaningfully at the exit and escorted me back along the hallway to the stairs, which we descended to the lobby.

At the doors he gently put a hand on my arm. "She means it," he said in a voice that was gravelly from a lifetime of smoking. "Don't come back."

"Thanks for the warning," I said, and went out. I'd done

everything I'd meant to do at PrestoCorp. Now it was all up to Dr. Hamish.

CHAPTER TWELVE
ENOUGH ROPE

I was halfway to Cal Thau when my cell phone played a few bars of the Sorcerer's Apprentice.

"Cronyn," I said into the cell phone.

"Turner Cronyn, the detective?" a woman's voice at the other end asked.

"That's me," I said. I hated to drive and talk on the cell phone at the same time, but I'd gotten the thing so clients could find me. I hoped the lady was a client and not just trying to sell a correspondence course in fingerprinting.

"Could you please come to Enough Rope in Venice as soon as possible?"

"What's your problem?"

"I'd rather discuss that with you in person, if you don't mind."

The secretive type. "All right," I said. "Give me the address."

She gave me an address on Abbot Kinney, and I told her I'd be there in half an hour or so, depending on traffic.

"Ask for Miss Rule," she said.

We wished each other a good day and hung up.

I still wanted to speak with a lord or two at Cal Thau and at least one of Misty's relatives, but now that I had the possibility of a paying gig they could wait. I didn't think Misty would mind. She would understand that even a detective has to eat.

I made surprisingly good time up the San Diego Freeway to Washington Boulevard and then went west. As I crossed the line into Mar Vista, the sky was suddenly covered with a gray overcast thick as a sweatshirt—no magic involved, just the traditional coastal low clouds and fog. I turned onto Abbot Kinney and found Enough Rope between a tiny restaurant with two tables out in front and a gallery that seemed to specialize in art made from brightly painted car parts.

I parked up the street and walked back. In the window of Enough Rope were wall hangings, plant holders, and other objects made from beads strung along rough brown lengths of rope all knotted together. I was a little surprised that a store specializing in macramé could stay in business. Macramé had been pretty popular about the time I'd been a student at Stilthins Mort but the craze had lasted no longer than the excitement over chia wizards.

I opened the door and was announced by the tinkle of a single bell. The dim place was crowded with more of the same kinds of hairy projects as those in the window. I picked up a flat and tightly wound coil of rope. Coaster? High fiber cookie?

"How may I help you today?"

I turned to see a woman standing just in front of a counter that divided the storefront from a back room. She was handsome rather than beautiful, with a face full of intelligence and a body that was not fat but substantial and solid. Jet-black hair fell in waves to her shoulders. She wore an elegant sky-blue dress that looked like a sheet that had been artistically draped around her.

"I'm Turner Cronyn," I said. "I'm here to see Miss Rule."

"I am Miss Rule," the woman said. The knowledge seemed to please her. She went to the front door of the shop, locked it, and turned over the card in the window so that it announced they were closed. "Come with me, please," she said, and led me around the counter. She held aside a curtain and let me walk ahead of her.

The back room was nearly bare and very clean, decorated with a few pieces of simple wooden furniture. The wooden floor shone in light from a chandelier that would have been more appropriate in a formal dining room. A beaded curtain hanging from another doorway told me there was at least one more room farther back. In the middle of the room was a table that was almost too large for it.

Sitting at the table were two more women. One might have been in high school except for her expression of calm wisdom. The other could have been anywhere from 60 to 105. Her hair was a luminescent white. She wore no glasses, but she didn't seem to have any trouble seeing. They were dressed in the same trick Greco-Roman origami-type blue dresses as Miss Rule and could have been her daughter and her mother. Miss Rule sat down between them. Unpleasantly, I was reminded of the board at Stilthins Mort.

"Mr. Cronyn," Miss Rule said, "this is Miss Spinner," pointing to the very young woman, "and this is Miss Cutter," pointing to the very old woman. The two nodded but said nothing. "We would like to hire you to help our granddaughter find the person who stole Eulalie Tortuga's soul."

"She's the granddaughter of all three of you?" I asked, confused.

"Yes," Miss Rule said. "Is the relationship of the clients to each other important?"

"I suppose not. How did you happen to choose me? Did I come recommended or did you throw a dart at the phone book?"

"One way is as good as another," Miss Rule said.

Her answer meant nothing, of course. I let it drift.

She spoke again. "What are your charges, Mr. Cronyn?"

"A hundred a day plus expenses."

Miss Spinner pushed a check across the table at me. I picked it up and saw that I had the same $700 back again.

"Something wrong, Mr. Cronyn?"

"No. Nothing. It's just funny how things work out, that's all. What makes you think somebody has stolen Eulalie Tortuga's soul?"

"This morning's paper suggested that Ms. Tortuga was now a zombie. If that is true, it means her soul has been taken."

"And what exactly is your granddaughter's interest?"

"She and Ms. Tortuga were very good friends."

I was about to explain that soul-searching was a little out of my line, which at best was a mediocre pun, when a fourth woman came in through the beaded curtain and stopped me. To say she was beautiful was to say the Taj Mahal was a building. Her off-white skin had no flaw that I could see, and I looked plenty close. Her features had been chiseled by a master, and thinking about a figure such as hers had driven mad better men than I. Her hair was a color of light not otherwise found in nature, but only because nature couldn't be that lucky twice. Usually, if only for my own amusement, I notice how a woman is dressed; but in this instance very little information got through to my brain except the experience of the astonishing woman herself. I'm afraid I gaped.

"This is our granddaughter, Astraea Scales," Miss Rule said. She didn't seem surprised by the effect her granddaughter had on me.

I nodded. Ms. Scales smiled. I had never received a gift half so wonderful. My body buzzed with good feelings. Whatever questions I'd been about to ask had evaporated with the woman's arrival.

"I will enjoy watching you work," Ms. Scales said.

I nodded.

"Shall we go?" she suggested. Her voice seemed to come from far away.

I nodded again.

Ms. Scales got her purse, then touched cheeks with each of the three women at the table.

Just walking Astraea Scales up the block to where I'd parked, I felt like a guy escorting the prom queen to the big dance. Nobody fainted on that short walk, but upon seeing Ms. Scales a couple of guys backed away clutching their hearts. They probably wouldn't die. Love can be troublesome, but it is rarely fatal.

I opened the passenger door for her and helped her get in before I slammed it. Damn! When had I washed the car last? I ran around the front of the car and got in. For the first time

I noticed her legs. Perfect, of course. Long, slim, and well-formed. A Mozart sonata in stockings.

CHAPTER THIRTEEN
JUSTICE

"So," I said, "Ms. Scales—"

"Please call me Astraea," she said.

I tried not to read too much into that. "Then you must call me Turner," I said with all the gallantry of a duke in a high school play.

We sat for a while, each of us bathing in the glow of the other's charm. "I think we should start by taking a look at the scene of the crime. Where did Eulalie Tortuga live?"

"I have no idea," Astraea said.

I wasn't in danger, and I was seven hundred bucks ahead, so I was surprised and suspicious but not yet upset. "Your three grandmothers said you and she were good friends."

"I am a friend of all who are victims."

"I get it," I said. "'A friend of those who have no friends,' like Boston Blackie." I wondered who was kidding whom.

"I don't understand."

I didn't like women who spoke in riddles, particularly when a couple of first-class riddles were already on the table. Particularly again when the woman was supposed to be on my side. If Astraea Scales was going to be a high-maintenance woman, not even her ethereal beauty and seven hundred bucks would make it worth my while to stick around. "Are you, in your own inimitable way, trying to tell me something?" I asked. She was still beautiful, but I was getting used to it—I could manage it now.

"I am Justice," Astraea said.

I blinked. "Justice?" I repeated.

"I am Justice," she said again, still very serious, "daughter of Zeus and Themis. But I am not a detective. Justice does not reach out and find people. People are brought to Justice. Bringing criminals to me will be your job."

"I see," I said while wondering how much trouble it would be to take her back to her grandmothers, if that's what they were. If I did, I would have lost fourteen hundred bucks in one day, which was pretty good even for me.

It was possible that she was Justice, but that was about as likely as my number coming up in the Lotto. Most people saw a fairy every now and then, if only from afar. But the ancient gods and goddesses were more like flying saucers. On the "where there's smoke, there's fire" theory, a few people believed that they walked among us, and a few more than that wanted to believe. But it was a very small crowd indeed that claimed to have actually seen one, actually talked to one, actually been given stock market tips by one—and most of those people were screwy: crackpots, shysters, freaks, and quarter-wits. The thought that I was about to join their cockeyed ranks was not appealing. Of course, I did not yet believe that Astraea Scales was anything but an extraordinarily beautiful woman with a rich fantasy life. I guess I didn't have to believe she was Justice in order to take her on as a client.

"You do not see, Turner, not yet. Eulalie Tortuga's present condition represents an impossibility. A zombie is a person who has had his or her soul removed. Making a zombie is not an easy operation, not even for one of your wizards. I suspect a keres."

"Keres?"

"One of the Dogs of Hades." She paused to see if I was following her. Then she explained further. "A keres is a minor god who carries the soul of a dead person to the underworld."

"It's a job, I guess," I said.

"You are correct. The time and circumstances of a person's death are determined by the Fates. If a soul is taken before the appointed hour, that person will become a zombie and stay that way until the soul returns. And that is certain to happen because a soul is not easy to dispose of. Just throwing it into the ocean will not avail you. It will seek out its body and reattach itself."

"Uh huh," was all I said. She was cute for a nut bar, but she was still a nut bar. "Somebody obviously managed the trick with Eulalie Tortuga's soul."

"Yes," she said. "It seems that someone has given substance to a keres legend."

Neither of us spoke for a moment. Astraea looked at me intently without smiling. Whatever she had just said, no matter how crazy, had great meaning for her and she wanted it to have great meaning for me. I was being paid to do a job and would try to satisfy her.

I tore my eyes away and started the engine, then drove back along Washington Boulevard looking for a place I'd heard of but had never been in. I should have won an award for keeping my eyes on the road.

"Where are we going?" Astraea asked.

"Maybe Vic Tortuga, Eulalie's estranged husband, knows where she lived," I said, answering her question, but sort of sideways.

"You know Vic Tortuga?" Astraea sounded surprised.

I guess she had a right to be surprised. Even to myself I didn't seem like the type who mixed with bestselling authors. "Of course not," I said. "But he's famous. That ought to buy us something."

She nodded, though I don't think she had any more idea what I was talking about than the flowers that bloom in the spring.

A few blocks later I pulled into a corner pod mall, and I ran around to the passenger's side to let her out of my car. We walked into a place called Jack's Magic Bean, a coffee joint where I could rent a skrying ball by the hour—or so I had heard.

Jack's was quaint. It smelled wonderful, as most coffee establishments do. A sack of beans leaned against the door holding it open, and a lot of original art by local artists hung on the walls.

As I had hoped, on each table was a skrying ball.

The place was nearly empty. A woman sitting in the window read a paperback novel between sips from her cup. A couple of guys in back were playing chess. They looked up when we came in as if they were expecting someone and kept watching us as we crossed to an empty table. I didn't think they were watching me.

A moment after Astraea and I sat down, a very thin woman wearing a black spandex top and black pants danced toward us as if she were auditioning for a musical. Astraea and I each ordered a mocha-something, and I asked for a key I could use to start the skrying ball.

After a few minutes, our waitress returned with a couple of steaming mugs and a spell packet. While the two guys in back watched Astraea drink her coffee, I emptied the glitter from the packet over the skrying ball, spoke the spell printed on the packet, and the globe came alive. The Microsoft genie appeared inside, lit from the bottom to make him appear wise and a little sinister.

"Give me the maJsys," I said softly.

The genie nodded and blinked and shrank to the size of a walnut down at the bottom of the globe. The maJsys magician appeared and asked me what I wanted. "Tell me about Vic Tortuga," I said.

The magician thought for a moment and began to talk about Vic Tortuga: his midwestern upbringing, his early success in publishing and TV, his list of books. None of it was useful.

"How are we doing?" Astraea asked.

"Fine," I said, a little irritably. "Would you like a muffin?"

"No, thanks. You didn't think his home address would be online, did you?"

"No," I said as I frowned at the globe. The magician stared back at me, his expression as flat and unreadable as ever. "Is Vic Tortuga appearing anywhere?" I asked him.

"Vic Tortuga will appear at thirty-five book stores in the next month where he will sign his latest book, *The Rack of Time:*

Looking for Pain in All the Right Places." The magician shrank and joined the genie at the bottom of the globe and was replaced by a list of bookstores along with dates and times. Many of the dates had already passed, but one of his signings would take place that evening at a store called Words, etc. in Sherman Oaks.

I took a pad from my pocket and quickly copied the information I wanted.

"Find something?" Astraea asked as she looked at me over her cup. She had large beautiful eyes. I think they were purple. Except that people don't have purple eyes, do they?

I held up a hand. "Thank you," I said to the skrying ball. "That'll be all." The genie expanded to full size again, winked at me, and the ball went blank. The glitter on the globe became gray ash that blew away in the timid breeze coming in the doorway. "He's going to have an autograph party this evening. We'll go."

"Why should he tell you anything?"

"Maybe he won't. Do you want to come and help me find out?"

"Yes, indeed. I am fascinated by your methods."

"Well, they're fascinating," I admitted. "Watch now, and you'll see more," I said as I took out my phone and used a simple spell to call my parents' number. While I listened to the ring, I put my hand over the mouthpiece. "Dad is a big fan of Vic Tortuga," I told Astraea. "He might know things that the maJsys didn't think to include."

Mom answered the phone, as she always does, and I lost ten minutes while she asked me how I was and then instead of listening told me how *she* was. Astraea watched me calmly while this went on, not bored, not anything. It takes a goddess, I guess. Eventually, I managed to get through to Dad, and I did the same dance with him as I'd done with Mom.

"What can I do you for?" Dad asked at last. "You didn't just call to find out how my geraniums are doing."

"You're right," I said, "though I'm always glad to hear the garden report. What do you know about Vic Tortuga?"

"Great writer."

"And?"

"And what? What do you really want to know?"

"I really want to know where he lives. Also I need to know what sort of guy he is. I'll want to put him into a frame of mind where he'll answer a lot of questions."

"You're working on that Eulalie Tortuga thing, aren't you?" he suggested.

The old man could still astonish me. "How did you know?"

"All that about Eulalie Tortuga was in the paper. Why else would you want to speak to Vic?"

"Maybe I just want his autograph."

"That reminds me," Dad exclaimed, "I just bought a copy of *The Rack of Time: Looking for Pain in All the Right Places.* Can you get it signed for me?"

"How would I—?"

"I know he lives somewhere in Los Angeles, but I have no details, so you'll have to go to his signing this evening at Words, etc."

"Why don't you—?"

"You were going to go anyway, weren't you? I'm leaving for the mystery convention this evening. I won't have time. Come and get the book. Words, etc. is almost around the corner."

We spoke for a few minutes longer, but I knew that visiting the parents was unavoidable.

"I have to visit my parents," I said. "Let me take you home first."

"No need," Astraea said. "Unless I embarrass you."

I decided not to try explaining that having her with me made me feel proud and conspicuous, as if I had 100-dollar bills hanging from my pockets. "No, no," I said quickly.

I was feeling in my pants for money to pay the bill when a man approached our table. He was short and square and dressed all in black except for white piping around the collar of his shirt. His head was not only as bald as a peanut, it was the same general shape. A tiny silver ring hung from his left earlobe. Sneering, he sat down across from me in the chair next to Astraea and put his hand into his pocket. He tried smiling at her, but the smile was less successful than the sneer.

"Cronyn?" he asked as if he wanted to know whether I had a disease by that name.

"Yeah?" I could be tough when necessary.

"You're off the case," the man said.

CHAPTER FOURTEEN
A BROKEN CHAIR

I stared at the man in surprise. "What case?" I asked. I knew what case. I also knew that Dr. Hamish had not disappointed me.

"The Misty Morning case. You're off it."

"Go peddle your papers," I said. "Tell Dr. Hamish that the next time she sends somebody around, I'll break his arm."

His eyes widened at that, then he relaxed into his chair. He even hung his elbow over the back. "You better talk nice to me, Cronyn. I have a gun in my pocket."

"Uh huh. I thought you were just glad to see me."

"What?"

"Never mind."

Without warning, the man's chair collapsed, dropping him to the floor. While he was still sitting there among the kindling, puffing and blowing and trying to figure out what had happened, Astraea felt around in his coat pocket and pulled out a pistol. She handed it to me. I put it into my coat pocket.

"Pretty lucky that happened," I said, contemplating Astraea in a whole new way.

"Coincidence," she replied suggesting it was no such thing.

Our waitress came over to see what the rumpus was. She looked a little worried. "That's never happened before," she said after she'd apologized quite a bit.

"Don't worry about it," I said. "My friend will survive."

"Oh sure," the man said as he climbed to his feet. He pulled over another chair, sat down in it kind of gingerly, and smiled at her.

"Free coffee and muffins all around," the waitress said and went away, taking our bill with her.

While he got comfortable with the idea of sitting, the man split his attention between Astraea and me.

"Let's start over again," I said. "You know my name. What's yours?"

"Nosmo King," the man said.

"And you work for Dr. Heather Hamish at PrestoCorp," I said.

King nodded. "I guess you think you're pretty smart," he said.

"About average. I guess despite her big talk Dr. Hamish doesn't like me sniffing around."

"That's right."

"I guess that means she has something to hide."

"She didn't kill Misty, if that's what you mean."

"What else might I mean?" I was slicker than a guy trying to sell himself insurance.

King thought that over while the waitress, smiling nervously, set down three cups of coffee and three muffins—cherry walnut by the look of them. King continued to think while he carefully peeled the paper from his muffin. Astraea and I didn't touch anything. We just watched him.

Eventually he made a decision. "Dr. Hamish hired me to find out what Misty was doing. That's all."

"And you failed or you two wouldn't be so sensitive about it."

"In a manner of speaking. I got so far as to make a copy of her laboratory log. Actually I made two copies, one for Dr. Hamish and one for me." He preened as if he'd just returned from the first flight to Mars.

"How did you do that? Imps were guarding the drawer in which she kept it." I was just guessing, but I thought it was a good guess. What else would the imps be guarding?

King enjoyed my curiosity while he chewed. He sipped his

coffee and leaned back in his chair again. "I dated her for a while. Sometimes she left stuff lying around."

Assuming what he told me was true, they were probably mercy dates. I hoped so. I hated to think of Misty falling for this guy.

"So are you off the case?" he went on.

"No. I still don't know who murdered her."

"All right, then," he said. "I see you're a pretty smart guy. I'm figuring that you and me should ought to work together. Whatever you learn about Misty's project you give to me so I can pass it along to Dr. Hamish. See?"

"If you have her log, don't you know everything there is to know about Misty's project?"

For some reason that question made King squirm. "Not exactly," he said.

"Meaning what?"

"It ain't important. What is important is that whatever information you get goes through me. See?"

"I don't give it away," I said, though at the moment I had nothing to sell. Then a clever idea struck me. "You stole her papers," I said. "Maybe you *killed* her, too." He goggled at me just as he had goggled at Astraea, but this time without the crooked smile.

"Maybe *you* killed her," King suggested right back at me.

"If you think you can make that stick, give it a try. But *I'm* not the one who dated Misty so I could get into her laboratory."

"Laboratory, pants—what's the diff?" he asked. He winked at Astraea. His sophistication seemed to have no effect on her.

"I'll explain it to you when you're older, if we're still acquainted then. Meanwhile, I believe you mentioned Misty's lab book."

"Did I?" he said off-handedly.

"Don't go simple on me, Nosmo," I said. "You want my cooperation. I'm willing to give it to you for a little reciprocation. You show me the book and I promise to go through you, should I ever again have the urge to report to Dr. Hamish at

PrestoCorp." I didn't think I ever would, but I could have been wrong.

"Why should I trust you?"

"Because you have no choice. Unless you'd like the police to come around with difficult questions. PI's license all up to date? Any outstanding parking tickets?"

He looked up at the corner of the room while he twisted his lip to help him think that over. "I don't carry the book with me," he said at last.

"Large, is it?"

He chuckled knowingly. "See you in an hour at Finks on LaBrea. Bring your friend." He winked at Astraea again. "Can I have my gun back?"

"Maybe later," I said. "You'd better go. We don't want to have to wait for you at Finks."

King nodded, got up and swaggered out of the restaurant.

* * * * * * *

"Thanks for disarming Mr. King," I said.

"I am Justice," she said. "You are the mechanism by which criminals are brought to me."

"That's all saving me meant to you?"

She grinned. Very nice. "You are a good man, Turner. I like you."

I nodded. I felt good. More than that, I felt that I could trust her, and that she would be a good person to bounce ideas off of. Maybe she would give me the morning line straight from the mouths of the gods. She was Justice, after all. *And* she liked me. Well, well.

"I like you, too," I said. "And if you're really interested in helping me you could share what the gods know about Eulalie Tortuga."

"What makes you think they know anything?"

"That's no answer. They wouldn't be gods if they didn't have special knowledge."

Astraea took some time touching her tongue to the tip of one finger, and using the wet tip to pick up a muffin crumb from her plate and putting it into her mouth. I liked watching her do it, but the performance wasn't getting us anywhere.

"Or," I went on, "we could just figure out what happened to Eulalie Tortuga the old-fashioned way—you know, using leg work and asking questions and being accosted by strangers in coffee shops."

Astraea smiled shyly. "I think the old-fashioned way would be best."

I sighed and shook my head.

She put her hand on my arm. "You might be surprised by the things the gods don't know," she said evenly.

"I might," I remarked, inviting her to tell me.

She said nothing. She'd even stopped playing with her muffin and only stared at me as impassively as a statue. I would have given a lot to know what thoughts were going through her mind at that moment—godlike thoughts or merely crazy ones?

I blinked before she did. "All right," I said. "We won't talk about what the gods know. Is it all right if we talk about what *I* know?"

Theoretically, I was supposed to keep one case separate from another. Anything that a client told me was supposed to be privileged information. Of course, strictly speaking, I didn't have a client in the Misty Morning murder case, so maybe I could stop agonizing over gumshoe ethics.

"Of course. Tell me about Misty Morning."

"How did...?" I began and interrupted myself. "Oh, sure. King and I mentioned her."

"That's right."

After a moment I began again. "Misty Morning was a talented graduate student at Stilthins Mort who was murdered yesterday afternoon. In her laboratory were these sort of space puckers. A pencil almost tore my arm off going into one; it should suck in air but it doesn't. It's possible that things that go in never come back out, but that's more a guess than a theory. The big question is, would the soul and the body stay separate if somebody threw a soul down this kind of transdimensional laundry chute?"

"It might if it was, as you describe it, a one-way chute. Do you believe it is possible that because of these 'puckers' the crime against Misty and the crime against Eulalie are connected?"

"It's possible." I scratched the back of my head. "I don't even know if the murderer noticed them. Certainly, the victim did not become a zombie. She was dead. Therefore, except for the long shot that the person who took Eulalie's soul had access to Misty's laboratory or access to the thing that made the puckers in Misty's laboratory or that the puckers are one-way, there isn't much of a connection."

"As Justice I am interested in the murder as well as in the stealing of Eulalie Tortuga's soul. You have suspects for Misty Morning's murder?"

"I have two so far, a guy wearing a Brent Martin spell and a little guy with a cauliflower nose. I don't think Herb Hillyer can be accused of anything more serious than puppy love."

"Who is Herb Hillyer?"

"Misty's assistant."

"People have killed for love before."

"Hillyer isn't the type." Even as I said it I thought I might be wrong.

"Is it possible the man wearing the Brent Martin spell and the little man with the cauliflower nose are the same man?" Astraea asked.

"I don't think so," I said. "The little guy had to arrive at Misty's house before Herb Hillyer or I did, or without Hillyer seeing him, anyway. That seems impossible given the traffic and the time of day, unless he could do some pretty sophisticated magic or use one of Misty's puckers."

"You can travel in these puckers?"

I shrugged. "Anyway, he could not have both come and gone if the puckers go only one way—which is still open to question. But okay, let's leave the puckers out of it for a moment. There was no sign of forced entry. Which means that somebody she knew could have killed her—almost everybody she knew had a key to her apartment."

"Did the murderer go in and out the back way?"

"There is no back way. I checked."

Astraea nodded.

"Meanwhile," I said, "we're stuck with the little guy and the guy in the Brent Martin spell. If the little guy could magically get into her apartment, he could probably magically get out. If he could magically get out, he had no need to masquerade as Brent Martin."

Astraea absorbed that while I continued.

"I found the little guy with the cauliflower nose in the bushes outside her apartment. He didn't kill her after I found him, and it is unlikely that he would have waited around if he'd killed her before. No, I think our main suspect is the guy in the Brent Martin spell."

"You said Misty lived in an apartment. Could Brent Martin have come out of some other apartment in the building?"

"It's possible. In which case he is not a suspect either."

"Which would leave us with Herb Hillyer," she pointed out agreeably.

"So far," I said. "And we still have all those other people with keys."

We sipped coffee and ate muffins for a while. I could have driven her home and investigated Eulalie Tortuga myself, or even driven her home and given back the money. But she was pleasant to talk to, and her Justice superpowers had already come in handy once. Plus the fact that giving back money is a bad habit to get into. I seemed to have acquired a partner.

"Are you really Justice?" I asked.

"Yes," she said, leaving me just where I'd been before I asked the question.

"Let's go," I said. "We have to be at Finks in forty-five minutes."

CHAPTER FIFTEEN
THE RACK OF TIME

Taking the freeway across town was almost worthwhile, but not quite, so I drove east on Washington Boulevard, the traffic thickening all the time. It got worse as I drove north. Astraea and I didn't talk, but she seemed to enjoy the ride.

At Melrose I turned past a sort of shed into the parking lot behind it. The lot was much bigger than the shed but it was full of vehicles, as it always was. I parked next to a streamlined model that seemed to be made of bronze and held together with thousands of rivets. It looked like a Victorian clothes dryer but was probably a two-man submarine. Amazing what people will take on the road.

When Astraea and I got out of the car, I was struck by the heavenly smell of grease and Fink's chili, the secret ingredient of which was probably more grease.

Astraea attracted the usual attention as we walked to the front of the shed, where the word FINK'S was painted on a billboard in big red letters. No explanation was offered, no explanation was needed. Up here the odors rising with the steam inside the shed were damned near strong enough to build on. The line was relatively short, for Fink's, and we stood in it.

"What are we doing here?" Astraea asked. "I am full of coffee and muffins."

I waved away her objection. "Think of what you had at Jack's Magic Bean as dessert," I explained. "This is an entirely different eating experience—heartburn city. You can order anything you want as long as you get chili on it. The rumor is that Orson Welles used to visit this place in his limo, his driver would order six chili dogs, and then they would tool around the city while Orson scarfed up the dogs in the back seat." I shrugged. "Cheaper than cocaine, I guess."

"It seems to be a popular place," Astraea admitted.

"There's always a line, even in the middle of the night. Gangs have declared it neutral territory. Nobody wants to be denied their fix."

When I got to the front of the line, I leaned on the counter and spoke to the counter man, ordering two chili dogs and two Mitz root beers. Mitz comes in a variety of flavors, and I believe that Fink's is the only place outside of Israel where you can get any of them. I paid for the food, gave Astraea the two bottles of Mitz, and carried the paper boats full of stomach corroder into a little bricked courtyard in back of the place, where there were a few picnic tables under umbrellas.

I bit into my dog immediately, and with a little encouragement Astraea did the same. She smiled and nodded as she chewed, just as anyone else might. I have never seen a woman look so good with a drip of chili on her chin.

I was thinking about seconds and trying not to burp when Nosmo King showed up carrying a Ralphs shopping bag in one hand and a chili dog in the other. Nobody got out of here without gas.

We waited while King ate his dog and drank his Mitz cola. People came and went. The smell of grease and chili was constant. In a disgusting display, King licked the remaining chili out of his paper boat, then swallowed the last of his Mitz. He used an untidy wad of napkins to wipe his face and hands. "Food of the gods," he remarked.

Astraea smiled. "Soon, perhaps," she said.

"Huh?"

"If your hands are clean, Nosmo, let's see it," I said.

He rubbed his hands together and thrust one of them into the bag. He pulled out a flat book with a black and white marbled cover. A brown stain that might have been coffee spread from the spine. The corners were worn and rounded, as if the book had been used a lot, and not carefully. He held it out as if offering his business card and folded his arms.

I opened the cover, allowing the light wind to riffle the pages like a magician about to do a card trick, and saw that Misty had wasted no time. The book began at the top of the first page with formulae and small paragraphs of words, all in tiny neat cursive writing.

I couldn't make out any of it. I had expected that I would not understand the formulae or her notes. But I couldn't even understand individual letters or symbols. I flipped through the rest of the book. A few pages at the end were empty, but the rest of it was the same kind of gibberish as the first page. I passed the book to Astraea. She studied it for less time than I had and put it down in a clean spot on the table.

"I'm generally pretty good with English," I said. "What's the gag?"

King leaned toward me on his arms and looked from side to side as if he were about to impart secret information. "I can't read it, and as far as I know Dr. Hamish can't read it either. But that doesn't change anything. I held up my end of the bargain. If you discover any information that might interest Dr. Hamish, it has to go through me."

I nodded while I thought about the book. I knew that wizards sometimes kept track of their experiments in code. If Misty was very clever, and she obviously was, maybe no one would ever know what the book said.

"All right," I said as I reached for the book and held it. "Anything I have for Dr. Hamish goes through you." Which was not exactly what he had proposed, but he didn't seem to notice. He folded up the shopping bag, saluted me with a single sharp nod, leered at Astraea, and strode away as if his pants were on fire.

"Can you read it?" I asked Astraea.

"No. Is it important?"

"It might be. Of course, if I can't figure out what it says, we'll never know. Do you want another dog?"

"No, thank you," she said and lifted one hand to stifle a small cute burp. "Perhaps some other time."

"Not the food of the gods?"

"Not exactly."

We walked back to my car, where I threw Misty's log book into the trunk. I drove us over to Crescent Heights, then north past small neat houses toward the Hollywood Hills. We crossed a street that led into a private community called Mount Olympus.

"Your people live in there?" I asked.

"Some," Astraea said, and refused to say more on the subject.

Crescent Heights became Laurel Canyon as we climbed. Soon we were swerving past houses and stores that would have looked more comfortable in a bucolic mountain village. The road straightened out as we dipped into the San Fernando Valley. We crossed Ventura and the traffic thinned again.

My parents still lived in the house where I grew up, a boxy and unpretentious affair with an attached garage at the front and all covered with a not very interesting shade of brown stucco. It was not exactly around the corner from Words, etc., but even so, getting to the bookstore wouldn't take more than fifteen minutes.

I parked, and we strolled up the cement walk to the front door.

"Nice geraniums," Astraea said.

"Don't forget to tell my dad," I said. "They're his pride and joy."

I was a little surprised that I had to knock on the door. Mom is usually right on top of things socially.

"Yes?" she said through the door.

"Don't be cute, Mom. It's me, Turner," I hesitated, "and friend." Astraea shined her smile on me. Then it occurred to me that my parents hadn't seen me since Lord Slex had changed my appearance. Mom probably thought I was selling brushes, at the very least. "How are Mortimer and James T?" I asked.

Behind the door all was silence. I could imagine the quick whispered conversation between Mom and Dad.

Mom opened the door a little and studied us. "Hurry," she said after a moment. "Don't let the cats out."

We slipped into the house as if we were anarchists arriving at a cell meeting. Inside, the house was nothing special either, except that I'd spent the first eighteen years of my life there and knew every board in the hardwood floor by name. Mom was a short woman, long past middle age, with a nimbus of white hair that looked as if it had been styled by the same person who did hair for George Washington.

Dad stood nearby, probably to make sure I didn't cold-cock Mom and head for the family silver. He was taller than Mom, and a little overweight. He had the profile of a cartoon bear. "Come into the light," he said. "I want to have a look at you."

With his hand gripping my arm, he escorted me along the narrow entryway and into the living room. Mortimer, the gray-and-white cat, was sleeping on the living room table. James T, who was orange with a white target on each side, was sitting in the kitchen doorway watching us solemnly.

"I'm sure you have a good reason for not looking like yourself," Dad said. "Let's have it." He sounded friendly, but he hadn't loosened the grip on my arm.

"One of my old instructors at Stilthins Mort put a spell on me."

"Why would he do that?" Mom asked, looking worried.

"It was part of a job," I said. "I'll change back when I get the chance, I guess. Maybe not. I'm getting used to looking like this."

Mom picked up a framed photo and showed it to Astraea. "Such a handsome boy," Mom said. "He doesn't need spells."

Astraea took the photo. While she studied it, Dad noticed Astraea for the first time. His eyes got wide, and they shifted to Mom and back to Astraea. I knew Astraea's virtue was safe, but that didn't prevent Dad from feeling guilty about what was probably the first thought that came into his head. As usual,

Astraea seemed not to notice. I was increasingly aware that the chances of her embarrassing me in public were remote.

"Who is this?" Dad asked.

"Astraea Scales," I said. "We're working on a case together." Dad nodded.

"Very handsome," Astraea said and handed back the photo.

"The wizard just firmed up my chin a little," I said.

Dad shook his head. "At least you had a haircut lately," he said. He was still holding my arm. I'd have to convince him to let go before it went numb.

"I can show you where the secret hiding place is," I said. There were removable floor boards in the corner of a back bedroom. Under them Dad kept a strongbox full of important papers and some cash. Theoretically nobody but my parents and I should even know of its existence.

"What did I promise to get you if you learned to tie your shoes?" Mom asked.

"Cowboy boots," I said. "But I never got them."

"That's him," Mom said. "He never could let that go," she explained to Astraea.

Dad released my arm and sat down heavily in an overstuffed chair.

"Please sit down," Mom said. "I'll get some fruit."

I knew protesting would do no good. "Thanks, Mom."

"Beautiful geraniums," Astraea said.

Dad beamed.

Astraea and I settled at opposite ends of the couch while Mom put a bowl of grapes in front of us on the coffee table and sat down in a chair she pulled away from the living room table. Idly she scratched Mortimer behind the ears. He turned his head and leaned into her hand. She began a story about the quality of the grapes and the good deal she had made purchasing them.

I let her continue while Astraea and I munched on fruit. "You're a demon shopper, all right," I said at last. "But as good as the grapes are, they're not why I'm here. We need to talk about Vic Tortuga."

"I'll get the book," Mom said, and rushed from the room.

"What do you have so far?" Dad asked.

"Not much," I said. "We suspect that somebody stole Eulalie Tortuga's soul, making her a zombie. We have a suspicion about who did it and how, but not why."

"Zombies aren't so common. What makes you think that's Eulalie Tortuga's problem?"

"Actually, Astraea suggested it," I said.

Dad leaned forward and plucked one grape from a bunch. "And what is Astraea's interest in all this?" he asked, being careful not to look at her.

Maybe Astraea would embarrass me after all. "I've taken her on as an assistant," I said before she could launch into her story about being Justice.

"You got good taste in assistants," Dad said. "And that might make things easier for you."

"How so?" I asked.

"Tortuga fancies himself quite a man with the ladies," Dad said. "You'll have more luck getting him to pay attention if Astraea is with you."

I nodded. Dad didn't need to know I was going to take her with me anyway.

Mom came back into the living room brandishing Dad's copy of *The Rack of Time* and handed it to me. I looked on the back flap where, as I'd hoped, I found a photograph of Vic Tortuga. He wore big dark-framed glasses on a square handsome face. A contrived curl of hair fell across his forehead, and he'd forgotten to button the top three buttons of his shirt. One open hand seemed to be attempting to grab a flying bird out of the air, but he probably was just making a point. I handed the book to Astraea. She studied the picture for a moment and then closed the book.

"We're having chicken," Mom said. "Stay and eat."

"Not tonight, Mom. Astraea and I have things to do." I stood up, hoping my parents would take the hint. Dad picked up a magazine; for him Astraea and I were no longer there.

"Of course," Mom said without a trace of sarcasm. "I understand. When you get work, you have to work."

She walked us back to the front door, and we had almost escaped when she called out to us. "Don't forget to pick your father up from the airport tomorrow."

"Right," I replied. "The mystery convention. The broom lands at four p.m."

"If I'm lucky," Dad called from the other room.

We all said good-bye again, and I managed to get to the car with Astraea. "Dinner?" I suggested when we were inside and the doors were locked.

"I think not. I am full of muffins and chili dogs."

"Me, too," I admitted. "Just checking. Don't want any of my clients starving."

"Not likely," she said.

We drove up to Ventura Boulevard, which was the usual conga line of heavy traffic. After creeping for a long block I found Words, etc. and was able to park in a big lot around back. It would be almost an hour before the signing began, and hanging out in my car seemed a little low-class.

As we walked to a nearby coffee joint we passed the bookstore window in which a banner announcing Vic Tortuga's appearance that evening was displayed along with a creative arrangement of his books. Eager-looking folks were already waiting in line for him.

Inside the coffee joint we found an empty table and sat down. After we ordered, the waiter stood for a moment more than he needed to just looking at Astraea, then remembered himself and headed for the kitchen.

"So," I said. "Tell me about yourself."

I didn't have to ask Astraea twice, but immediately got an earful. She had two sisters, Eunomia and Irene. Eunomia's job was to see that laws were observed, and Irene was in charge of peace.

"Hmm," I remarked as I built a fanciful wall from individually wrapped sugar cubes. "What do you do when you're not running around with private investigators?" I asked.

"My sisters and I dance with the Graces."

"That sounds like fun," I said. "Anywhere special? Some club in Hollywood?" I immediately wanted to reach into the air and grab back that sarcastic crack, but it was too fast for me. I was glad to see that it left no mark on Astraea.

"You don't believe me," she said evenly. It was just a statement of fact.

"I don't know, myself," I said. "I saw that chair collapse under Nosmo King. Did you do it, or was I just lucky?"

"I am Justice," she said.

"I've never met a goddess before. I don't suppose many people have."

"We're around," she said.

Our steaming coffee mugs came and the discussion stopped until the waiter went away, which took a while. He seemed very concerned about whether Astraea had enough cream and sugar.

"Do you know how your grandmothers chose me for this job?" I asked as I stirred my coffee with a wooden stick.

"It was fated," Astraea said.

I nodded. Given what I knew—or what I thought I knew— about Astraea, her answer didn't exactly surprise me.

"Well," I said, "bringing folks to justice is my business. If you're Justice, we'll get along fine."

"It's true," she said.

While we sipped, the counter did a swift take-out business, mostly selling to people carrying Vic Tortuga's book. When we were done with our coffee, I paid up, and we walked down to see the man himself.

CHAPTER SIXTEEN
MEETING THE NEW TOLSTOY

With the lowering of the sun, the day had cooled considerably. I loaned Astraea a not-very-fashionable jacket that had been balled up in the trunk of my car. She made it look like a designer original going to the Oscars.

I got Dad's copy of *The Rack of Time* from the front seat, took a moment to scrawl something on the title page, then joined Astraea in the line outside the bookstore. It now extended down the block past the coffee store that was doing terrific business and a stationers that was not.

Getting into the bookstore took about twenty minutes. Before Astraea and I walked through the door three different guys asked me if I had any spare change, and a car full of college guys whistled and made remarks about Astraea as they cruised by. I didn't have any spare change, but Astraea gave each panhandler a quarter. She smiled at the guys in the car, embarrassing them. I thought they might come around the block again, but they didn't.

Astraea and I were quiet, but the people around us had no trouble finding things to talk about. Apparently, many of them had met Vic Tortuga before at other public events. He was something of a local character, known to have a smart mouth and quite a high opinion of himself. A tall, pretty blonde in jeans and a sweater that fit her like a second skin claimed to have had at least one run-in with Mr. Tortuga. To hear her tell it, he'd said to her, "Hey, baby, what do you say to a little fuck?"

And she had replied to him, "Hello, little fuck." She and her two male friends could barely contain their laughter until she'd finished, and when she did they howled like wild things out of the Mato Grosso.

Inside, the store had the heavy comfortable smell of new paper. It was warm, too, and Astraea soon took off the jacket I'd loaned her and hung it over one arm. The autograph line wound among the stacks, giving everyone an opportunity to get a good look at the stock. Somewhere up ahead Vic Tortuga was holding forth. He made passes at the women in the voice of W. C. Fields so that nobody would take offense. Often, laughter spumed into the air as if from a fountain.

The line curled around a bookcase, and I saw Vic Tortuga for the first time. In person he looked a lot like the guy in the photo on the back flap of the book. The main difference was that the curl of hair on the real Vic was plastered by sweat against his forehead, and his face was a little flushed with excitement. Yes, he was a man who liked to meet his public.

Another difference was that he had a companion, a tall rangy woman with short dark hair. Her jeans were fawn colored, and her blue top clung as if it were wet, though I don't think it was. The plunge of her neckline wasn't exactly in good taste, but it was mighty interesting. She had a hard face that was beautiful in a conventional Hollywood way. If she were in the movies, she would play the best friend of the hooker with the heart of gold.

The companion waved her hand over each book as the customer placed it on the table, causing the book to open to the title page by itself and slide across the table to where Vic could reach it. Once he asked her for a glass of water, and she made it appear from a fall of fairy dust. Parlor tricks, the kind of stuff people learn in night school.

Vic Tortuga noticed Astraea when there were still five people ahead of us in line. He kept looking up at her and smiling his most winning famous-author smile. Astraea smiled back, of course. Vic was encouraged by this. He didn't know that she smiled back at everybody. Vic's dark-haired companion glanced at Astraea, frowned as if she'd detected a bad smell.

When my turn came, I set the book down on the table. The companion didn't bother to do her magic over it, and Vic had to grab it with a boardinghouse reach. "Who would you like this to?" he asked me while looking at Astraea. Then he looked down at the book. "What the hell is this?" he asked.

"Just a question," I said. I had written "Where is Eulalie Tortuga?" on the title page just about where Vic Tortuga would normally sign his name. "Do you know the answer?" I asked.

He got a cagey expression on his face, as if he'd just thought of an angle. "I might," he said. "Who wants to know?"

By this time the people behind Astraea and me were rubbernecking to see what the holdup was and grumbling to themselves.

"I'm a detective," I said, "but this is not the time or the place for a discussion. You're disappointing your public."

He looked back along the line. "I guess I am." He nodded at Astraea. "Is she with you?"

"That's right."

"Lyda," he said to the dark-haired companion, "give these nice people my home address. We'll all have a drink together when this is over."

"Is that wise, Vic?" Lyda asked.

"Let me do the thinking, honey," Vic said. "Just give 'em the address."

"Are you going to sign that guy's book?" a man about three back asked in a high voice. Rarely had I seen a man so thin.

"I was waiting for *you* to sign it," Vic said nastily, and the people in line laughed. Even the thin guy laughed. "Do you really want this signed?" Vic asked me.

"Sure," I said. "It's for my father. He thinks you're the new Tolstoy."

"Some people are easily amused. What's his name?"

I told him, and Vic scrawled something in the book. "Later," he said and gestured me aside.

Astraea and I went over to where Lyda was waiting in the

cookbook section. She had written an address on a scrap of paper that had been in the depths of her purse for a few months. "It's near the top of Beverly Glen," she said as she handed the address to me.

"Thanks," I said. I could see something was eating her.

Lyda took a long speculative look at Astraea. "You're the type," she said.

"What type?" Astraea asked.

"The type," she repeated. "His type. I'm his type, too. The world is full of his type." She didn't sound happy about what the world was full of.

"That's good, isn't it?" Astraea asked. "He'll never be lonely."

"I guess you don't know much about loneliness."

"Excuse me?"

"Look, Lyda," I said, "I don't know what sort of cozy little setup you and Vic Tortuga have going, but we're not here to throw any sort of wrench into it. I'm a private detective working on a case. Astraea is my assistant. We want to ask Mr. Tortuga a few questions. That's all."

"That might not be all Vic has in mind."

Astraea and I watched her march back to the table where Vic Tortuga was signing books. She was not quite the stunner that Astraea was, but that didn't mean she was difficult to look at. Walks like hers started fires.

"What was that all about?" Astraea asked.

"She thinks that Vic has a romantic interest in you."

"Vic's with her, isn't he?"

"That's right. I guess she thinks that might not make any difference to Vic."

"It makes a difference to me," she explained firmly.

"I thought it might. Let's get some air."

We left the store, and I took Dad's book back to my car, where I locked it in the trunk along with Misty's log. For a while we browsed up and down the shopping center. In the supermarket Astraea caused two guys to crash their shopping carts together, but that was the only excitement. After a while we wound up sitting behind Vic as he signed books for a few stragglers.

When he was done, he stretched mightily and yawned. "You have the address?" he asked.

I gave him the number. "Top of Beverly Glen."

"Right," he said. "You can follow me. Let's go."

We didn't leave right away, of course. Vic signed a stack of books the store manager had ready for him, then the two of them spent some time pulling each other's legs and laughing about it.

When we went out to the parking lot at last, Vic and Lyda got into a small sporty jelly-bean of a car. A moment later, two industrial strength will o' the wisps ignited over the front bumper. Astraea and I got to my car as quickly as we could, started it, and pulled in behind Vic's car. It had the license VT, which probably didn't mean Vermont.

Vic took off with a roar, and for a minute or two I was close behind him. He couldn't maneuver much on Ventura Boulevard, crowded as it was. But as soon as he turned left onto Beverly Glen, he was off like a shot. He seemed a lot more interested in showing me what a hot driver he was than in making it easy for me to follow him.

I decided that playing his game was pointless, even if my car could have kept up. Astraea reminded me of the address, and some time later we found it, as advertised, near Mulholland, which ran across the spine at the top of the Hollywood Hills. I parked. Inhaling the dry spicy perfume of the hills at night, I walked next to Astraea back along a high hedge to Vic's house, which was just a mass of shadows against the deeper darkness of the hills. We walked up a path set with brick in a herring-bone pattern to the front door, where he'd left the porch light on, which was nice of him. It illuminated the three steps up to the big wooden slab that served as a front door. I knocked.

CHAPTER SEVENTEEN
DIALOG OVER A PB
& J SANDWICH

Lyda opened the door wide and seemed not very happy to be doing it. We walked into an entryway paved with black stone and filled with soft jazzy music. Apparently speakers were hidden everywhere because the music stayed with us as we followed Lyda into the black and pink kitchen, where Vic Tortuga was standing at a counter building himself a peanut butter and jelly sandwich on a saucer. Lyda sat down on a stool near the breakfast nook with her knees almost up to her chin, no more interested in what we said or did than she was in the social life of the paint on the walls.

The kitchen was neat, almost neurotically so, and well-lit by indirect fixtures that artistically tossed the light around. Vic ignored us while he methodically finished making the sandwich. He put away the jelly and the peanut butter and the bread, and dropped a knife and a spoon into the aluminum sink.

"You know who I am," he said. "The cute-as-a-button lady on the stool is Lyda Firebough. And who the hell are you?"

"My name is Turner Cronyn. As I told you at the bookstore, I'm a private detective. This is Astraea Scales, my assistant."

"Interesting name, Astraea. Greek?"

"Latin," Astraea replied.

"Of course," he said as if he'd known it all along.

He lifted the saucer to his mouth to catch the crumbs and took a bite out of his sandwich. "P B and J?" he offered while chomping on it with satisfaction.

"We can see that you're busy, Mr. Tortuga," I said. "If you'll just answer a few questions, Ms. Scales and I will be on our way."

Vic nodded with his mouth full and made a magnanimous gesture with one hand that I took to mean that he was ready to cooperate in any way he could.

"We are investigating the Eulalie Tortuga case. If you can tell us where she lived, we won't trouble you any further."

While he nodded, Vic continued to eat. He poured himself a glass of milk and drank about half of it before he answered. "Who's your client, shamus?"

"Nix," I said. "Confidential."

"I don't have to tell you anything."

"That's right. Except that you and Eulalie were married once. I assume you still have some feeling for her. You might want to know who made her a zombie, and why, and whether she can be cured."

"The police are already on the case. That's why I pay taxes."

"I have advantages the police don't have."

"Such as?"

I smiled at him.

For a moment he didn't like that. He took a lot of trouble setting the empty saucer carefully in the sink, then brushing the crumbs off his hands over the saucer. He grinned at Astraea. "Maybe advantages such as your lovely assistant?"

Now that the conversation had gotten around to Astraea, Lyda began to smolder.

I knew Vic was just shooting in the dark, but if talking to Astraea would make him more cooperative, I could go along with the gag. "Maybe. She has a strong interest in justice."

"I see. Well." He suddenly put his arm through Astraea's and guided her out of the room. "I have a strong interest in justice myself."

When they were gone, Lyda sighed but otherwise didn't move.

"Mr. Tortuga seems to be something of a free thinker," I said.

"He's free with his hands, too. And he cares more about Eulalie than he pretends."

I was pretty sure Astraea could take care of herself, but I moseyed out of the kitchen anyway and followed the sound of their voices to the living room—a large room with an enormous TV sphere at one end. Books crowded floor-to-ceiling bookcases everywhere except where there were windows. Vic and Astraea sat together knee to knee at the corner of the big L of a nubbly maroon couch that took up most of the floor space. I sat down on a matching lounger to one side and let my fingers play with the tiny knots on the fabric. Vic and Astraea pretended I wasn't there and I let them pretend.

"You mean she's here?" Astraea asked, astonished.

"Of course," Vic said. Silly Astraea.

Lyda leaned against the entry to the living room with her arms crossed. She did not give off little puffs of smoke, but she wanted to.

"May I see her?" Astraea asked.

"Come on," Vic invited. "You, too, Cronyn."

As he passed her, Vic tried to pinch Lyda's cheek, but she hit his hand away. He chuckled.

Vic led us along a short hallway to a closed door. "I hope you have a strong stomach," he said. His expression was serious now, and he was sweating as he had been in the bookstore, though the air was not warm.

I just nodded, not knowing what to expect. I guessed that he was going to introduce us to Eulalie Tortuga, but I had no idea what condition she might be in now. Astraea looked interested but untroubled. Whatever she'd said to Vic had worked. As sometimes happens, Dad had been right about bringing her along.

Vic passed his hand over the cheap interior door lock, causing it to flicker briefly. He seemed nervous about actually opening the door. I wondered if my stomach was strong enough for whatever that room contained.

CHAPTER EIGHTEEN
AN ENTERTAINING EVENING

Vic turned the handle and pushed open the door. Inside was a guest room lit by a single hurricane-style lamp standing on a bedside table. As in the living room, every wall not used for something else was a bookcase. The bed was empty and smooth, as if it had just been made. Sitting in a chair to one side, her face sculpted by heavy shadows, was a woman wearing white flannel pajamas covered with tiny pink roses. Long red hair hung down around her shoulders. Her face was relaxed and held no expression. She might have been sleeping except that her eyes were open and the little finger of her left hand was vibrating. It never stopped the entire time we were in the room. I knew this woman. I'd met her once before.

"Eulalie Tortuga," Vic said as if introducing the Queen of England. "You wouldn't know it to look at her now but she was the hottest art dealer in town."

"How did she get here?" I asked.

"Walked, I guess," Vic said. "She showed up very early this morning."

"Funny she should come here."

"Not so funny," Vic said angrily. "We were not able to live together, but that doesn't mean we hated each other, or even disliked each other. She just came to the place she knew they'd take her in."

"In her present condition I'm surprised she knew anything."

"You know what her condition is?"

"The paper said she was a zombie."

"The paper!" Vic exclaimed with contempt.

We stood in the doorway for a few more seconds watching her. No part of her moved except that little finger. She must have been breathing, but I couldn't see her do it.

"Hello, Eulalie," I said.

No response. I would have been surprised if I'd gotten one, but I had to try.

"I've seen enough," I said, making Vic smile. He liked people who said "when" before he did.

He closed the door gently and carefully locked it. We all went back to the living room where Lyda Firebough was sitting on the lounger I had been sitting in before. Vic and Astraea sat at one end of the big L and I sat at the other.

"So, Mr. Detective," Vic said, "do you know any more now than you did before?"

"A little," I said. "A day or two ago I saw Eulalie Tortuga coming out of the office of Lord Zorn Slex at Stilthins Mort."

Vic seemed surprised by that. "What was she doing there?"

"Having an argument. She seemed to think that whatever relationship she and Lord Slex had was now ended. He disagreed with her."

Vic's face clouded over.

"Come on, Vic," Lyda said. "For all practical purposes you two weren't married any more. You can't have expected her to stay celibate. You certainly didn't stay that way."

"Keep out of this."

Lyda seemed pleased to have gotten a rise out of him.

"Do you know how zombies are made?" I asked.

"Voodoo or something. Does it matter?" He was still angry about Lord Slex.

"Astraea tells me that zombies are made when a soul is removed from the body of a person before its time."

Vic pursed his lips. I could see he wanted to say something clever and insulting. But all he did was glance at Astraea. "Is that so?" he said.

"But when a soul is removed early," Astraea said, "keeping it away from its body is impossible. It always finds a way back."

"Then if you're right about Eulalie being a zombie, all we have to do is wait."

"No," Astraea went on. "It would have returned already, immediately after it had been removed."

"Then she's not a zombie," Lyda said.

"Very good, schutzie-putz," Vic said sarcastically.

"Or," I said, "someone has found a way to dispose of souls permanently."

Everybody thought about that. Especially Astraea, who knew more about lost souls than anyone, thought about that.

"That doesn't sound likely," Vic said.

"No, it doesn't," I said. "But a grad student at Stilthins Mort was murdered yesterday. Her name was Misty Morning. She had things in her laboratory that might have done the trick."

"Misty? Dead?" Vic's cool supercilious attitude cracked. He seemed genuinely astonished and horrified.

I was surprised, myself. I hadn't expected my announcement to have that effect on him. "I guess you didn't see this morning's paper," I said.

He and Lyda Firebough shook their heads.

"I'm afraid it's true," I went on. "How did you know her?"

"She was Vic's girlfriend before me," Lyda said in an unsteady voice. "Even so, we were friends. How was it done?"

"A rat-killing spell."

"Oh," Lyda exclaimed as she put a hand to her mouth.

"Who did it?" Vic asked, his voice tight with control.

"I don't know. It doesn't take any special skill to use a spell like that. It is pretty cheap stuff that would be purchased for the very reason that it would not differentiate between rats and other living things—like people. Did Misty have any enemies— a wizard, maybe, or a guy with a cauliflower nose?"

Both Vic and Lyda studied the sea-green carpeting as if clues were hidden in the weave. "Misty was a terrific person," Vic said. "A lot of people had keys to her place, I suppose, but none that I know of would want to hurt her. Of course, I didn't know everybody who had a key. A cauliflower nose?"

"That's what it looked like to me," I said. "Do you have a key, Mr. Tortuga?"

That shocked him back to his old self. "No. Why? Do you think I killed her?"

I shrugged. "Your estranged wife is now a zombie and your former girlfriend is dead. That's quite a coincidence."

"And my motive would be?"

"I don't know, but it would be fun to guess."

Vic made a noise of disgust way back in his throat and made a slashing motion with one open hand. "With an imagination like that you should be writing books. Besides, as I said, I don't have a key to Misty's apartment."

"That's refreshing," I said. "You seem to be one of the select few."

"But he could have used mine," Lyda suggested. "He knows I keep it in my purse."

"I don't," Vic said, coming to a boil.

Lyda smiled and said nothing.

"What about Lord Slex?" Astraea asked. "Like Mr. Tortuga, he had a connection to both Misty and Eulalie. And, I understand that, unlike Mr. Tortuga, he did have a key to Misty's apartment."

I shook my head. "Sure. A lot of people had keys. The real problem is that not one of them, not even Lord Slex, seems to have the skill to remove a soul and keep it long enough to get it to Misty's apartment, where he could use one of those space puckers."

"Space puckers?" Lyda asked.

"Those things in Misty's lab where a person might permanently dispose of a soul. I don't know that one of them could keep a soul any more than a sieve could hold water, but no other possibility has yet presented itself. Of course," I went on, "anybody could hire a soul removed. If they knew who to hire."

"Lyda might," Vic said, smiling broadly. "She has a lot of

experience with illegal magic."

"Vic," Lyda said, warning him.

"Oh, didn't you know?" Vic asked innocently. "During Prohibition she helped Eddie 'The Ender' Tips and Louie 'The Mouth' Stuckler, and a magician—who, for the purposes of Prohibition, called himself Merlin—to smuggle bootleg magic. Merlin was their magic connection. Lyda was a runner, delivering the magic and collecting money for it."

Lyda buried her head in her hands. She and Vic seemed to snipe at each other a lot—not everybody's cup of tea, but they seemed to enjoy it. Only this time Vic may have gone too far.

"After Prohibition," Vic jiggled on happily, "she did time and because of it couldn't get a wizard's license even though she'd been through the regular course at Stilthins Mort."

I looked at Lyda. "You were doing magic at the bookstore," I said, hoping to get her back into the conversation. "Lyda?" I said when she didn't answer.

When she lifted her head, her eyes were dry, but terrible anger showed on her face. "You don't need a license to do magic," she said in a voice that was too composed, "just to get caught."

After that the living room was so quiet I could hear a clock ticking in another part of the house. A car swished by outside like the ghost of a car. My shoes squeaked when I moved in them a little. Vic continued smiling.

"Did Misty or Eulalie have anything to do with your Prohibition activities?" Astraea asked. She spoke softly, but her voice seemed to boom in the silent room.

To Lyda, the idea seemed to be a new one. "Why, no. For one thing, fifteen years ago Misty was barely a kid. In any case, she and Eulalie never had any criminal connections at any time, that I know of. Except him," she flopped her hand in Vic's direction, causing him to briefly laugh like a lunatic.

I stood up, and Astraea did the same. Vic's eyes followed her as she walked across the room to stand next to me. Lyda made no move to join him, but she looked at us with interest.

"I can't tell you what an entertaining evening it's been, Mr.

Tortuga. And thanks for the autograph for my father. Now, if you'll just give me Eulalie Tortuga's address, Astraea and I will be on our way."

"I hope I'll be seeing both of you again," Vic said, though he was looking at Astraea.

"We may have more questions," I suggested agreeably.

Vic nodded and asked us to wait here. While he was gone, Astraea asked Lyda if she was all right and she claimed that she was. "I don't know why I get like that," she said, "Vic flirts with everybody."

"I didn't flirt back," Astraea said.

"I noticed. Thanks."

"If you're worried that someone might hear about your activities during Prohibition," I said, "don't be. I am the graveyard of your secrets."

"Thanks," she said again. "Living here, it's easy to forget there are nice people in the world."

Vic may have been listening beyond the bend in the hallway because he came back then with a slip of paper that he handed me. Written on it in neat block letters was an address on Highland. He'd also given me his telephone number. "In case you come up with something," he said.

"You never know," I said. "Sometimes I get lucky."

We all had a good laugh over that.

I thanked Vic again, while he and Lyda walked us across the black stone entryway to the front door. Astraea let him take her hand and kiss it gently, but it seemed to have as much effect on her as a feather has on a wrecking ball.

Outside, the evening had turned cold. Astraea and I hurried along the high hedge without speaking, and I let us into my car. The seats were even colder than the air and Astraea shivered. The heater blew warm air at us as I rolled back down the hill on the LA side.

"What do you think?" I asked when Astraea had stopped shivering.

"You are the detective," she said. "I am Justice."

"I know," I said thoughtfully. "You're just some goddess. I bring the criminals to you. But you protest too much. You asked some good questions in there. And you got Vic Tortuga to show us Eulalie."

"Any pretty woman could have done it."

"Maybe."

We passed Rigby Court on the way down the hill, and I turned onto it so Astraea could see the scene of the crime—or the outside of it, anyway. A blue neon address flickered and buzzed on the outside wall as if it were full of insects. The rest of the building might have been taken to the Moon for all we could see of it in that light.

"Misty lived here?"

"Yes."

Without another word she got out of the car and walked under the bougainvillaea into the courtyard. I hurriedly followed her. The courtyard was fragrant with night-blooming flowers. The perfume and the hulking shadows cast by the trees made the whole place seem even less real than it had during the day. Astraea stood outside Misty's apartment with her hands raised, palms outward, like a mime feeling his way around the inside of an imaginary box. Red words floated in the air: Police Line—Do Not Cross.

"Not much to see," I said after we'd stood there for a while.

"No," she said. "But sometimes I get feelings."

"Tonight?"

"Not so much. Just what we already know. She was fundamentally a good person."

"And the murderer?"

"Probably somebody she knew. But you already guessed that."

I nodded there in the dark, which seemed pointless, so I stopped.

She shivered once, not necessarily from the cold, and let me escort her back along the cement path, then out to the car. We started down the hill again.

"Do you think either one of the Stilthins Mort board members or Vic Tortuga is a keres?" I asked, just supposing out loud. The question whether any of them had the supernatural power to kidnap a soul had been burning a hole in my brain for some hours.

"I haven't met any member of the board," Astraea reminded me, "but I am sure Vic Tortuga is not. I would know."

I ignored the fact that I had forgotten who had met whom. "Tortuga suggested that Lyda Firebough might know where to hire somebody to steal a soul," I said. "I think he was just yanking her chain, but it seems like a real possibility. What do you think?"

"Yanking her chain?"

"Trying to get a rise out of her, to make her angry for the entertainment value. It's not important. Could anybody but a keres steal a soul?"

"Maybe. The world is full of gods, goddesses, and demi-urges. But certainly no human could do it. And to answer your next question, yes, I do believe it is possible to hire a keres to do the job for you."

"It seems to me finding a keres would be almost as diffi-cult as separating a soul from a body. You can't just search for 'demons' in the maJsys."

"True."

"Could you find one if you had to?"

"I would have to go through channels, and even then my request might not be granted."

"Channels?"

I glanced at her and saw a soft smile flicker on her face. "It is not important," she said.

"Yanking my chain?"

"I would not do such a thing."

Soon we were at the bottom of the hill, and I was able to think about something besides my driving. I still didn't know who killed Misty Morning, but if someone had used one of her space puckers to dispose of a soul, then her murder and

Eulalie Tortuga's current situation might be connected. Which might mean that the person or persons unknown who had taken Eulalie's soul had also murdered Misty to get the pucker.

I found Enough Rope again and stopped the car. The street was empty, tourists having gone wherever they go at night. I half-turned toward Astraea and she half-turned toward me. Her lips were a little parted and I thought I could smell her jasmine-scented breath. Slowly I leaned closer to her, and I thought I was going to touchdown when she stuck out her hand at me. "Thank you for your help," she said. "Please keep me informed."

"Sure," I said, my head spinning.

Before I had a chance to at least be gentleman enough to walk her to her door, she was out of the car and into the small store. I sat for a moment trying to catch my breath. I had apparently misread all the signs. Well, it wouldn't be the first time.

I had a long lonely drive home in the cold thinking about Astraea and about Misty and about Eulalie. If I'd done anything differently, would Astraea have kissed me? I also wondered whether Lord Slex had done me a favor by altering my face. When I had a free minute I'd get some Spell-Be-Gone and change back. What I looked like didn't seem important at the moment. No useful thoughts about murder or the stealing of souls came to me that hadn't come to me before.

For once I found a place to park right in front of my building. I took the elevator to my floor and let myself into my apartment. Thoughts continued to swirl in my head while I got ready for bed, and I was actually horizontal for all of a minute when I had an idea. I leaped from the warm nest I'd made and went to the corner of my room where I sat down in front of my skrying ball and spoke my spell code at it. I got the maJsys from the Microsoft genie and looked up the mythology of Justice.

Everything Astraea said about Justice and her sisters was true, or at least documented. They did dance with the Graces. The maJsys article also said that she was a relative of the Three Fates. If the three women at Enough Rope were the Fates, that would fit in nicely. Or was I merely crazy? Astraea, if that was her real name, could have done the same research I was doing, discovered the same ancient knowledge I had discovered. And the three women could be just that, three women.

One fact about Justice that Astraea had not shared with me was that she was a professional virgin, often associated with the constellation Virgo. That explained the handshake, if nothing else did. Even if Astraea only *believed* she was Justice, I guessed I would have to get my kicks elsewhere.

I shut down the skrying ball and went back to bed, where I attempted to think professional thoughts.

CHAPTER NINETEEN
MAKE THE CALL

The sun touched my face and I awoke. Or maybe what did it was the sound of a jackhammer breaking up concrete many floors below, a sound like a bumblebee in a tin can. In any case I lay there for a while with my eyes closed against the glare coming in through the windows, thinking.

For some reason my mind kept returning to Merlin—the guy who'd supplied illegal magic to Eddie 'The Ender' Tips, Louie 'The Mouth' Stuckler, and Lyda Firebough during Prohibition. Lyda seemed sure that neither Misty Morning nor Eulalie Tortuga had ever been involved with any of the gentlemen. However, like a lot of professions, wizardry is a pretty small pond. It was possible that entirely by accident Misty had stumbled across Merlin's true identity. I was not reaching very far to think that Merlin would have murdered Misty to keep the secret a secret, especially if he had a lot to lose.

It was also possible that my theory was a bucket of swill, but I wasn't doing anything else that day so I would invest a little time looking under rocks to see what damp nasty things skittered away from the light.

I got up, washed, dressed, and breakfasted. I burned an hour that way, then called Vic Tortuga's private number.

"What?" a voice demanded. It was Vic himself.

"It's Turner Cronyn, Mr. Tortuga."

"You know who took Eulalie's soul?"

"Not yet, Mr. Tortuga. Might I speak with Ms. Firebough?"

"Ms. Firebough is busy," Vic said. "She has her finger in her nose." Vic laughed. I let him. He finished and yelled for Lyda. Soon there was the click of heels on a hard surface and a moment later Lyda came on the line.

"Turner Cronyn, Ms. Firebough."

"I recognize the voice. What can I do for you?"

"Last night there was some talk about Merlin—"

"Do we have to talk about that?"

"It might help."

Lyda breathed gently into the phone. "All right, then," she said. "What do you want to know?"

"Did you ever learn who Merlin really was?"

"No. I never had much to do with him. I worked through Eddie and Louie."

"I see. Thank you, Ms. Firebough."

"Lyda. And while I have you—you know, I've been thinking."

Which was a straight line if I ever heard one, but this didn't seem to be the time for cleverness. "What have you been thinking, Lyda?" I asked.

"With all that talk about Misty last night I forgot to tell you something that may be important. Before she went with Vic, back when she was an undergrad, she dated Lord Philpot for a while. Nobody's supposed to know, but I'm thinking that Lord Philpot might be able to tell you something useful."

"He certainly might," I said. "Do you have any other random thoughts?"

"Not about Misty, no," she replied as if she were really sorry.

"Thanks for your time, then," I said and hung up. Her second-hand relationship to Merlin didn't surprise me. If I'd thought a little longer that morning, I wouldn't even have called her to ask the question. Assuming Merlin had killed Misty because she knew his real identity, then if Lyda knew, she would have been dead long since. So either Merlin believed that Lyda didn't know or my entire theory was thinner than diner coffee.

I didn't think it would do any good, but I used the number Lord Slex had given me to call the Morning family back in Chicago.

After three rings a female voice answered. She sounded old and very tired, as if I had awakened her from a deep sleep.

"Mrs. Morning?" I asked gently.

"Yes. Who is this, please?"

"My name is Turner Cronyn, Mrs. Morning. I am investigating the death of your daughter."

There was a long silence during which tiny electronic tones came to me from the other end of the universe.

"I already spoke to the police, and to those lords at the school where she worked."

"I understand how unpleasant this must be for you, Mrs. Morning, but it's possible you can be a great help to me finding out who did it."

"Who is this?" a man's voice yelled at me. Too late I held the receiver away from my ear.

"This is Turner Cro—"

"I don't care who the hell you are. My wife and I have been harassed enough by you people. We're bringing Misty home where she belongs, and that's the end of it."

Somebody had obviously rubbed him the wrong way. Maybe there wasn't a right way. "Don't you want to know who—?"

"We don't use magic, whoever-you-are. We don't believe in it and we don't approve of it. Lord knows what made Misty the way she was, but we always told her she'd come to a bad end. Talking about it won't help. We're bringing her home and that's the end of it."

By this time I had the receiver a good six inches from my head so that when he slammed down the phone the crash did only minor damage to my eardrum.

After speaking with Misty's parents I felt a little less sorry for them. Misty hadn't just come to Los Angeles to work, she'd come to escape from Chicago. I hoped she could rest easy back there.

Next I called Lord Philpot. Talking to him couldn't be any more useless than talking to Misty's parents.

A young girl answered the phone at Lord Philpot's home.

I recognized her voice, which was a surprise, but it gave me something new to think about. I told her I wanted to speak with Lord Philpot. She claimed not to know where he was or when he'd be back.

"It's important," I said. "I want to talk to him about Misty Morning."

"Poor Misty," the girl said. There was a scratching sound and then complete silence, as if she had put her hand over the receiver. She seemed to be gone for a long time. While she was gone I drew a sphere and shaded it carefully. "He isn't here right now," she told me again when she came back. "But he often spends the evening at the Magic Vault. You might run into him there."

I thanked her and she thanked me, all very polite, and I hung up.

I pushed the switch hook on the telephone and held it down while I tried to predict the future. I had no idea whether Lord Philpot would actually make it to the Magic Vault this evening. I tried to make that mean something, but couldn't decide either way.

During these pointless thoughts I released the switch hook and spoke the spell for Harold Silverwhite. While the phone rang I thought about the large favor I had once done him. Helping him had been a pleasure, but Silverwhite felt he was still paying me off. Going to him when I needed his help did us both some good.

"Acme Magic," a cultured voice announced. It wasn't quite British—mid-Atlantic I think the accent was called.

"How's the boy?" I asked.

"Is that you, Cronyn?" Silverwhite asked. "What a pleasure. How is my favorite consulting detective?"

"That was Sherlock Holmes. I'm just a regular old PI. Remember?"

"You'll always be a consulting detective to me. What may I do for you, old chum?"

"Did that guy who attacked me ever come back?"

"He did not, I'm sorry to say. He could have helped me clean up the lab. It took hours."

"Sorry."

"Not your fault, old chum. What about you? Any unpleasant visitations?"

"No. I guess whatever was bothering him stopped bothering him. Right now I have a different problem."

"No favor too large, old chum. No favor too small."

"Thanks. I have a little something I'd like you to take a look at. Will you be at the Magic Vault this evening?"

"I can be, of course. Shall we say nine-ish?"

"Let us say nine-ish."

"I'll pencil you in," Silverwhite said.

Two guys at the club, that was us. We said our good-byes and hung up. Having spoken to him, I felt as if I'd made some progress. He was intuitive about anything magical, which Misty's code probably was. Some jealous people claimed he was part elf. It might even be true. If he'd been with me at Misty's laboratory, I probably could have gotten into that empty drawer before the police arrived.

I went to get the morning paper from outside my door, and sat down with it in the kitchen. I stared at it for a long time without anything registering, then something snapped inside me and a photograph I'd been staring at made me shiver and blink.

The headline said Second Zombie Found, which in itself was worth noting. But the photo next to it was a head shot of a guy named Joe Flynn, a small business man who, except for a thin mustache that was no more than twin Ls back to back under his nose, could have been my brother.

"Coincidence," I said out loud, hoping it was true. But I generally don't believe in coincidences. The way Joe Flynn tied me to the stealing of Eulalie's soul made me nervous. I let the queasy feeling work in me for a while then turned the paper over and went back to the telephone to call Detective Fotheringay downtown.

"Siltz," the voice at the other end of the line growled at

me when I connected. I told him that I wanted to speak to Fotheringay and he asked me who was calling. I didn't feel like having an argument that morning, but I told him anyway. "Imagine," Siltz said, and left me on hold.

"Fotheringay."

"Cronyn," I said.

"I'm dancing," Fotheringay said. "What can I do for you?"

"I see you have another zombie on your hands."

"You're a little behind," Fotheringay said, "We have three new zombies."

"Oh?" I said, not knowing whether I wanted to hear more or not. "You fascinate me strangely."

"Joe Flynn was only the first. Early this morning—but too late for the papers, I guess—two more showed up."

"Anything in common with Eulalie Tortuga?"

"Not a thing that we can see. Renaldo Duncan owned a restaurant in Culver City. Merv Lupinsky was a technical writer who lived in an apartment near Fairfax High. As far as we can tell they didn't know each other. Neither one of them knew Flynn. But they all still had something in common."

I waited, fearing that I knew what he was going to say.

"Given differences in facial hair and glasses and such, each of them resembled the others physically."

Though I had been mentally braced, Fotheringay's confirmation was still a shock. Bizarre and unpleasant possibilities rolled through my mind with the anonymous evil intent of enemy tanks. I said nothing.

"Cronyn?"

"What are the chances?" I remarked, just to be saying something. I needed to get a grip. "Do these victims have addresses?" I asked.

"That's police business," Fotheringay said. "Besides," he went on, "my team and I have been all over those places, just as we've been all over Eulalie Tortuga's place, and we found nothing anybody would call a clue."

"I'd like to take a look, even so. If you've already been there, you can't be worried about me muddying the water."

"Hell," he said softly. There was a long open space during which I heard a radio playing elevator music softly, people talking, and telephones ringing—office noises. Fotheringay came back and gave me three addresses. He was about to tell me where Eulalie Tortuga's house was but I stopped him. "I already know that one," I said, having some pride.

"Maybe you are a detective after all," he said. "She's unlisted."

"If you get an outfit you can be a detective, too. Do you have time to answer another question?"

"Sure. Down at headquarters we like nothing better than to do research for you private guys."

"Cop humor," I remarked playfully.

"Get on with it," Fotheringay said, "or I'll let you talk to Siltz again."

"The question is this," I said. "Do you have any magic stuff from Prohibition lying around in a dark dusty corner of your evidence room?"

There was a short silence. "I assume you're not just taking a poll," Fotheringay said.

"No. In particular I'm looking for a spell put together by a Prohibition magician known as Merlin."

I imagined him nodding into the telephone. "Is this maybe a bright idea connected with the murder of Misty Morning?" he asked.

"Someday it could be," I said. "But right now it's just a hunch on a very short leash."

"It doesn't matter. All the Prohibition stuff we ever had was taken to the La Brea Tar Pits years ago, either dumped into the pits themselves, or put on display at the Prohibition Museum. Why is this important?"

"I was just thinking that spells have characteristics, like fingerprints, depending on where the magician who made them up learned his magic. If one of Merlin's spells still existed, an expert could tell me where he went to school."

"That might be useful," Fotheringay allowed grudgingly.

"But I still don't see what that has to do with Misty Morning."

"I'll let you know if anything comes of my hunch."

A vast sigh came at me through the telephone. "All right. I don't know why, but all right. Call Mr. Samuel Quandum at the Prohibition Museum. Tell him I sent you."

"Thanks. By the way, how are *you* doing on the case?"

He laughed at me and hung up.

CHAPTER TWENTY
THAT OLD BLACK MAGIC

A minute later I was riding down in the coffin-like elevator with a big woman who had a jaw like a satchel. She was a neighbor but I didn't know her name. We both nodded and smiled before ignoring each other completely the rest of the way down.

I crossed Sixth Street and entered the La Brea Tar Pits. It was a beautiful park, a city block square, one thick side of which was burdened with art museums. Tar pits of varying sizes dotted the landscape, each surrounded by a municipal spell to keep out the curious and the stupid. A couple of kids were trying to get a kite into the air using only the wind, and not having much luck. A man and a woman sat on a bench beneath tall trees sniffing at each other's throats. Following an asphalt path, I found what I was looking for—a small round building made of white-painted brick.

The inside was mostly taken up with exhibits telling the story of Prohibition; Prohibition was one of those ideas that seemed so good to some people that they decided God must be on their side. A woman named Anna Montaigne started the movement by single-handedly destroying a mom-and-pop spell store in Clarion, Pennsylvania. Ms. Montaigne was uglier than a dried-up apple and had no talent for magic herself, though her enemies claimed she was a witch. Her talent lay in public speaking. And before long she'd convinced a lot of people that all magic, no matter how innocuous, was the work of the devil.

"Pick a card, any card," became an obscenity. It meant the political life of any public servant to oppose Ms. Montaigne. Then rumors leaked out that Ms. Montaigne's rhetorical talent came from a spell cast by her second in command, a tall thin geek named Charles W. McGonigal. The rumors increased both in frequency and severity until one day Montaigne and McGonigal failed to show up for an anti-magic rally. Neither they nor the movement's operating funds were ever seen again. After that, the forces opposing Ms. Montaigne had no trouble pulling Repeal out of a hat.

Other exhibits showed examples of Prohibition magic, and pictures of guys like Al Capone, who in their own public-spirited way had supplied magic where it was needed. Nowhere was there any mention of Merlin.

On one side of the room was Ye Olde Gift Shoppe, where you could purchase souvenirs of your day at the Prohibition Museum. In the center of the room was a big square pit, which at the moment was lined with squirming little kids and a couple of harassed-looking women. The kids were leaning over a low wall and pointing things out to each other. "Cool," seemed to be the most common exclamation, though I heard an occasional "awesome!" A man the shape of a bowling pin was talking to the kids in a high, nearly feminine voice.

I went to look over the heads of the kids into the pit. Below was a lake of tar. In the center of it, books, wands, cauldrons, bags of leaves and roots, capes covered with stars and moons, and other magical paraphernalia were glued into a mound by ancient black goo. In one place bubbles continued to rise, and when each one broke, it released a little cloud of sparkling dust that quickly fell onto the tar—the entire surface glittered with the stuff.

Behind the cash register in the gift shop was a young woman wearing a black gown that was bulky enough to hide a multitude of sins. I sidled over to her and we watched the kids together. "I'm looking for Samuel Quandum," I said.

"That's him," she said in a warm pleasant voice and nodded

in the direction of the fat guy lecturing to the kids. "Is there something I could help you with?"

"Not unless you're an expert on Prohibition magic."

She shrugged. "I just work the cash register," she said. "Would you like a bag of talcum powder that looks like the spell that got Al Capone? Only five bucks plus tax."

"Maybe later," I said. I turned, and together the woman and I watched Samuel Quandum go through his spiel for the kids. They liked it well enough to stay quiet through most of it. I didn't hear anything that was useful to me. Now and then my eyes met those of Mr. Quandum, and his brows would turn up into a questioning expression. Then he would start talking again, and the expression would disappear.

The two women looked even more harassed when the kids invaded the gift shop, but the lady behind the cash register remained calm. While they were at it, Mr. Quandum walked over to me. I introduced myself and asked if I could speak with him alone.

"I have to be available to answer questions," Mr. Quandum said.

"I have a question," I said. "Detective Fotheringay downtown thought you might be able to answer it. I won't trouble you very long."

"Very well, then," he said, and led me back to a small cluttered office at the end of the building opposite the gift shop. He moved a pile of back numbers of a newspaper called That Old Black Magic from a chair to the floor and asked me to sit down.

"You don't seem to use much magic yourself," I said as I looked around.

"It clashes with the exhibits," Mr. Quandum explained. "What can I do for you, Mr. Cronyn? You're a detective, you say? I'm afraid the crimes I know most about are much too old to interest you."

"Oldies but goodies, Mr. Quandum. I'd like to hear about a Prohibition magician named Merlin."

Mr. Quandum smiled. "Merlin was a fairly common name

for a Prohibition magician who wanted to keep his or her true identity a secret."

"This Merlin would have worked locally with a couple of jokers named Eddie 'The Ender' Tips and Louie 'The Mouth' Stuckler."

Mr. Quandum scowled. Or maybe he was just concentrating. Still at it, he rose and began walking his fingers through a filing cabinet. "We don't display everything," he said with his back to me, "there isn't room. But it's all been identified and cataloged. I did most of the work myself."

I made a noise showing that I was listening.

"Here it is," he said triumphantly in his shrill voice and turned to me with a folder in his hands. He set it down on top of the papers on his desk and opened it. Inside were some typed pages and a cellophane bag with gray powder in it. The gray meant the spell's power had expired. In this case it had probably expired some years ago. He sat down and I stood to look over his shoulder.

"This is very nice," he said. "A spell made by one of the six Los Angeles Merlins, this one found in the hideout of Mr. Tips and Mr. Stuckler. Fairly typical of Prohibition magic. This spell was used to keep the house clean and orderly."

"Sounds wicked," I remarked.

"Apparently Anna Montaigne and the government thought so."

"Were you able to determine where this particular Merlin was trained?"

"I believe so," Mr. Quandum said as he shuffled through the typed sheets. "Ah," he said at last. "It was put together by someone using the Stilthins Mort method."

I nodded. What Mr. Quandum told me was very much what I'd expected. "Does your folder happen to give Merlin's real name?"

Mr. Quandum shuffled papers for a while. "Nothing about that here, I'm afraid. All we know is that Merlin frequently took the form of Brent Martin, that musical actor. Anything else?"

Mr. Quandum prepared to close his folder while he glanced past me out the door.

"Do you know the whereabouts of Tips or Stuckler?" I asked.

He hurriedly checked his papers again. "No. Like Merlin, they were never caught. Only some woman named Lyda Firebough. Is that helpful?"

"Not much," I said truthfully. "But the other, about Stilthins Mort, is very helpful." I stood up. "Thanks for your time." He blinked at me as I walked out the door.

Over in the gift shop the kids were all lined up with their books and bags and wands and cone-shaped wizard's hats—today's mementos, tomorrow's trash.

I stepped outside the museum and called Fotheringay on my cell phone. Siltz answered again and acted as if I'd ruined his day by asking him to take a message. "Tell Fotheringay that Merlin learned his magic at Stilthins Mort."

"Meaning what?"

"I'm not sure yet. It might have something to do with Misty Morning's murder."

"How would it do that?"

"Just give him the message, OK?" I suggested, cooling my usual warm manner by about twenty degrees.

Siltz hung up, leaving me with an ear full of nothing. I held the phone for a moment while I looked across a grassy field at the traffic on Sixth Street. Behind me the kids continued to yammer at each other while one of the two women tried ineffectually to make them quiet. I was about to put the phone back into my pocket, but instead dialed Stilthins Mort and asked for Lord Slex. I walked to a bench and sat down in the shade of a big tree with my phone against my ear.

The professional female voice that answered told me that Lord Slex was in a meeting, so I asked if either of the other two board members was available. "It's about Misty Morning," I said.

She did not speak for what seemed to be a long time. "Just a moment, please," she said.

"Lord Trask." His voice came on without any sound to indicate that he'd picked up a receiver.

"Turner Cronyn here, sir," I said.

"Hilda says you wish to speak to me about Misty Morning. I was under the distinct impression that we had released you from the case." I imagined him removing his monocle for emphasis while his mustache twitched, rabbit-like.

"Yes, sir, you did. But I decided to stay on the case for my own reasons. As you might imagine, I feel that I owe something to Ms. Morning."

"That, of course, is your business. Why did you wish to speak with me?"

"Did you ever hear of a magician who, during Prohibition, was known as Merlin?"

"I've heard of him, yes." Lord Trask's voice had backed away from me a few miles. Either he didn't know there were at least six local Merlins—or maybe he just liked the fact that *I* didn't seem to know.

"Do you happen to know his real identity?"

"I understand he died," Lord Trask said—a little too quickly, I thought.

"Understand how? From where?"

"I don't remember," he said irritably. "It was a long time ago. Are you quite finished?"

"Almost," I said. "Just one more question."

"And that is?"

"Do you think a master wizard would know how to separate a soul from its body?" Ace Cronyn, getting 'em right between the eyes.

Lord Trask waited so long to answer that I began to think he'd put the receiver down as soundlessly as he'd picked it up. When he spoke at last, it was with exaggerated courtesy and a cold controlled fury. "Mr. Cronyn," he said, "you seem to have a talent for asking insulting questions. But in this case, because the answer is so simple and obvious, I will answer your question. I am a master wizard, Mr. Cronyn, and I know of no such method. Does that answer your question, Mr. Cronyn?"

"Yes, sir. Have a nice day, sir."

"It's much too late for that," Lord Trask said. There was no mistaking when he hung up.

I sat for a few minutes with the telephone in my lap, just enjoying the early fall day. A light wind rustled the leaves. Somewhere birds argued. Except for the boom of the traffic I might have been out in the country. The two women hustled the kids across the park and soon they were gone, leaving the day peaceful again.

I had succeeded in confirming that Merlin was associated with Stilthins Mort, and that he and two members of his gang had never been captured. I had also managed to annoy Lord Trask, though it was still not clear to me why my question about souls had had that effect on him.

I sat there a while longer playing catch with one idea and then another, and then I heard a shriek that raised the hair on the back of my neck.

CHAPTER TWENTY-ONE
BUSY MORNING

I looked to one side and saw a huge flying beast gliding toward me on leathery wings, each of which had a sharp finger of bone at the tip. Its mouth was wide open in a toothy and most unpleasant grin. I sweated as I let it get closer. When it shrieked again and I smelled breath that would peel paint, I rolled forward off the bench, coming to my feet ten or fifteen steps away. With a rush of air the thing roared like a Wilshire bus as it zoomed through the space where I'd been sitting, sending the bench tumbling, and then swooped far up into the sky.

I ran. I didn't know if it would do any good, but I could think of doing nothing else. I ran. I took a moment to look over my shoulder and saw the beast make a wide slow graceful wheel in the sky and come at me again. I ran.

It was pretty obvious that the thing was an old piece of magic that had bubbled up from a tar pit. I was just lucky enough to be there at the wrong moment. Closer now, it shrieked again. I couldn't keep this up for long. Eventually that thing, that refugee from a bad time for wizards, would crunch me in the big scissors of its jaws. I would feel brief but excruciating pain, and tomorrow morning I would be a small poignant item in the papers. Politicians would fulminate, but nobody would really care except my parents; they would care a lot. I didn't want to put them through that, so I ran a little faster.

When I judged that the beast was pretty close, I suddenly dropped to the turf and was once again pummeled by the hard wind of its passing. I got up and, while the thing was making its turn in the sky, I looked around the park. I was in the middle of a big grassy field—nothing to hide behind or under for hundreds of feet in any direction. A man strolled onto the field from a copse of big trees, coming toward me with a couple of kids dancing around him.

"Go back!" I called to him.

"What?" he asked.

He and the beast saw each other at the same second. He grabbed his kids and took off. I didn't think he was going to make it back to the trees in time, particularly because those kids must have looked so tasty to a predator, but the beast flew over them as if they weren't there and came ahead at me. I started to run again, once again fell at what I judged to be the right moment, and once again the beast glided inches above me in its jet-powered way.

While my face was mashed into the grass, I had an idea. I got up and ran toward the nearest tar pit. Why hadn't the beast attacked the guy and his two kids? I didn't want it to attack them, I just wondered. Soon the municipal spell around the pit slowed me down, but I pushed through it with big wading motions, getting as close to the big pool of tar as I could. The beast dived at me. I ducked and it missed. I looked up just in time to see it float over the tar pit with all the ease of an autumn leaf. Suddenly it got all over sparkly, closed up like an umbrella, and was sucked down into the tar pit as if by a vacuum cleaner.

I turned and walked out of the municipal spell. When I was entirely free of it, I allowed myself to collapse on the grass, breathing hard. I almost went back into the museum to tell Samuel Quandum what had happened, but right then it seemed more important that I rest. Besides, I got claustrophobic just thinking about becoming one more neatly typed page of data in Mr. Quandum's filing cabinet.

When I was breathing normally, I got up to go home. As I passed it, I glanced suspiciously at the tar pit into which the beast had disappeared. At the Sixth Street stoplight, a man looked at me. I was worth a look, I guess—I wasn't my usual dapper self. My knees were grassy green, and I had ripped my shirt. I was covered in grass clippings. I was dripping sweat, too. I probably looked as if I'd slept in a dumpster. Personally, I was just glad to be alive.

Upstairs in my apartment I bathed in hot water rather than using magic. Using water took longer and was a little more complicated, but ultimately was a lot more satisfying. I dressed again, very stylish in brown this time, and sat down at my telephone enjoying the feeling of clean clothes against my skin.

I looked up the main number for the California Institute of Thaumaturgy. When I called it, I got a sweet young voice that said the name of the school back at me. I asked for Lord Meston. "Just a moment." I waited.

"Lord Meston," a voice answered. It was a big round voice—not loud, but booming even so, and mellow, like an expertly played cello in a hall with perfect acoustics. I told him who I was and that I was working on the Misty Morning murder case.

"I heard about that," he said sadly. Without using much imagination I could see him shaking his head in sorrow. "How can I help you?"

"Did you know Ms. Morning?" I asked.

"We met once or twice, the first time at the party Cal Thau threw when I arrived to take a position on their board. I don't actually remember what the second occasion was. There may not have been one."

"Arrived from where?" I asked.

"I went to school at Conjure Hall in New York, and after I graduated I taught there for many years."

"Then you came here for the climate," I suggested.

"Doesn't everybody?" he asked.

"What was your impression of Ms. Morning?"

"She was beautiful, smart, and talented. I liked her."

"Did you discuss her leaving Stilthins Mort and coming to teach at Cal Thau?"

"I may have said that we would be delighted to have her, but

I didn't actually make an offer."

"Why not? You said yourself she was pretty good."

Lord Meston laughed heartily and with appreciation. "It wouldn't have been ethical," he said. "She was under contract to Stilthins Mort at the time. Besides, she was not the only pretty good wizard in town. We have a few at Cal Thau, too."

"Yeah," I said noncommittally. "I bet you're one of them."

"You'd win that bet," Lord Meston said, and laughed again.

"Do you know what she was working on just before she was murdered?"

Lord Meston did not speak for a long time. Somewhere not far away someone was having a conversation. I heard the twang of only one voice and then silences, so it was probably a telephone conversation.

"Do you think I killed her?" Lord Meston asked.

"The lords at Stilthins Mort hired me to protect her from educational and industrial spies. They wouldn't have done that unless they had a reason."

"Oh, those guys," Lord Meston said as if he were discussing the Three Stooges.

"Do you know what she was working on?"

"I have no idea. What was she working on?"

"Nobody knows," I said. "Not even Dr. Heather Hamish."

"How is Dr. Hamish these days?"

"Busy feeding her fish."

"Ah. I thought so." He laughed again.

"Thanks for your help, Lord Meston."

"You're quite welcome. Delighted to help. Call again any time."

I hung up and for some reason left my hand resting on the receiver. I'd gotten as much information out of him as I would have gotten from a brick wall. He didn't seem the type to commit murder, but lots of guys who didn't seem the type—desperate guys, guys who had been pushed too far, guys with tempers— did the deed. If I didn't learn a reason why not, eventually I would have to go visit him.

Then I knew why I hadn't taken my hand off the receiver. I needed to call Astraea Scales. She was still my client and she deserved a call, but not being sure of my own motives I didn't know what to say to her. I shrugged. What the hell. I dialed the only number I had, Enough Rope.

"Hello?" It was one of the three women in the back room, an old lady's voice. I could almost see her wattles shake as she spoke.

"I'd like to speak with Astraea."

"Of course," she said, delighted as if I were that nice boy who was going to ask Astraea on a date.

Astraea came on the line sounding very much as if she'd lingered over a second cup of coffee and the funnies rather than being chased by a flying dragon. I told her what I had accomplished that morning—not bad considering it was almost noon. "It's just a theory, of course," I said finally. "It's entirely possible that Merlin had nothing to do with Misty's death."

"I suppose it is," she said, reluctant to give up the idea. "What do you think of Lord Trask's reaction to your question about souls? Do you think he has anything to do with Eulalie Tortuga?"

"I didn't expect him to explode into my face, if that's what you mean. Maybe he still has some paranoia left over from Prohibition."

"Paranoia? But what has he to be afraid of?"

"Maybe nothing—nothing that still exists, anyway. Just because a guy is smart doesn't mean he's sane. I don't know what he went through during Prohibition. And Slex might have answered my question the same way if I'd put it to him, I don't know. Slex wanting to take Eulalie's soul would certainly make more sense than Trask's wanting it, for a moment putting aside the question of whether a wizard could really do it at all."

"Hmm," Astraea said. "There must be a renegade keres in the mix somewhere."

I could only agree.

"Maybe," she went on, still thinking, "one of the Stilthins

Mort lords is Merlin."

"Could be. But a lot of people do magic using the Stilthins Mort method. Look, Astraea," I went on quickly, "how would you like to go out with me tonight?"

"Is this part of the case?" she asked warily.

Sure. She was a professional virgin. She wanted to know whether she was still a client or had become the object of my desire. I guess I *could* get too clever. Reining in my silver tongue just a little, I explained about Harold Silverwhite and Lord Philpot.

Astraea seemed to understand. "I will dress to kill," she said.

"Maybe just to injure," I suggested. "We have to get some work done. We don't want every man in the place fainting."

"All right."

"Right now, I'm going to Eulalie Tortuga's house. I'll let you know if I learn anything."

"I will come there, too."

"No need for that. Take it easy. I'll keep you informed. That's why your three grandmothers pay me the big bucks."

I expected her to argue with me but for some reason she did not. "Very well," she said.

I hung up feeling as if I'd thrown dirt into her face. But I had feelings too, and knowing what I'd learned about her on the maJsys the night before I wasn't yet prepared to drive around with her all day pretending she had all the sex appeal of a wad of chewed gum. I'd been entirely professional on the phone, but that didn't help. My chances of getting to know her more intimately were the same as I had of successfully juggling anvils.

When I'd sat there long enough to feel silly about pouting, I got up and went out. Downstairs I strolled to my car through the perfect air, through the kind of day even Los Angeles gets only two or three times a year. I felt better just walking around in it.

Not far away I heard idiotic laughter, but it's no crime to laugh so I didn't think much about it. Too late I heard footsteps run up behind me.

Before I could turn to see what was going on, someone threw

a sack over my head. The foul smell of fertilizer clotted in my lungs as I struggled. But the sack already held my arms tightly against my sides, so all I could do was wriggle like a caught fish. I yelled for help but doubted whether anybody heard me.

Muffled idiotic laughter came through the sack again as somebody knocked me over. Somebody caught me by the shoulders and somebody else picked up my feet. I kicked out as hard as I could but hit nothing. I continued trying to make life difficult for my captors, but in less than a minute I was thrown into the back seat of a car. Somebody knocked all the wind out of me when he sat on me. The giggling continued as the car started with a squeal of tires, and we were on our way.

CHAPTER TWENTY-TWO
TRAPPED

Sherlock Holmes might have been able to keep track of left and right turns, but I was not the iron man he was. I had a hard time just breathing. Whoever was sitting on me now seemed to weigh as much as a buffalo and was quickly moving into elephant territory. When I managed to take a breath, all I got was fertilizer. By the time we arrived where we were going, I'd lost a lot of my fight.

I had a moment of comfort when the elephant weight lifted. Then somebody picked me up, put me over his shoulder like a sack of potatoes, and carried me up some steps into a building. I heard a game show on a TV, and a few heckling male voices asked Rudy what he was carrying. Rudy, who I assumed was carrying me, didn't answer.

I could tell by the sound of Rudy's footsteps that we moved through several rooms and then along a hallway. He carried me down a flight of stairs and dumped me onto a cold cement floor. Rudy trudged up the stairs, shut the door at the top, and locked it with an old-fashioned mechanical lock.

When nothing else happened for a minute or two, I managed to weasel out of the fertilizer bag. I was on the floor of a small room lit by a single fluorescent tube of the kind you don't see much any more because will o' the wisps put out a more flattering light. Down here the quality of the light didn't matter. The room was obviously used for storage, filled as it was with unmatched tables and chairs and hundreds of cardboard boxes.

The air was musty, but after the fertilizer it smelled like spring-time. The place had no windows, and the only door was the one at the top of the narrow wooden staircase Rudy had carried me down.

I walked up the stairs feeling as if I were carrying a safe on my back, and carefully reached out for the handle that would move the deadbolt. Something slowed my hand down and prevented it from reaching the door. As I'd expected, the door had a fortification spell on it to prevent me from doing exactly what I was trying to do. "Hey," I called out.

A moment later footsteps approached.

"Pipe down or we'll put leeches on you," a guy called through the door. He strolled away laughing.

I didn't think Rudy really had leeches available, but I also didn't think that calling through the door would do anything but make my throat sore. I went back down the stairs and sat on the second step from the bottom. I pulled out my telephone and experimentally spoke Harold Silverwhite's phone code. I suspected I would miss our appointment at the Magic Vault that evening. I should probably have called Lord Philpot and Astraea too, just to be polite, but all my good intentions went for nothing. I might as well have been holding a bar of soap. My phone was dead; I heard neither buzzing nor static. Apparently abducting me had not been a spur-of-the-moment decision. Someone had taken the trouble to set fortification spells on the door lock and dampening spells that would prevent anyone in this basement from using a cell phone. I spent quite a bit of time wondering who that person might be and whether I would leave the base-ment alive.

In a corner crowded with mops and brooms I used a tiny, fragrant, and none-too-clean bathroom, then looked for a place to sit that would be a little more comfortable than a wooden step. Among the furniture I found an easy chair with gritty tufts of ancient cotton batting escaping from places on the arms where hands had rested for years. But it was good enough for me. I was a man who'd spent the past hour in an old fertilizer sack.

I loosened my tie and waited to see what would happen.

* * * * * *

When I awoke the next morning, the basement had not changed. My watch said it was six-thirty, meaning the sky would be fairly bright by now. Something might happen at any minute, or it could be days before anybody looked in on me.

Except for a couple of minutes when herds of some animal galloped up and back along the floor above me playing basketball, I'd spent a quiet day and even quieter night. I'd done a lot of thinking and had been able to make connections I'd been too busy to see before.

I tried my phone again with the same disappointing result, then sat in my trusty armchair for a while, dozing and thinking about how hungry I was. Breakfast was very important, and I'd be more than a little cranky if I missed it, especially because I had sucked on my tie for dinner. At exactly seven by my watch someone turned the lock in the door at the top of the stairs. I stood up and watched the door swing open. A man descended the stairs carrying a covered tray. The aroma of coffee made me want to float up to meet him. He looked familiar but at the moment I couldn't remember why.

The man carrying the tray was a little shorter than I was. He wore gray work clothes and heavy, blotchy work shoes that looked as if they'd seen a lot of use. A thin frizz of white hair stood up from his head as if he were perpetually frightened. The wrinkles on his big-featured brown face were deep enough for agriculture.

He noticed me watching him and smiled with embarrassment as he descended the last few steps. Then the smile went away, and he wrinkled his nose. "You smell as if you spent the night in a field," he said as he put the tray on a stack of cardboard boxes.

"Fertilizer bag," I said. "Almost the same thing."

He shrugged and turned to go.

"Not so fast," I said.

"I got work to do," he said without looking at me. "Plugged sink upstairs." He sounded worried and defensive.

"The sink's not going anywhere," I said. "What is this place? What am I doing here?"

He shuffled in place. "I'm not supposed to talk to you," he said and put one foot on the lowest stair.

"I promise not to tell," I said.

He sighed. "A couple of the frat boys picked you up," he said. "Just youthful high spirits, you know?"

"Sure. I'm kinda cute sometimes. But which frat boys? What fraternity? And were they really just feeling their oats, or is something else going on?"

"I don't know. I'm just the janitor, you know?"

"I know. When you don't know, you don't know."

He turned and tried a smile on me. "Yeah. That's right."

I had the beginnings of an idea how to get out. "Wait for the tray," I said. "I can have a little company and you can take the tray back with you."

"I don't know anything," the janitor reminded me.

"That's fine. You can tell me baseball scores or something."

His eyes looked all over as if searching for an escape route, but at last he agreed. With a great show of heartiness, I pulled the cloth from the tray and discovered that it carried an individual serving box of corn flakes and a small carton of milk in addition to the coffee in a foam cup—not exactly my dream breakfast, but better than an empty stomach.

I opened the cereal box along a scored line and poured in the milk. While I ate with a plastic spoon, the janitor told me about the plugged sink and the broken window and the loose carpeting. I nodded and grunted amazement at appropriate moments, and he seemed satisfied. Soon the cereal was gone. I swallowed the last of the coffee, now tepid, and covered the remaining mess with the cloth.

"Thanks," I said.

"No problem," he said, and picked up the tray. "I'm sure somebody'll be down soon to tell you what's going on."

I nodded and waved. "Thanks again," I said as he ascended the stairs. At the top he turned the knob on the door to pull back the dead bolt. Obviously the fortification spell worked only on me. He went out and I heard him turn the lock on the other side of the door.

I waited exactly five minutes by my watch. Then I skulked up the stairs to the door, got as close to it as I could, and listened. I heard all the activity one might expect in a crypt.

I took a step back and studied the door. I had never been much of magician, but one thing Lord Slex had always said stuck with me—"Remember your basic fundamentals. The most complicated magic problem can be broken down into smaller simpler problems."

That's what I had done. I hadn't wanted the janitor to stay just because I was starved for company. I wanted him to stay because he would take the remains of my breakfast away when he left, long before he might take them otherwise. Those utensils I'd used, infected with whatever makes me me, were now fairly nearby on the other side of the door. By the law of contagion and using the right spells, I would act on them at a distance and they would act on me.

I grumbled my spell—all I wanted was to hook up with my trash on the other side of the door—and pushed against the fortification spell. Nothing happened, but I may have pronounced some of the words wrong. I tried again, grumbling a little louder. This time when I pushed against the fortification spell I sank through it as if through molasses. I felt the fortification spell circling my wrist and then farther up my arm as I pushed ahead and at last touched the knob that moved the deadbolt. I turned it and had the satisfaction of hearing the deadbolt slam back into its groove.

I waited to see if I had attracted any attention. When nothing continued to happen, I slowly pulled the door open and looked through a long hallway that had been painted landlord-white before I was born. A single will o' the wisp in the ceiling, faded with long use, did its best to illuminate the area. The surface tension of the fortification spell slid across my body as I stepped into the hallway. I moved along it without any trouble to a kitchen full of dirty dishes and old food, some of it so dry it no longer smelled. For some reason the place looked familiar. While I tried to figure out why, I moved through the kitchen to the next room. Though for my own protection I didn't touch anything, I did surprise a roach, which scuttled under a drift of ancient pizza cartons.

The doorway on the other side of the kitchen let me into what may have once been a formal dining room. It looked as if chimpanzees had been having a party there for some months. On the wall were posters of sports figures and naked women, sometimes posing together. Outside, branches of camellia bushes brushed against the windows like people trying to see in through the dirty panes of glass.

I heard a sound coming from the room beyond the dining room and froze. It was a dry sound, the kind a grasshopper might make turning over in bed. It came again, and then a grunt. I tiptoed across the floor and glanced sideways into the next room. A boy was sitting reading in a wingback chair that had seen better days, though by far it was the nicest piece of furniture in the room. A pair of brown oxfords rested on the floor next to the chair. Using one finger he pushed a pair of glasses up his nose, then turned a page of the book he was reading, making the grasshopper sound again.

The chair was one of half a dozen in front of a fireplace full of old fast-food wrappers. On the mantle were a crowd of loving cups and trophies. Over them, instead of a naked girl or a football player, was a framed painting of Lord Trask solemnly pulling a rabbit from a top hat. The artist who'd painted the portrait had tried to improve Lord Trask's appearance, but he still looked like a stately prune wearing a monocle and a thin mustache. Over the portrait was a metal plate with words engraved on it: Our Founder. Now I knew why the place looked familiar. Having been abducted and taken here fit nicely into what I'd been thinking during the night.

The nose of the lad in the chair twitched, and he looked up with surprise. "What's that smell?" he asked pleasantly.

"My sparkling personality," I said.

"Oh, a wise guy," he remarked. He looked at the dining room door through which I'd come. "I thought I was alone," he said with sudden suspicion.

"I was in the basement," I said. "That probably doesn't count."

"What were you doing in the basement?" he asked. "For that matter, what are you doing here at all? You're not a brother."

"I was, though, some years go," I said.

"Oh, an old boy," he said, liking the idea. He smiled again. "Reliving former Abracadabra glories?" he asked.

"Not exactly," I said. "I was brought here."

"By whom?" The lad was now entirely mystified. I didn't think I'd be able to help him much.

"A group of your frat brothers," I said.

"But why?"

"Just high spirits?" I suggested.

"Huh?" he replied.

"Nothing," I said as I walked quickly to the front door. "Sorry to have disturbed you."

He pondered me as I crossed the room, but he lost more interest with every step I took. When I reached the front door, I looked back at him. He was reading quietly again as if nothing had happened. Strange men emerging from the basement may have been fairly common occurrences for the current Abracadabra House. Not like in the good old days.

Once outside I stood on a cement porch looking up and down the block, which was crowded with big old two-story Craftsman houses, many flying colorful fraternity flags. Across the street a few houses down, five or six guys in shorts were sitting on their own front porch proving their manhood by drinking beer for breakfast.

I moseyed to the end of the block, the corner of Sorrento and Franklin. I pulled out my phone and was pleased to hear a dial tone. A two-word spell brought up my personal directory and I made it dial a number. One of Astraea's grandmothers answered the phone. She didn't seem surprised to hear from me, and she put Astraea on immediately.

I apologized for standing her up the night before, and suggested that if she picked me up and gave me a ride home, I would explain all.

"This is good," she said. "I will be there soon."

CHAPTER TWENTY-THREE
DIRTY LITTLE SECRETS

About ten minutes after I disconnected, a sedan chair floated to a stop in front of me. It was draped in various shades of orange that varied from tangerine to the color inside a conch shell. It was carried by four small white horses, none bigger than a standard poodle, each with a pair of wings growing from its withers. The feet of each horse trotted in its own small apricot cloud. I had seen fancier rigs, but not often.

Astraea leaned out at me and smiled, giving me that warm and fuzzily embarrassed feeling I found so pleasant. "Get in," she said.

I got in and reclined next to her on a lot of puffy pillows. Astraea grabbed a set of golden reins that waited for her in midair, and the sedan chair floated away.

Astraea looked terrific, as usual. She wore tight pants of some buttery yellow leather, with a matching jacket. Under the jacket was a white satin blouse with a deep V neck. Her sunlight-colored hair was tousled, which somehow only added to its perfection. It would still be nice to make love to this woman, but I'd gotten used to the idea that it would probably not be possible. Or I'd convinced myself that I'd gotten used to the idea, which was much the same thing.

I told her where I lived, and she nodded. "You have a peculiar smell," she said as she maneuvered through traffic easily, using the golden reins as if they controlled a single horse.

"It's a long story. But that smell is the reason you and I didn't go to the Magic Vault last night."

"I was worried. I did not like to think of you as unreliable."

"Thanks. I don't like to think of myself that way either. But you knew I would show up at last, didn't you?"

"I hoped."

I guess she wasn't going to say anything about her grandmothers and the information they could have given her if they were the Fates. "What kind of a vehicle is this?" I asked instead of digging further.

"It is this year's Bellerophon," she said proudly.

"Never heard of it," I admitted. "Import?"

"It has a limited availability," she said.

We were moving along at a good but normal clip. For a moment I watched the muscles in the backs of the front two horses moving under their skins. "How did you get here so fast?" I asked. "I couldn't have made it from Venice in less than forty minutes."

"I am Justice," she said. "I have ways. Tell me about the smell."

We should all have such useful ways. What she had done was impossible at any time of the day or night. I told her about being taken to the Abracadabra House in a fertilizer bag and spending many hours in the basement. I tried to make the story funny and was rewarded with occasional laughter like cold water over smooth stones.

"The dragon attack yesterday morning might be coincidental," Astraea said, musing. "Old magic does rise from the tar pits occasionally. But your abduction to the fraternity house seems directed at you specifically. And taken together, these two events seem even more suspicious."

"Do you believe in coincidences?" I asked.

"Not very much," she said.

"Me neither." I flicked a speck of fertilizer out the window. "I think Lord Philpot and Lord Trask were responsible for my most recent adventures."

"Many people at PrestoCorp could manifest a dragon,"

Astraea reminded me. "And not a few at Cal Thau or at Thau Tech could do it."

I nodded. "That already occurred to me. But to use the magic in the tar pits you need a connection with it. That means whoever conjured up that dragon had to be doing magic during Prohibition. Dr. Hamish at PrestoCorp and members of her staff I saw were just kids back then. And I checked on the lords at Cal Thau and Thau Tech. Every one of them was back east during Prohibition. The chance they would have magic in the tar pits is slim."

She said nothing until we pulled up for a red light. Then she looked at me and raised an elegant eyebrow. "Did one of them kill Misty, and the other steal Eulalie Tortuga's soul? Or did they do both together?"

"None of the above, I think. I think both of them are running scared about other things entirely—things I was getting close to without even trying."

"What other things?"

She turned back to the traffic as we began to move again. "Things," I said. "For instance, Lord Philpot enjoys extracurricular activities with his students."

"They do not visit museums together, I suppose," Astraea said, and she smiled in a way women have been smiling since the dawn of time.

"No. He sleeps with his students—at the moment with a good-looking blonde lady named Marjory. I was introduced to her at the Broken Wand, a student hangout. Yesterday, when I called Lord Philpot to make an appointment to see him, she answered his phone."

"Perhaps she is his assistant."

"Perhaps," I admitted. "And perhaps he helps Marjory with her homework, too. She's cute, but she has no more talent for magic than a couple of crossed sticks. Why would Lord Philpot chose someone so magically inept for an assistant unless he had something besides magic in mind? For that matter, without his help how would she become a student at Stilthins Mort in the first place?"

"It is unethical, yes?"

"Yes. And apparently Marjory is just part of a pattern. Lyda Firebough tells me that Lord Philpot dated Misty while she was an undergraduate student."

Astraea carefully considered this piece of news. "Misty was not inept," Astraea said. "My understanding is that few were more ept."

I chuckled. "You're beginning to talk like me," I said. "She was still his student," I went on more seriously. "And also a blonde babe—he seems to have a weakness for blondes. It would be difficult to believe he kept her around just for her magical abilities."

"But he did not kill her?"

"It's possible, but no. First, so far I haven't heard anything like a motive. Second, a man in his position would be afraid that a murder investigation would shine a bright light onto his whole life, maybe revealing his dirty little secret."

Astraea nodded. "We will speak to him this evening at the Magic Vault."

"If he's there. And we'll talk to Lord Trask, too."

Astraea turned south on LaBrea. "Lord Trask also has a dirty little secret?"

"Yes, indeed. Even dirtier, maybe, depending on your point of view. But let me start at the beginning. After spending the night in the basement of the Abracadabra frat house, the janitor brought me breakfast. I knew who he was because I eventually remembered seeing his photo in the newspapers a few years ago. His name is X Marks, and he's a notorious small-time pen man last caught working in San Francisco."

"What is a pen man?" Astraea asked.

"A specialist in counterfeiting signatures and other fancy artwork. He was working with a man named Ian Tahern, currently known as Lord Trask, a con man who is no more a wizard than he is a doctor or an oil baron. I'm still trying to figure out how he got onto the board of Stilthins Mort. Did he drop a big donation of worthless stocks and bonds on the school, or did he cut to the chase and invent a background paper trail? According to the San Francisco cops, he can be very convincing."

"He arranged for some of his fraternity boys to abduct you," Astraea said as she turned right onto Sixth Street and we tooled west past four-story brick apartment buildings that looked as permanent as redwood trees. Immediately the air seemed cooler, though I probably just imagined it.

"He did. What concerns me personally is how long he was going to keep me in that basement."

"Maybe he thought he could eventually convince you that investigating the people closest to Misty was not in your best interest. Eventually, perhaps he would kill you."

"Then I must be a real disappointment to him," I said. The white buildings of the La Brea Towers came up on our right. After another block or two I had Astraea turn into the complex. It had taken about half an hour to get me home, so apparently she hadn't used any of her "ways" to get us there. She found a place to park, but neither of us got out of the sedan chair.

"If those two lords hadn't been so damned paranoid and cagey I might not have bothered to make all these connections. But the dragon coming out of the tar pits suggested that if I was wrong about any little detail in their backgrounds, that detail would be replaced by something even worse. The whole kidnapping scene convinced me that I was right."

"You have no need to call the police," she announced. "I am Justice."

"Reading my mind?" I asked with surprise. I had, in fact, been thinking about turning in the lords Trask and Philpot.

"No. Just guessing."

"The police might have a different viewpoint," I suggested.

"They might. Ultimately it will not matter. I am Justice. Now that you have revealed criminals to me, I will take care of everything."

"We still don't know who killed Misty or who stole Eulalie's soul," I reminded her.

"Everything in its time."

I chuckled a little. "I guess if you live with the Fates long enough, you learn to be philosophical."

"Go. You have things to do, as do I," Astraea said with sudden energy.

I pushed back the peach-colored curtain on my side. Around us life went on: old folks tottered along with shopping bags, kids chased each other and played ball, gardeners herded their enchanted sheep. "I'll pick you up at eight," I said.

"The Magic Vault. Of course," she said as if she had forgotten.

I got out of the sedan chair, and it soared away, gone in no time. I entered my building under the appraising eyes of some old folks sitting on a sunny bench at the building's entrance. In my apartment I did a few personal hygiene spells—I would rather have used hot water, but there wasn't time—and then changed clothes.

When I was once again clean and splendid I called Silverwhite to apologize for not appearing last night, and suggested that we try again this evening. I spoke to his phone imp. Hoping for the best, I left my message and went out again.

CHAPTER TWENTY-FOUR
PUCKER UP

Eulalie Tortuga's home was nearby in miles, almost walking distance, but measured in terms of class and style it might as well have been in Oz. It was between Third and Beverly on a block of Highland that was divided by a grassy median. Down the center of the median a row of tall old palm trees grew like a picket fence.

Like a lot of dwellings in that neighborhood, Eulalie's was a weathered pile of red brick that was too big to be a house and too small to be a mansion. It was wrapped as a gift in thick tattered layers of ivy tinted a million shades of green, leaving only the doors and windows uncovered. I took a chance and parked in the half-moon of cement driveway that had replaced the front lawn.

As I approached the front door I ran into an invisible wall and red letters appeared in the air saying Police Line—Do Not Cross. With one hand on the invisible wall I followed it around the side of the house, looking in through windows as I passed them. Some were curtained, but others were clear and let me look into big rooms with hardwood floors; hanging from walls were fanciful paintings full of brush strokes and color, and resting on tables were odd bits of metal, glass, and wood that didn't look like anything and so must have been art, too. Probably important, expensive art—right up to the minute stuff. I had to wonder who was kidding who.

The backyard was a square plot of grass that hadn't been cut in a week or two. In one corner of the yard was a forlorn tree that was so twisted and gnarled, it looked as if it had dropped in from the fairy kingdom of Griffith Park. Under it was a wrought-iron bench one would sit on only as penance. In the other corner was a two-car garage that was closed and padlocked. At the back of the main house I came to a pair of French doors through which I could see the machinery of a home gymnasium. I crossed the flagstones, getting as close to the house as the police line would let me, and peered into the room.

A treadmill, a stairstep machine, and a couple of weight-lifting gadgets rested on gray indoor-outdoor carpeting. The machines were dark now, their spells faded. The wall opposite the French doors was all mirrored so that I could look at myself looking in. I was about to continue on to the other side of the house when I caught a distortion in the air up in one corner of the gym. I wasn't surprised the police had missed it. I would never have seen it myself if I hadn't known exactly what to look for.

It was one of those space puckers I'd seen in Misty Morning's laboratory, but there was something different about it, too. I stared at it trying to decide what the difference was. Suddenly, I noticed that the pucker was bigger than the others I'd seen. Assuming they all started out the same size, and that the ones in Misty's lab were the oldest, the difference in size might mean the puckers slowly dissipated over time. Great. Disappearing evidence.

I crossed the grass to sit on the wrought iron bench, which was as cold and uncomfortable as it appeared. The bench fit my mood exactly. I didn't want to be comfortable, I wanted to think.

Either the thing that made the puckers was portable or Eulalie owned one. If she owned one, had she gotten the machine from Misty, or had they each gotten one from somewhere else? How many pucker-makers were there? Was some underworld character turning out puckers like fake ID? I hadn't ever heard of such a thing, but you never know. I may have missed the memo.

Of course, Misty had not had her soul stolen, she had been murdered. Why would somebody bother to create a pucker if he or she wasn't going to use it? To confuse the police? If so, the criminal would have made the puckers more obvious. No. Misty had made the puckers herself using some method of her own, for reasons of her own. The person who stole the method could have killed her to get it. That would make a nice motive. Okay. One pucker-maker, then, and somebody had stolen it.

Was the person who stole the pucker-maker the same person who had taken the souls of Eulalie and the three guys? That would make sense. Who else would want it? Had this person also murdered Misty? Probably, but not necessarily. Like Lord Slex and Vic Tortuga, the space puckers seemed to be a connection between Misty's murder and the taking of the souls. But even with access to the space puckers, removing a soul in the first place seemed impossible for anybody but a keres. The only suspect I knew for sure wasn't a keres was Vic Tortuga—and even he might have hired one if he'd had the chance.

The longer I sat on the iron bench, the less I thought about the case and the more I thought about how hard the bench was. I went back to my car still turning things over in my mind but not making much progress.

As I drove around the driveway and out onto Highland, I noticed a car begin to move at nearly the same time. It was a small sporty Circe painted a deep purple. The driver seemed to be a big mouse—which couldn't be right. I looked again while I waited for the traffic to clear and it was still a mouse: big ears like ping-pong paddles, long nose with a thing like a black olive at the tip, bristly whiskers. Whoever was driving was wearing a masquerade spell, of course: Fashion victim.

I drove up to Melrose Avenue and turned left. Starting in the mid 1980s the hipper element had slowly migrated up there from Fairfax. Now Melrose was crowded with stores full of outrageous clothing for the youth market and holes in the wall where, for a price, one could get any part of the body pierced or tattooed, even parts I didn't care to think about. Spells that would horrify the parents were also available. Above it all the Hollywood Hills continued looking down without concern. The occasional white stucco house glared out from the hillside like a hunk of ice.

I turned onto Genesee, a street so narrow a car with an extra coat of paint would have trouble passing a car going the other way. Four-story buildings in fruit colors lined it like teeth, each one squatting on a lot that fit it exactly. Nobody had died and left me a parking space at the crowded curb, and I eventually had to put money into a meter on Melrose.

I walked back to the building I wanted, a dusty lime-green cube. I mounted three red steps and walked into the cool dim hallway. A heavy odor compounded partly of aging wood and plaster, and partly of immigrant cooking, gathered me into a warm paw. Rising to the second floor was a long stairway carpeted with the same aggressive pattern of big flowers that covered the first floor hall. Under the stairway I found a row of mailboxes. Lupinsky was in number 27.

While I walked up the creaking stairs, a woman behind one of the doors below yelled angrily in a guttural language. A child shrieked and began to cry. A door slammed and all noise stopped as if a playback had been interrupted. On the second floor I knocked on a wide brown door with a 27 on it.

The door was opened by a tall, fat man with a great fuzzy black beard. His features were large and fleshy. He scowled at me, which didn't make him any more beautiful. Suspenders rolled like tire tracks over his sparkling white shirt, the ends hooked to the waistband that rode high over his big belly.

"Yes?" he said as if I'd already insulted him.

"My name is Turner Cronyn. I'm investigating what happened to Merv Lupinsky."

"The police were already here."

"I'm making an independent investigation connected with another matter."

"What other matter?"

I saw that he and I could play Twenty Questions all afternoon. I was about to push past him into the apartment when an older woman came up behind him wiping her hands with a dishrag. Time had not been kind to her. She rubbed her nose with a tissue she took from a pocket in an apron that looked as if it had once been part of a cheap cotton dress very much like the one she now wore. "Let the man in, Irv," she said in a tired voice. "Maybe he can help."

After a moment Irv stood aside, allowing me to enter a living room full of old furniture covered in plastic. "Thank you, Mrs. Lupinsky," I said, guessing who she was. Two floor-to-ceiling windows, now open to let in a slight breeze, looked down on the street. Mrs. Lupinsky settled with a sigh onto the couch, crackling the plastic that covered it, and immediately began to sniffle. Tears welled in her eyes.

"My son didn't know me this morning," the woman said. "He didn't know anything. Why would anybody do that to Merv?"

Irv stared at me angrily. "This guy doesn't know anything either, Mama," he said accusingly.

I tried a smile on him, without effect. "Irv is almost right," I said. "I know very little. If you read the papers, you know as much as I do. That's why I need your help. Did Merv know anybody named Renaldo Duncan, Joe Flynn, or Eulalie Tortuga?"

Mrs. Lupinsky worried over that question. Slowly, she shook her head.

"Tortuga?" Irv asked. "Does she have something to do with that writer, Vic Tortuga? He writes smut. Nobody in this family would have anything to do with him; no good person would."

"Understandable," I said, just trying to get along. I opened my hands. "You see how little I know? That's why I was hoping you could tell me something about your son, anything that might give me a clue who did this to him and why."

"We already talked to the police," Irv reminded me.

Going around that particular mulberry bush again seemed pointless. I looked at Mrs. Lupinsky. "Anything you could tell me might help."

The old woman opened up, then. Trivial information gushed from her—little domestic details about what a swell person Merv was, how he was kind to animals and to his mother, and did his best to get along with his brother, Irv. At the moment he was under observation at Cedars-Sinai Hospital. "He was a technical writer, you know."

"So I understand. Do you know what he was working on?"

She looked at Irv with her sad watery eyes. "Please, Irv."

Without a word Irv stalked heavily from the room and returned a moment later with a manila folder that he thrust into my hands.

The plastic couch cover crinkled beneath me as I sat down to read the contents of the folder. But I didn't even have to open the cover to be jolted. Stamped in big red letters on the front were the words PROPERTY OF PRESTOCORP. PRIVILEGED INFORMATION FOR THOSE WHO NEED TO KNOW ONLY. The fact that Merv had been working for PrestoCorp when his soul was stolen may have been only a coincidence, but it was interesting—perhaps even suggestive. That was something else I'd have to discuss with Harold Silverwhite.

Obviously the folder had a security spell on it because I couldn't open it. Even if I could have taken a look at the papers inside I probably wouldn't get more than a general drift. I set the folder onto a coffee table that ran the length of the couch and was covered for most of that length with old women's magazines.

Mrs. Lupinsky held up a framed photograph. "Such a good boy," she said. "So smart and good-natured."

Like his brother, Merv was a chubby boy with a black beard. I stared at the photo and tried to mentally subtract the beard and add some hair atop his head. I'm not that good. He might have looked like me, maybe not.

I thanked her for showing me the picture. She turned it around and, looking at it herself, got a little hysterical. She pleaded with me to find out what had happened to her boy and to make him the way he had been.

"Look," Irv shouted. "You made her cry! Get out! Get out!" He pulled open the front door so hard that it banged against the wall and swung back the other way.

I was already moving toward the doorway when I noticed something near the corner of the ceiling. It was a space pucker, of course, the biggest one I'd seen so far. Which might mean it was also the newest. I don't think they'd noticed it or Mrs. Lupinsky, at least, would have mentioned it. I went out without mentioning it either. If Irv climbed a ladder to get a better look at it before it faded back into the fabric of the universe, Mrs. Lupinsky would probably lose another son.

* * * * * *

A guy with a green Mohawk haircut and an extra set of eyes looking out of his forehead was leaning against my car smoking a cigarette. His earlobes dripped like water from a leaky faucet into nothing at all, to make a nice ripple effect at the level of his chin. When I got into my car, he saluted me and walked off without a word, clip-clopping like a horse. Wearing shorts to show them off, he had the hooves and shaggy legs of a goat— even his knees were on backward. On Melrose he wasn't worth a second look.

A car waited behind me, blocking traffic as I pulled out. I thought it would dive into the space I'd just vacated but instead it followed me up the street. It was a Circe, similar to the car I'd seen outside Eulalie Tortuga's house, but cornflower blue instead of purple, and the driver was a woman, a little over-made-up, with hair so blonde it was incandescent.

The Circe stuck within a block of me as I drove across town to Renaldo Duncan's restaurant in Culver City. Whether it was the same car and the same driver I'd seen before was difficult to know in a world where spells to make cars a different color, and to disguise one's self, are available to anybody with a few extra bucks.

I parked in the lot next to Renaldo's and waited a moment for the Circe, now blue, to pull in after me. But it went on down the block and rounded the corner. I shrugged. It wasn't the first time I'd been wrong about somebody following me.

Renaldo's, a one-room place with stucco walls, specialized in Mexican food. There were thousands of joints like it all over town. Good smells floated in the air, and I remembered that I hadn't eaten since breakfast. I sat down at a Formica-topped table.

Soon a pretty dark-haired girl in a dress encircled with colorful flounces took up the classic position near my table with book in hand and pencil poised. I ordered the *plato de enchiladas*, and when she came back with it a few minutes later, I asked her about the boss. She didn't know much about him, being new on the job, but she described him as "a nice man." To her knowledge he had nothing to do with any of the other names I mentioned.

The enchiladas were good, and when I got up to pay the bill she showed me a photograph hanging over the cash register. In the photograph a man in a black charro outfit stood next to a man in a business suit. The man in the business suit was clean shaven, and except for the slightly pudgy cheeks and the tan, he looked a lot like I had before Lord Slex put a spell on me.

I thanked the girl and went outside sucking on a toothpick. A bottle-green Circe was parked at the end of the block.

The air had been warming up all afternoon, and now it was hot enough that I was uncomfortable in my jacket. When I put the jacket into the trunk of my car, I noticed the copy of *The Rack of Time* I'd gotten signed for my father the night before. It reminded me that I had to pick Dad up from the airport at four. That gave me just enough time to visit Joe Flynn's house, with maybe a little over.

In my shirtsleeves I strolled down to have a look at the Circe. Now the driver was a television alien, with a lot of extra bumps on its face and long stringy orange hair. The alien didn't look at me as I passed. I quickly walked around to the driver's side and leaned in at the open window.

"Everything all right here?" I asked.

The alien looked astonished. "What?" it croaked in what may or may not have been the real voice of the person inside.

"Are you a fan, or are you just tailing me for practice?"

"I haven't been—" the alien said.

"That's all right," I said. "I just wanted you to know that I'm now going to the airport to pick up my dad. After I take him home, I'll be going home myself. It's been a long tiring day, what with being followed and all."

Without another word the alien started the bottle-green Circe and drove away. I had to leap back or be run over. I watched the car scuttle to the end of the block and turn right.

I walked back to my car wondering whether Herb Hillyer was in the alien suit. But he had been driving a Honda, and I didn't think he could afford even the basic Circe, let alone a Circe equipped with options like a car-of-a-different-color. Of course it could have been somebody else entirely, somebody else with an interest in Misty Morning or Eulalie Tortuga. I was pretty sure I would find out. The tailer almost always crosses paths with the tailee eventually.

Joe Flynn lived nearby. I suspected that visiting his house would be pointless, but I had to do it anyway, just for the sake of completeness.

Joe lived in a small house on a wide street full of small houses, none of them with walls thicker than cardboard. A square of anemic-looking grass lay defeated in front of each one. I put on my coat again, so as to look more respectable-like, and walked up the cement path to the front door. I knocked on the door and shortly spoke with a plain woman dressed in jeans and a colorful shirt that was frayed at the cuffs and elbows, the kind of outfit a woman might wear to do her chores. When I told her why I was there, all the life drained from her face but she invited me in. We talked for a while, she nervously and on the edge of tears. Nothing that she told me seemed useful. While she went on, I looked for a space pucker but failed to see one. When she was finished, I asked if I could see the rest of the house.

"Why?"

"Clues," I answered vaguely.

She nodded.

The place was full of plastic curtains and cheap furniture, but it was fairly clean. In the bedroom, Joe Flynn was lying flat on his back on his side of the bed, looking as if he were asleep. He was even snoring. On the dresser was a photograph of the woman, much younger and happier, standing next to a man who looked like a younger version of the guy on the bed. "Handsome dude," I said. She got all dreamy-eyed and dabbed at her eyes as if she were about to cry. When we got back to the living room, I told her that I was sorry about her husband, and she nodded again.

I thanked her for her time and went out to my car feeling generally crummy about getting up the hopes of people who would probably never again have a meaningful relationship with their loved ones. I had seen a big space pucker near the ceiling in the bedroom but had not mentioned it. I had learned as little as I had feared. That space pucker and our similar looks was all these guys had to do with either Misty Morning or Eulalie Tortuga. I shook my head.

The airport was a straight shot down the San Diego Freeway. On the way I saw a few Circes of various colors, each driven by a person who looked more or less normal. I couldn't even guess whether I was being followed.

CHAPTER TWENTY-FIVE
HOUNDS OF HELL

When I got within spelling distance of the airport, every surface in my car sparkled briefly. Seconds later, like a trained pig, I took my place in line with about a thousand other cars. I was behind three men in a rowboat that carried a few square feet of calm water around it. The airport spell shunted each vehicle to where it needed to go. When my turn came, a ramp dropped in front of me and I drove up it to the lot where people picking up passengers parked.

The federally mandated traffic spells around the airport were a real pleasure. It was too bad the voters were too cheap to pay for enchanting the freeways and surface streets.

I found the Golden Broom terminal and walked inside as a broomstick boomed overhead and shook the windows. The terminal was filled with large black cats. One of them waved its tail as it rubbed against my leg. I wasn't carrying anything more dangerous than a ring of keys, so the cat soon trotted off to pass another customer through security.

I walked along the crowded concourse, following arrows to the Golden Broom waiting area while trying to avoid suitcases floating behind people hurrying to their brooms.

After a long hike I found the gate through which Dad would come and sat down to wait. While I had nothing better to do, I studied the people around me. No mice. No ladies with hair the color of white-hot metal. Not even a TV alien. Just a lot of blank expressions on people waiting for somebody or something that could not come soon enough.

Outside the big windows a broom slid in for a landing across the tarmac and taxied up to the gate. Even in the slanting late-afternoon sunlight a golden halo showed around its brush. A few minutes later the door into the waiting room opened and people poured eagerly out of the broomway. Some were met; others walked off while attempting to get their luggage into the air with a wave of a hand and a packet of commercial spell dust.

Dad strolled through the doorway schlepping his overnight bag. I was afraid he might have forgotten that I didn't look the way I normally did, but he smiled when he saw me, and I went over to greet him. Suddenly I was struck with a dismaying idea so obvious I was horrified that I had not considered it before. I swear that it was not until I saw Dad step off the broomway that it occurred to me how much I normally resembled him and, therefore, how much danger he was in.

My smile was friendly enough as I approached him—I was genuinely pleased to see him, after all. "Trouble," I whispered hoarsely when I got close enough that only he would hear me. "Let's blow this Popsicle stand."

His smile fell as if someone had let the air out, and his eyes shifted up and back. He nodded once, and we marched from the waiting area.

As we entered the concourse, a man fell into step beside us. He wore a red satin baseball jacket with the words "Hounds of Hell" stitched across the back. His black hair stuck up in untidy spikes above a square face that was ugly in a heavy, determined way.

I was so surprised that it took a moment for me to process what I was seeing: it was the same guy who'd attacked me at Harold Silverwhite's cottage! Before I could do anything, even warn Dad, the guy grabbed him by the arm and pulled him away from me. Though Dad struggled, he had no more chance of escaping than a mouse has when caught in a spring trap.

"Hey," I cried while I reached out for Dad's other arm and grabbed air.

Shooting dirty looks, people dived out of our way as I hurried after Dad and his captor. I heard a police whistle, but it was too far away to do me any good. The guy pulled Dad through a door with a stenciled number on it. I got to the door just before it clicked closed behind them. By the time I got through, the two of them were far down a long empty cement corridor lit by tubes of industrial fairy dust. Our racing footsteps echoed into the hot heavy air.

When they exited through a swinging metal door at the other end, I was right behind them—so close I could see the acne pits on the back of the guy's hairy neck. Dad was sweating but still struggling, bless him. We entered a large room where big muscular men lifted impedimenta from rolling green conveyer lawns and dropped it through a hole in the floor.

Three airport security officers were waiting for us. My friend in the red jacket didn't even slow down. He dragged Dad across the room as if he were a doll and jumped into the hole while the luggage handlers watched with amazement. I made a small animal noise and leaped down the hole myself. The officers may have followed—I didn't know.

A moment later I was falling through a baggage cyclone, one more clumsy, oddly shaped package dropping from the sky. I almost lost my enchiladas. At the bottom, the baggage cyclone whirled me around, and through the dizziness I got a quick impression of people waiting for their luggage, now surprised by the sudden appearance of yet another man. I leaped over bags, suitcases, and trunks, then across an expanse of open floor to an escalator where Dad and the guy were already halfway up to the next level. At the top I found myself on another concourse. Neither Dad nor the guy in the red jacket was anywhere in sight.

People shrieked, getting out of the way as more security officers approached at a gallop. While I waited for them to arrive I turned my head, hoping to spot Dad and his buddy. All I saw was a fist the size of City Hall slicing toward my chin. I felt momentary pain and saw a bright hard flash, then knew nothing but darkness.

* * * * * * *

I awakened to harsh medicinal smells and bright light that came through my eyelids. My jaw throbbed, but that was OK. It was my jaw and I was glad to have it. I moved a little and stiff paper rattled under me.

"He's moving," a female voice said. I had heard it before but couldn't place it. There were a lot of things I couldn't place right at that moment.

"How are you feeling?" Dad said, and I opened my eyes. He was looking at me with concern.

I made some experimental sounds, which didn't do my jaw any good. "Fine," I managed after a while and passed out.

When I opened my eyes again, I was in the same place, but this time I was alone. I sat up on the edge of the bed, making it rattle again, dangling my feet and supporting my head with my right hand. I was in a small clean room, probably part of the airport infirmary. Through the open door I saw a waiting room from which three concerned faces looked at me.

Dad rushed into the infirmary with two women close behind. One was obviously a nurse, a middle-aged woman with a face that was not beautiful but full of kindness. The other was wearing a denim outfit and motorcycle boots—it was Lyda Firebough, Vic Tortuga's current squeeze. Even if I hadn't just been slugged by a guy in a red satin jacket, you could have blown me over with a summer breeze.

"How are you feeling?" the nurse asked professionally.

"Like the inside of a cement mixer," I said.

That made her smile. "He'll live," she said to Dad. "Don't leave without seeing me," she requested. "You'll have to sign some papers." She left.

"Who was that guy?" Dad asked.

Before I could answer, a short man in a blue blazer and white turtleneck entered. He had an enormous prow of a nose, and his skin was dark, as if he were always standing in shadow. On the pocket of his blazer was a complicated insignia involving a lot of keys and firearms.

"I am Stan Perisegian," he said in a somewhat foreign but melodious voice. "I am head of security here at the airport. As you might expect, I have a few questions."

I nodded, wished I hadn't, and grabbed my head again to keep it from rolling across the floor.

"You and your playmate caused quite a disturbance," he said.

I said nothing, just waiting for the good parts to come.

Mr. Perisegian shifted his weight. "Your father, here, tells me he has no idea who tried to abduct him or why. Do you know?"

"It involves a case I'm working on."

"Oh? Police?"

"Private."

He nodded but did not seem impressed. "You'll have to give me a little more than that," Mr. Perisegian said. "I have a report to fill out."

I had as much interest in his report as he had in the pain in my head, but I also knew he could give me a hard time if he thought I was hiding something that might endanger his airport.

"I'd like to know who the guy is, myself," I said. "He could probably help me solve my case." Which was true as far as it went. I assumed that the guy in the red satin jacket was the same joker who had been stealing souls all over town and shoving them down the oubliette of the space pucker. I was sure knowing that would not help Mr. Perisegian write his report.

"And he wanted what?"

"My father," I replied. "Or somebody who looked like him."

Mr. Perisegian smiled. "With those cagey answers you probably think you're protecting a client or some other ethical garbage, but really all you're doing is making trouble for yourself. If I don't get the answers I want, I intend to call the police."

"It'll be nice to see them again."

His smile wilted a little, but he was still game.

"Look," I said, "I know you have an airport to protect. And you believe I can tell you something that will help you do your job. But I don't think so. It's true that guy in the red jacket might return and cause more trouble if somebody who looks like my father passes through. But I have no idea how to stop him. I didn't stop him this time. I don't know how he was stopped."

"This young lady here seemed to surprise him," Dad said.

I looked at Lyda Firebough. She appeared to be a little tired, but she tried a smile on me. "We used to know each other," she said.

"And his name is?" Mr. Perisegian asked.

"Eddie 'The Ender' Tips," Lyda said.

"Sounds like a wrestler," Mr. Perisegian remarked. "What do you think he wanted with Mr. Cronyn?"

"I couldn't say. He never showed any particular interest in guys when I knew him."

Mr. Perisegian sighed. "Would you care to press charges, Mr. Cronyn? Either of you?" He looked from me to Dad.

"Against whom, for instance?" I asked. "You don't need my permission to look for the guy. I wish you luck. I've been looking for him for a few days and haven't found him yet."

Mr. Perisegian nodded as if that was just the sort of answer he had been expecting to hear. "Why don't you nice people just kind of scram? Okay with you, nurse?"

"Somebody has to sign the release."

Mr. Perisegian stayed in the small, clean room and watched us through the doorway while I signed the release form and we filed out onto another crowded concourse.

CHAPTER TWENTY-SIX
THE BLUE DIAMOND

Lyda walked arm in arm between us. Mostly for my benefit, we walked slowly. I ached all over, as if I had taken Eddie's punch with my entire body. In a sense I guess I had.

"How are you feeling, Dad?" I asked.

He shrugged. "Pretty good, actually. I haven't had that much exercise since the last time I let your mother take me grocery shopping."

I smiled, understanding.

A little farther down was a small, sparsely attended bar. Nobody paid attention to the TV on a high shelf mumbling to itself about sports.

The short walk had tired me out, but I felt better than I had. Lyda and I settled at a metal table far away from the other customers and not much larger than a dime, while Dad went to get three beers.

"You look like hell," Lyda said.

"Thanks," I said. "Nice to see you again, too."

She nodded. "Where's your partner?"

"Home, I guess. And Astraea and I are not exactly partners."

"Somebody should tell her."

"I see," I said. "Guilt by association."

A hefty security woman sauntered by and took up a station between the two doors of the men's room across the way. She began picking at one hand with the other. When she caught me staring at her, I smiled and waved. She didn't seem surprised.

She didn't seem anything. She went back to picking at her thumb.

Dad came back to the table with three beers in plastic steins and set them down, leaving just enough room on the table for our elbows, if any of us wanted to be so crude. We all did. Between sips we spoke softly into each others' faces.

The first tide of cold bitter taste swept mental cobwebs before it. Feeling a little more alert, I put down the stein and leaned forward. "Before we discuss my professional connections, Lyda, perhaps you can tell us how you come to be here. It must be quite a story."

She shrugged. "It's simple, really. I've been following you all day."

"That must have been you in the Circe-of-a-different color—the mouse, the blonde, and even the TV alien."

"I just hoped to keep you a little off-balance."

"You had me guessing, that's for sure. I'm just dying to hear your motive." I snapped my fingers. "Or did Vic Tortuga send you?"

"Good writer," Dad stated.

Disgust crossed Lyda's face. "He doesn't know where I am. And he doesn't know anything about the Blue Diamond."

Blue Diamond? Dad was about to ask the obvious question, but he thought better of it. "Um," was all I said.

Lyda stared at me until a grin split her face. She had a nice grin. "You have no idea what I'm talking about."

I nodded. "Just this once. Enjoy it while you can."

She shook her head. "And to think I was following you to—" She stopped and shook her head again.

Dad put down his beer. "The guy in the red satin jacket had something that looked like a blue diamond."

"I assume you're talking about the guy who hit me," I said.
Dad nodded.

"Eddie 'The Ender' Tips," I went on. "Any minute now we'll be getting around to Ms. Firebough's professional connections."

She attempted to cover her discomfort by taking a big swig

of her drink.

"What did Eddie do with this blue diamond?"

When Lyda said nothing, Dad explained. "After he knocked you out, Eddie shoved me into a room not much larger than a broom closet—it may have been a broom closet for all I know. He took this blue diamond thing from his pocket, pointed it up at a corner of the closet, said a couple of words I didn't catch, and a blue beam shot out. When it was gone, kind of a lens was left behind, as if the air had somehow thickened."

"Ah," I said with satisfaction.

"Meaning what?"

"Meaning that my theory about Eddie is probably correct. He's the guy who's been going around town stealing the souls of guys who look like me."

"He found me pretty quick," Dad pointed out. "I hadn't been on the ground more than five minutes."

"You don't look like any of the guys whose pictures I've seen in the paper," Lyda said to me. She glanced at Dad. "You don't even look much like your father."

"I've had a little work done," I said, unaccountably embarrassed.

She gave me a sidelong look through her lashes. "I'd like to see the original some day."

I nodded, thinking that she was not the only one. But I wasn't ready to have the simple spell removed from my face. Not yet. I had too much to do.

"Would anybody like to hear the rest of my story?" Dad asked.

Lyda and I looked at him expectantly.

"I didn't think I would like what was going to happen next, but I never found out for sure because at that moment a silver-haired movie star entered the broom closet. When she got a good look at Eddie, her disguise popped like a long electric spark, revealing Ms. Firebough, here. Eddie took one look at her, threw his hands into the air, and shrank to a point of light that faded over the next few seconds. Ms. Firebough and I went to look for you. The rest you know."

We were all quiet while commuters hurried by out on the concourse.

"Do I have to convince you I'm intrigued?" I said. "Tell me about the Blue Diamond."

"Misty showed it to me a week or two ago," Lyda said. "It makes those space puckers, as you call them. Misty called them knots. That's why I didn't know what you were talking about when you mentioned 'space puckers' at Vic's house."

"What did Misty use them for?"

"Nothing yet. When I talked to her, the knot was just a scientific curiosity." Her eyes got large and frightened. "Do you think Eddie is stealing souls and using the knots to dispose of them? Is that what happened to Eulalie?"

"That would be my guess."

"But she doesn't look at all like those other guys or your father. She's not even male."

"I haven't worked that part out yet," I admitted.

"I seem to have fallen a little behind here," Dad said. "Would one of you care to explain how anybody could steal a soul?"

I explained all I knew about keres, about how their job was to take the souls of people who had died according to universal plan, about how if one of them took a soul on his own initiative the soul would hurry to reattach itself to the body it came from unless it could be disposed of quickly in some permanent way—using one of Misty Morning's knots, for instance.

"And he finds guys who look like you—how?" Dad asked.

"As I said, he's a keres. He has talents unknown to magicians."

"That's quite a fable," Dad said.

"That's the story as I know it," I said. "Take it or leave it."

"All right, then," Dad said. "Maybe whoever is stealing souls—Eddie, say—isn't stealing all of them for the same reason. Trying to shoehorn all the crimes into the same box is preventing you from seeing the separate truths."

"Which are?" I asked.

"As far as you know," Dad said, "you have no connection with Eddie 'The Ender' Tips. Why Eddie is stealing the souls of men who look like your unenchanted self remains to be revealed. But the other truth...." He stared at Lyda Firebough, and I soon joined him.

"Did Eddie know Eulalie Tortuga?" I asked her.

Lyda shuddered as she sighed. "He knew her," she said. "He was in love with her, but she wouldn't have anything to do with him. She and Vic had just broken up, and she might have thought she could still win him back. Hah!" The exclamation exploded out of her. It was nasty. "I had a little crush on Eddie myself," A tiny smile came and went like waves on a still pond. "I guess I've always had a weakness for the bad boys."

"Eulalie's rejecting Eddie would explain a lot," I said.

"I hope you catch him and arrest him," she said. "If he's a keres, it might not be possible. But if you can get him, I hope you do." She sounded bitter now, bitter as day-old coffee at the bottom of a pot. "I could have supplied the magic during Prohibition. We didn't need Merlin. But my magic wasn't fancy enough for Eddie. And none of them, not Eddie or Louie or Merlin, lifted a finger when the police picked me up. When Eddie saw me in the broom closet just now, I guess I surprised him. I guess he thought I might still be a little angry." She laughed ruefully. "I know I was surprised when I got a close look at who had bundled your father into that broom closet."

"If he has the Blue Diamond, Eddie probably killed Misty, too," I said. "But did he just kill her for the dingus, or because he had some personal argument with her the way he had one against Eulalie?"

"I don't think Eddie knew Misty," Lyda said.

"Then he didn't have one of her famous house keys." I pondered. "Not that he'd need one. As a keres he could get in and out of anywhere—he wouldn't need to leave by the front door, disguised or not. But if he didn't know Misty, he probably didn't know about the Blue Diamond, either. Unless you told him about it."

"I didn't. I have no idea where Eddie lives or how to contact him. Until I saw Eddie today, I hadn't had anything to do with him since the old days. I had no reason to."

"Then it was all coincidental. Eddie or somebody else killed Misty, and Eddie did his job. Maybe he showed up a little early and saw Misty playing with the Blue Diamond. The possibilities occurred to him, and he took it when he took Misty's soul."

"It might have happened that way," Dad agreed.

And, I continued in my head, if any of this conjecture was worth the hot air that saying it took, everything must have happened after Eddie attacked me at Harold Silverwhite's laboratory or he would have taken my soul when he had the chance. If. And his motive still seemed a little unclear, too. By the time Eddie had the Blue Diamond I looked like somebody else and he couldn't find me again. As good a reason as any for keeping my disguise for a while.

"Let's put that aside for a moment," I said. "Earlier you were about to explain why you were following me."

"I thought you might lead me to the Blue Diamond. And I guess you did." Lyda got philosophical and took a slow sip of her drink. "I just wanted Misty to get credit for inventing the thing," she went on, "whatever it turned out to do."

Dad looked at her out of the tip of his eye. "And make a buck or two on the side?" he suggested.

"Is that so bad? Being Vic's girlfriend is hard work. There are fringe benefits, of course, but it doesn't really pay very well."

"I'm sure that's true," I said. "Despite what a good writer he is."

Dad scowled at me.

"A detective more suspicious than I am might suspect that you killed Misty to get the Blue Diamond for yourself. The police said that anyone with two hands and a voice could have done it."

Lyda seemed so surprised I was almost sorry I had brought it up—almost. "Well, if I did, I botched the job. I didn't get the Blue Diamond—Eddie seems to have it."

"Fair enough," I said and took a drink. I hated a case where everybody knew everybody else—there were too many suspects. "Do you know Misty's mentor, Lord Slex?"

"Who?"

Her ignorance was a relief, but no surprise. "What about Louie 'The Mouth' Stuckler?"

"I figured we'd get around to him eventually," Lyda said. "As you may recall from Vic's lecture in his living room the other night, Louie was the fourth person in our happy bootleg quartet. When I got arrested, he didn't help me either, but I don't hold it against him. He did the best he could. He wasn't very bright, but he was a much nicer guy than Eddie. And he wouldn't need a key to Misty's apartment, either. He's a keres, too. He has a cauliflower nose, just like the guy you mentioned at Vic's."

I almost fell off my chair. "Is that so?" I said. "You might have said something earlier."

"When we talked at Vic's, you asked if Misty had any enemies that I knew of. I knew Louie wasn't an enemy, so when we got distracted by other things I kind of let it go. As far as I know, Louie and Misty never even met. And if he heard about the Blue Diamond, he didn't hear it from me."

"If they never met, why was he following her around?"

"He was following her around?"

I told Lyda and my father about meeting Louie at Stilthins Mort and then outside Misty's apartment.

"It makes no sense to me," Lyda admitted.

"Do you know where I can find him?" I asked.

"Sort of. I know he lives in an abandoned amusement park."

I stood up. "Thanks for your help, Lyda."

"That's it?" She sounded surprised and a little hurt.

"What more should there be?"

"Nothing, I guess," she said. "See ya round, shamus."

Dad and I watched her walk away, her black boots ticking against the marble floor.

"What was that all about?" I asked.

"I'm the wrong person to ask. Even your mother mystifies

me." He shook his head, stood up, and drained his stein. "Let's go see Louie."

"You're not coming with me," I said as I picked up his bag.

"Of course I am."

"We're already late. Mom'll be out of her mind. Besides, I have a few things to do first."

The security woman fell in a few yards behind us. She seemed to be just dawdling along, but she had no trouble keeping up with us.

"Call your mother on your cell phone," Dad said.

"You can't come with me," I said as we marched down the concourse toward the waning daylight. "It's too dangerous. What if Louie and Eddie are working together stealing souls?"

"What if they are?"

We reached the doors that led outside. I looked over my shoulder as Dad and I pushed through the spell. The security woman had stopped just within the concourse and was watching us the way she might watch rain fall. Apparently her interest, and probably the interest of Mr. Perisegian, ended at the door.

The argument I had with Dad continued until we found my car. It continued as I negotiated the ramps and tunnels out of the airport. It continued as we rolled up the San Diego Freeway slowly enough for sight-seeing. By the time I got him home, I'd convinced Dad that leaving town for a while would be a good idea. Even if he wasn't afraid of what a keres might do to him, his safety would comfort Mom. Comforting Mom was an argument for which he had no defense.

"Stay to dinner," Mom suggested at the front door. "We're having chicken."

"Yes, do stay," Dad said and smiled innocently.

"After I solve this case," I said, "I'll spend the day."

Mom nodded sadly, but I don't think she was convinced.

I backed out of the driveway feeling as if I was abandoning her. I liked my parents, but if I didn't live my own life they would be delighted to let me help them live theirs. Maybe they understood intellectually my need to make my own decisions, but letting their little sonny-boy go was always difficult for them—and going was always difficult for me. Still, by the time I got to the freeway, I was all right again. I had business at the Magic Vault.

CHAPTER TWENTY-SEVEN
THE MAGIC VAULT

The freeway was pretty sluggish at that hour, so getting to Venice took a little longer than I expected. When I got there Enough Rope was dark. I tapped on the door and Ms. Rule emerged from the gloom to let me in. She was wearing jeans and an Enough Rope t-shirt. Her attire seemed a little informal for one of the Fates, but I was no expert on what goddesses wore in their time off.

As before, Astraea emerged from behind the beaded curtain. With all the light behind her she looked even more like an angel than usual. She wore a silver dress with blue highlights, her blue stilettos matching the highlights. The dress was long, but slit nearly to her hips on both sides.

In a moment we were back out in my car. Her grandmothers had not suggested a curfew, which was just as well. Murder investigations keep their own hours.

During rush hour, which seems to add about twenty minutes at each end every year, there is no good way to drive from Venice to Hollywood. We had plenty of time to talk but not much to talk about.

"Did you do what you needed to do?" I asked.

"It has been done. And you?"

I told her about the phone calls I'd made that morning and the legwork I'd done that afternoon.

"What about Merv Lupinsky?" Astraea asked.

"He could work for PrestoCorp a long time without running

into Misty," I said. "It's a big place. Besides, if she was just selling them patents, she probably didn't go down there much."

"You believe their connection is coincidental?"

"I don't know enough yet to believe anything. That's one of the reasons we're going to the Magic Vault this evening—to visit with Harold Silverwhite. He knows people who know people."

"And Lord Philpot will be there, too?"

"Yes, if we're lucky. He may not show up."

"Would that mean he was afraid of you?"

"Not necessarily. It might mean he has better things to do than talk to a cheap shamus."

"Cheap shamus. Is that you?"

"Unfortunately, yes."

With the perseverance of pioneers crossing the plains, we eventually closed in on Hollywood. We passed the small mansions on Franklin—a street that was attempting, like an old dowager down on her luck, to maintain her dignity—and turned left into a driveway that took us up a steep hill to a very polished-looking monkey who relieved me of eight bucks, buying me the privilege of having my car professionally parked.

The carhop almost broke his neck pretending he was not watching Astraea walk from the car to the massive front door of the Magic Vault. The doorman, a man no bigger than a bread truck, smiled and welcomed us as he pulled open the vault-like door with a stainless steel handle the size of a baseball bat. Inside, the lobby was decorated to within an inch of its life by magical artifacts from all through history—many of them looking like instruments of torture. In the center of the big room was a well from which smoke rose and then disappeared as it twisted toward the ceiling.

"Good evening," said a pretty woman wearing a rather old-fashioned gown. "Is this your first visit to the Magic Vault?" She smiled as if she meant it. She was good.

"I've been here before." I said.

"Very good," she said. "Give your password to the man at the door at the bottom of the stairs. And have a lovely evening."

She was now smiling at the giggling couple that had come in behind us.

Astraea glanced at me with concern.

"Come on," I said and without thinking took her hand. Without thinking, I guess, she let me.

I escorted her down a curved staircase to a heavy wooden door. I knocked twice, three times, then twice again.

"What—?" Astraea began, but was interrupted by a square panel in the door sliding open. A pair of dark eyes under bushy brows glared out at us.

"Swordfish," I said, and wiggled my eyebrows at him, Groucho-like.

The panel slammed shut and the door swung open on creaky hinges, releasing hot jazz, the rumble of conversation, and the smell of expensive alcohol—all air-conditioned for the comfort of polar bears. I led Astraea inside.

The main room was the size of a skating rink, and wide doorways hung with red velvet led to smaller rooms at the sides. Tables were scattered about and people in evening dress were scattered about the tables. A few of the customers wore wizard's robes. Everybody seemed to be having a good time. The bustling waiters wore tuxedoes with gleaming white aprons pulled up snug under their armpits. Grim-looking men, also in tuxes, stood in corners watching everything, and occasionally reached into their coats—a performance designed to suggest they were checking to make sure their gats were primed and ready, but they were probably just scratching.

"What sort of place is this?" Astraea asked.

"It's a magician's bar designed to look like a shuffleasy, one of the illegal magic clubs that opened during Prohibition."

"A bad time for wizards," Astraea remarked. "Why would any of them want to come here and relive all that?"

The couple that had come in behind us trotted down the stairs, still giggling, and we got out of their way as they hurried into the main room.

"For the same reason people go see World War II pictures—

because it's over and the good guys won. It's a safe thrill. You can knock any number of times on the front door and give any word for a password, they always let you in. The whole joint is show biz. Come on, I'll buy you a drink."

We walked across the room to a long bar heavily-carved with famous wizards doing famous tricks. The back bar, as carefully lit as a movie set, was crowded with bottles of varying size, shape, and obscurity. We strolled down to the end of the bar where Harold Silverwhite should have been stationed and found a stranger with a frizz of lifeless brown hair that was trying to find a foothold on his noggin.

"Harold's not here yet," I told Astraea, then ordered a gin and tonic for myself, and chardonnay for her. I was carrying the glasses to an empty table I had spotted when I saw two men sitting in a corner. It was the handsome Lord Philpot and the pruney Lord Trask, of course. I had not expected to see Lord Trask that evening, but his presence didn't bother me. They watched me come as I carried the glasses to their table.

"May Ms. Scales and I join you?" I asked.

"Of course," Lord Philpot said, and gestured to two empty chairs while Lord Trask watched us with something like horror. I could imagine why. Nobody had bothered to tell him that I'd escaped from the basement of Abracadabra House. Maybe nobody knew—I didn't know how often a frat boy would check.

Astraea and I settled. She sipped her wine while I made introductions all around. The three of them nodded at each other like bobble-head dolls. Philpot took her hand gently in his and over it said he was delighted to meet her. He glanced up at me. "We waited for you last night," he remarked casually.

I looked at Lord Trask. "Something came up," I said. "A personal matter."

Neither of the lords bit on that. "Nice place," I went on in a conversational tone, glancing around as if I owned it and was thinking of turning it into a parking lot.

Lord Trask grunted and drank from a glass that looked as if it contained ice water but probably did not. He shrank into himself, as wrinkled and unhappy as an old faded paper flower. He wasn't glad to see me, but he didn't know that I suspected him of having me abducted. It was to his advantage not to ask questions.

"I was told you wanted to speak to me about Misty Morning," Lord Philpot said. "I don't know why. I told you everything I knew in the board room the other day."

"Then why are you here?" I asked.

He shrugged. "As a courtesy to you," he said. "Besides, I come here often. It is like spitting in Anna Montaigne's eye and giving Charles W. McGonigal a hot foot."

Astraea and I nodded.

"I assume you have an idea," he went on. "I am curious to hear what it is."

"You seem to have a lot more confidence in me than Lord Slex does."

"Perhaps it is because I don't know you as well."

I laughed at that, and Astraea smiled.

"What is your idea, Mr. Cronyn?"

"Just that you and Misty were closer than I, and perhaps the other members of the board, were led to believe."

"This idea comes to you how, Mr. Cronyn?"

"I have to protect my sources, sir."

"Of course."

We drank while good times raged around us. A grotesque crone in an evening dress walked through the room on the arm of a beanpole of a man in a coat and tie. They were angry about something. "I'll get you!" the woman cried and pointed at individuals in the crowd. They laughed at her and made rude remarks. "I'll get you all! Magic is sinful!" I was reminded unpleasantly of Eddie "The Ender" Tips.

"Go back to Hell where you came from," Lord Trask cried and threw a wadded-up paper napkin at the women. It fell between the tables far short of its target. The couple didn't even slow down, and soon went out a side door that said Employees Only.

"Anna Montaigne and Charles W. McGonigal," Astraea said.

"Appearing nightly," I explained. "Every forty-five minutes until closing."

"They don't get any respect," Lord Philpot said. "Those of us who suffered through Prohibition with the original cast find the performance quite satisfying."

"Tell me about your relationship with Misty."

"There is no law against seeing one's students socially."

"No," I admitted. "But the fact that you neglected to mention your relationship earlier is a little suspicious."

"It is not suspicious," Lord Philpot said. "It is only private. Besides, there was no relationship, not in the objectionable sense you mean."

I nodded as if I believed him. "Were you angry when she dropped you?" I asked suddenly.

"She didn't—"

I held up one hand. "All right. Was *she* angry?"

"Neither of us dropped the other. There was no relationship."

I'd have more luck carving marble with my teeth. I tried a different tack. "Like the other lords, you were sure that Misty had no enemies. Was that your private idea, too?"

"I don't know who killed her, if that's what you are asking."

"Always the same questions," Lord Trask grumbled, his diction a little loose. Now I was sure the clear liquid in his glass was not water. His statement startled me. Maybe he was right. I seemed to be going in circles. Each of these birds had his own dirty little secret, but neither of them seemed to have much to do with Misty's murder. I stood up and Astraea rose beside me. "Have a lovely evening," I said and made a short bow. Astraea and I got away from the table with as much grace as we could.

"Tomorrow morning nothing they say or do will matter," Astraea said to me softly.

"No?" I raised an eyebrow at her.

"You brought them to Justice. Their fall will be in all the papers."

"I still think the police—"

"Fear not."

"What did you actually do?" I asked.

"Encouraged the universe to follow its course."

"That's pretty ambiguous."

By this time we were back at the bar. The depressed little man was gone and in his place was Harold Silverwhite. Tonight he wore a fawn gray Edwardian suit—a little tighter style than was fashionable at the moment, but very natty all the same. A cold beer stood before him sweating on a paper coaster. "Turner, old chum!" he exclaimed. "How nice to see you." He smiled at Astraea. The smile was genuine and had a lot of heat behind it. I knew Silverwhite well enough to know that he would have smiled the same way if she'd looked like a walrus. "Who is this charming person?" he asked.

I introduced them to each other and they shook hands.

"What can I do for you, old chum?" he asked.

CHAPTER TWENTY-EIGHT
A DELICATE CONSTITUTION

The joint was filling up, and the bar, which had been half empty when we walked in, had almost every seat filled. In some popular locations people were two and three deep.

"Come join me in my private thinking parlor," I said, and led them to an strangely empty table in the middle of the room. I thought Philpot and Trask were watching us, but when I smiled in their direction they ignored me.

"Have you heard about the Misty Morning case?" I asked Silverwhite when we were settled.

"Only what I read in the papers, old chum."

"I don't think the papers mentioned her latest project—some kind of thickening of the air into lens shapes. I'm told that Ms. Morning called them knots. Each knot sucks things in, even souls, and doesn't let them out. I don't think so, anyway. Do you like it so far?"

"Tickety boo, old chum. But souls?"

"Maybe you haven't read in the papers about how Eulalie Tortuga and some other people are suddenly without intelligence or personality—zombies, the paper said."

"Ah. You believe there is a connection between these zombies and the death of Ms. Morning," Silverwhite suggested.

"We believe so," Astraea said.

Astraea and I drank while Silverwhite rocked in his chair a little, a thoughtful expression on his face.

"Anything about it on the jungle telegraph?" I asked.

He frowned, considering. "Not a thing. And keeping a project like that quiet would be difficult. There would be rumors, if nothing else. I'm quite interested. Tell on, old chum."

"I was hoping you'd say that. I have a copy of Ms. Morning's laboratory log out in the trunk of my car. The only problem is that it's in code. Nobody can read it."

"You've brought me a challenge, old chum!" Silverwhite said with delight. "My van is here and at your service."

"Van?" Astraea asked.

"I will personally give you the two-shilling tour," Silverwhite assured her.

"Hang on, Blackstone," I said. "Before you begin showing Ms. Scales how to pull rabbits from hats, I have another question. Ever hear of a fellow named Merv Lupinsky? He was a tech writer recently working for PrestoCorp."

"I'm afraid I don't know Mr. Lupinsky. Sorry."

"Ms. Morning had sold some patents to PrestoCorp—her car-of-different-color, for one. I'm thinking she and Mr. Lupinsky might have known each other."

"They worked together?"

"I have no idea. I was hoping you and your sources would surprise me."

Silverwhite checked the spelling of the name with me and made a note on his paper coaster. "Anything else?" he asked.

"Just the log," I said.

"Very well, then," he said as he stood up, "let us adjourn to the parking lot."

Getting out of the Magic Vault was a lot simpler than getting in. We merely walked out a door marked EXIT and found ourselves back in the lobby. "Have a *bueno* evening," the hostess called gaily as we left.

Outside, the gentle air was a little warmer than the processed stuff inside. It touched us with silky fingers and sent us the sweet perfume of night-blooming flowers. The carhops were gathered around a small lighted sentry box listening to a radio that gave out plenty of static along with the *mariachi* music. Silverwhite told the carhops we weren't leaving, just getting items from our cars. We showed our claim tickets and got our keys back, each hooked to a paper tag with the number of the spot where our car was parked.

At the bottom of a long steep driveway we came to the parking lot. Another carhop straightened to attention, hid a cigarette behind his back, and asked if we required assistance. We didn't and he relaxed.

We found my car and I got the log book. The three of us walked it to Silverwhite's van, which was parked the next aisle over and down a ways.

He used his keys to open the double back doors, releasing the pent-up smell of chemicals and herbs. The whole inside of the van contained a complete chemical laboratory, with a specialty in magic. It was crowded but neat—it had to be neat to get everything in.

"Wonderful," Astraea remarked, awed.

"Thanks," Silverwhite said. "I've been a consultant for a long time, and early in my career I never had what I needed when I wanted it, so I designed this van. Over the years I refined the design until I came to the magnificent organization you see before you. There is very little I can do in my laboratory at home that I can't do in this bit of rolling stock."

"But he's just being modest," I said.

"Wonderful," Astraea remarked again.

"I have a lot to be modest about, old chum," Silverwhite said as he climbed up into a space that was just big enough for him, sat facing us on a stool, and pulled a table down in front of him. "Let's have it," he said and held out his hand. I gave him the log book.

He conjured up a will o' the wisp that shined a bright light onto the table top. He inspected the outside of the log, then opened it and inspected that. He turned pages with fingers that were nearly as rakish and elegant as Astraea's legs, stopping now and then to fire fairy dust from the tip of his index finger at a particular word or phrase. Through it all he hummed selections from *The Mikado*. It was a performance as much as it was an analysis. I wondered if the performance was for our benefit or his own.

When he'd been through the log once he put it down, stared at it, and drummed on it with those long amazing fingers of his. He rolled backwards into the van on his stool, collecting leaves and bits of bark from shelves as he went. Seconds later he returned and made a tiny bonfire next to the book on the table. He held the log book over the bonfire, allowing the smoke to gather around it like a ball of dirty yarn. Silverwhite waved the smoke away, opened the book again, and frowned at a few pages. By this time he'd stopped humming.

Suddenly he waved his hand over the bonfire, making it disappear, then closed the book and gave it back to me. I'd rarely seen a man more defeated.

"Well?" I asked.

"No charge," Silverwhite said.

"You weren't going to charge me anyway," I said. "You couldn't read it, could you?"

"No."

"And that bothers you."

"You make me sound like a man with a very fragile ego, old chum." He spoke carefully, like someone walking on a wet floor.

"Nothing like that," I told him. "It's just that I know you hate to leave a problem unsolved."

He inclined his head once.

He was still thinking when he climbed down from his van and locked the doors—considering alternatives, remembering old spells he may not have used in years. "A pleasure to have met you," he told Astraea.

"And you." She rested her hand on his wrist. "You are not dead yet," she said. "Call Turner if something occurs to you."

He gave her a creaky smile. He was looking at her, but not seeing her. His mind was elsewhere. "Thank you, my dear," he said.

"Let me know if you learn anything about Merv Lupinsky,"

I said.

"All right," he said. It was just something to say while he shook hands with me. He quickly got into his van and drove away, his engine noise soon lost in the rumble of traffic on Franklin Avenue.

Astraea and I strolled back to my car. I wasn't feeling very jaunty myself. I'd learned nothing new from Lord Philpot—or from Harold Silverwhite either, for that matter. If Silverwhite couldn't decode Misty's log book, maybe nobody could. Of course, the news was not all bad. If Silverwhite couldn't do it, Dr. Hamish probably couldn't do it, either.

"I like him," Astraea said.

"I like him, too," I replied. "Though he does seem to have a delicate constitution."

"Like some detectives I know," she said.

"That's not nice."

She smiled. "Just yanking your chain," she said. Her laughter invited me to laugh along with her.

I had one more thing to do this evening. All might not be lost. "It's a beautiful night for a drive along the coast," I said. "Want to come?" I remembered the smell of fresh ocean air that had remained behind when Louie 'The Mouth' Stuckler disappeared at the dead end of Misty's street. Lyda Firebough told me that Louie lived in an abandoned amusement park. Lucky for me there was only one abandoned amusement park within a hundred miles, and that one happened to be in Santa Monica, right on the ocean. Louie might be there.

"I think this is not a casual invitation," Astraea said.

"No. I'm going to visit Louie 'The Mouth' Stuckler."

"It is a beautiful night," Astraea said. "I will go with you."

We got into my car and I drove us west. When we arrived at the beach, the air was cold and the night sky was a swatch of gray corduroy. Orange lights shone down onto the pier from tall poles, and it was easy enough to find a parking place. Only a few spaces were taken, and those by early-evening smoochers who had no interest in anything but each other.

Astraea and I walked through the cold damp air to a high chain-link fence, each of us happy to be wearing a coat. The freshness of the ocean mixed, as it always does, with the stink of dead fish and seaweed, giving the beach an odor like no other.

We looked through the fence at the dark sinister jumble beyond, and over it at the big block letters, now gray with expired magic dust, that spelled out SNAP: SANTA MONICA NAUTICAL AMUSEMENT PIER, and wondered how we were going to get in.

CHAPTER TWENTY-NINE
A NICE HOVEL

"I remember this place," Astraea said, pleased.

"You came here often?" I asked with surprise.

"Once," she said. "I was curious."

"I'd think that an amusement park like this would be pretty dull for gods and goddesses. I heard they played chess using real people, mortals, for pieces."

"Being a god is not always as much fun as you may believe," Astraea said gravely.

I shrugged. "Few things are," I said. "I guess this place wasn't or it would still be in business."

The fence was bent away from one of the posts where thrill-seekers who'd come before us had snuck inside. We stood silently in the dark, invisible as a couple of black cats in a coal bin, until a crowd of noisy kids had passed at the land end of the pier. I ducked under the fence and stopped a few feet inside behind a fiberglass fish as big as my automobile. A sharp protrusion on the fence had snagged my shirt, ripping it. But I was a he-man and didn't care. Astraea appeared beside me. In that light I could not tell whether she had walked or arrived magically.

I recited a spell and a will o' the wisp collected itself out of reflected moonshine and floated before us. In the cold white light I saw six entrances, each blocked by a rickety sawhorse that was no more than a suggestion to keep out.

I chose an entrance, moved a sawhorse, and motioned the will o' the wisp ahead of us. Like a faithful dog on the scent, it led Astraea and me through a long tunnel decorated with paintings of fanciful sea creatures that once must have been pretty gaudy. At the other end of the tunnel we walked out into an enormous open space that was a Hollywood designer's idea of a quaint fishing village. A sign that said Admiral Benbow Inn creaked when it swayed. Ragged netting moved in the fresh ocean breeze. The place looked new in the near darkness, but where the will o' the wisp light touched walls I saw flaking paint, rotting wood, and rusting metal.

The main street of the village wandered off into the shadows. Below us, the ocean grumbled and crashed against the pier's pilings. I was suddenly taken with the immensity of the job I wanted to do. "This is a big place," I said, sounding worried even to myself. "Louie could be anywhere, if he's here at all."

"He's here," Astraea said.

"Where?" I asked.

"Close," she said.

Encouraged by Astraea's certainty, I knocked over a big metal drum full of trash. It clattered, breaking the night into a million pieces. Or maybe it just made a loud noise. A sheet of old newspaper skidded down the street like a crippled ghost and wrapped itself around a drainpipe. Astraea followed me when I strolled down a path whistling "The Caissons Go Rolling Along" as if I hadn't a care in the world. I stopped at a door or two and shook each one by the handle, then knocked like a brush salesman with a quota. I looked around and saw nothing but the old buildings and my will o' the wisp and Astraea. Standing still, and in that light, she didn't just look like a goddess, but like a statue of a goddess—unchanged and unchanging after a thousand years.

We passed a rollercoaster that had cars like little rowboats lined up at the bottom, and a restaurant in the shape of a whale. At the far end of the street was a rail fence and beyond that the wet blackness of the big petulant ocean. As we passed a carousel decked with seahorses a raspy voice called out to us.

"Hey, you."

I turned slowly, my body suddenly icy. Standing next to a

yogurt shack was a short man wearing red pants and a white shirt open at the neck. He had spiky hair, a red face, and a cauliflower nose. He held no weapon in his hands, but he didn't seem to be afraid.

"Louie 'The Mouth' Stuckler," I said.

He reeled back into the shadows as if I'd struck him, but was back in a moment. I was very careful not to have moved. Astraea had not moved either—a statue again.

"Says who?"

"My name is Turner Cronyn. I'm a detective. Lyda Firebough sent me."

He smiled. "You know Lyda? Gee."

"Yeah, gee," I agreed. "This is Ms. Scales, my associate."

He enjoyed taking a good long look at her.

"Can we go somewhere and talk?" I asked.

He nodded, hooked a thumb and walked off without waiting to see if we would follow. My will o' the wisp bobbed along next to me while we hurried to keep up with him. "Don't I know you?" he asked over his shoulder.

"We met a couple of times," I said. "Once outside the administration building of Stilthins Mort, and the other time just outside Misty Morning's apartment after she was murdered."

He stopped and looked at us with shock that seemed real enough for the emotion to be genuine. "Somebody whacked the babe?" he asked. He made wet noises with his mouth. "Who done it?"

"I thought you done it," I said.

He stared at me, then looked away immediately. He eventually led us to a high clapboard fence and pushed near the top of one of the boards. The bottom pivoted upward and he ducked under. The will o' the wisp and Astraea and I followed him.

The will o' the wisp made sharp sinister shadows in the area beyond the fence, a giant's playground of half-demolished buildings. Scattered around were mounds of dirt, stacks of splinter-like lumber, and piles of bricks with the corners broken off. Ancient pipes stuck out from the piles like the bones of prehistoric birds. I was glad for the will o' the wisp as we followed Louie along a downward-slanting path into a hovel beneath a mountain of rubble that looked as if it might collapse at any moment.

Actually, Louie's quarters were rather nice for a hovel. They contained a wing-backed chair designed to look as if it were made of coral, and a dinette set that had been new when Formica was the latest thing. Near the dinette set was a stove made from a big iron fish, and across from it was a huge soft bed that was lumpy with pillows, each of which had the sentiment "I Got Dunked At SNAP" stitched on it. The colors of anything were impossible to determine. The will o' the wisp made no headway against the light coming from a TV set that faced the coral chair. On the screen, shapely women in a rainbow of short snug dresses were dancing with enthusiasm to an orchestra that had been wound up too tight. The place smelled of steamed cabbage and wet earth.

The will o' the wisp floated over to the far wall where the entrance to a huge pipe made of corrugated metal led back into the mountain of rubble. Like a curious animal the will o' the wisp looked into the dark tunnel and lit the first few feet of it.

"Get away from there," Louie shouted in a voice much too loud for that small room.

I waved a hand, said a spell, and the will o' the wisp dissolved into the air with a small sigh.

With the will o' the wisp gone, the TV seemed much brighter. Louie stared at the TV sadly for a moment, then made a dismissive wave in its direction causing the picture to collapse and the music to stop in mid-squeal. With the TV off the room went black for a moment, and I stiffened, but then Louie stirred up his own will o' the wisp, which cast watery yellow light from its place in the center of the ceiling. He swaggered to the coral throne, leaving Astraea with one of the kitchen chairs. It swayed a little as she sat down, but it held her. I stood behind her.

"How is Lyda?" Louie asked.

"Pretty good, I guess. She's living with Vic Tortuga."

"Who's that?"

"Some writer."

He nodded as if I'd really explained. "I love musicals," he said with the enthusiasm of a man who could eat them for breakfast, lunch, and dinner. "The one I had on was 'Feathers.' Do you know it?"

"No."

Astraea didn't know it either.

Our answer disappointed him. His face curled up as if he was wondering if he could talk to people who didn't know their musicals.

"Look, Louie, I want to talk to you about Misty Morning."

He nodded, suddenly serious. "The dead babe. What is she to you?"

"I was hired to protect her, but I kind of muffed the job. Finding out who killed her seems to be the least I can do. How well did you know Misty?"

"I didn't know her at all."

His answer surprised me and I watched it drop to the floor like a rock. Astraea glanced around at me, eyebrows up. "Then why were you stalking her?" I asked.

Louie got comfortable on his throne. My line of questioning didn't seem to upset him. Maybe he hadn't killed her after all. "I wasn't stalking her, not exactly. I was just watching her."

"Why?"

"I was hired by a guy. He paid me off in musicals. I used to didn't know 'The Rains of Ranchipur' from 'Singin' in the Rain.' He gave me the good stuff. You know 'Singin' in the Rain,' miss?"

"I may have seen it once or twice," Astraea said. "Tell us about the man who hired you."

Louie shrugged. "The guy seemed to know me, but I never seen him before."

"What did he look like?" she asked, doing pretty well for a woman who claimed not to know anything about detective work.

Louie thought for a moment. "Just some guy," he said.

"Tall, short?" I prodded. "Fat, thin? Did he have a mustache or beard? Was he bald? Two heads? Three eyes?"

Bewildered by my rapid-fire suggestions, Louie tried to tie his fingers into knots. "Just some guy," he said again, this time with less certainty.

Lyda had been right: Louie was no brighter than a guttering candle. But I was already here, so I kept pitching. "Does this guy have a name?" I asked.

"Probably. Everybody has a name, huh?"

"You got me," I admitted.

"You wanta see the end of 'Feathers'?" Louie asked after a quiet moment during which no good ideas came to me. He stood up and stepped toward the TV.

"No, thanks. I won't be in your way much longer. Do you know Eddie 'The Ender' Tips?"

"Sure. Everybody knows Eddie." The thought pleased him.

"If you didn't kill Misty, maybe he did it."

"Neither one of us killed nobody," Louie stated.

"How can you be so sure?"

"Because keres don't kill people. It ain't our job. You know what a keres is?"

"Sure. Ms. Scales told me," I remarked. "Ms. Astraea Scales."

"Astraea?" he said as if I'd confused him again. He stared hard at her. "It *is* you, ain't it?" he exclaimed.

"Yes," she said.

"I didn't recognize you at first. I guess nobody expects to see no celebs in their own neighborhood."

"No need to apologize," she said kindly, and waved away his discomfort.

He smiled shyly and looked at the floor.

"I hired Mr. Cronyn to find out how Eulalie Tortuga became a zombie," she explained.

"You know," Louie said, "just like I know. To make a zombie you have to remove the soul of a person who ain't scheduled to die and somehow keep it removed. It ain't possible."

"You sound like a man who's tried," she remarked.

Louie said nothing, but looked mournfully at the blank TV screen.

"Eddie found a way," I said.

"Yeah, right."

"He killed Misty Morning to get her Blue Diamond, a dingus that makes what Misty called a knot. You shove a soul into the knot and it doesn't come out."

"Really?"

"It's a theory, anyway."

Louie considered the possibilities. "Eddie might have taken the Blue Diamond thing, but he didn't kill Misty. No keres could. I told you that."

"They can't or they wouldn't?"

"We can't. I told you it ain't our job." Louie sounded pretty certain of this. And though he wasn't very smart, the chances were good that he knew a lot more about his own business than I did. Besides, I didn't think he had the nerve to lie about it in front of Astraea. "Misty ain't a zombie, is she?" he asked.

"No," I said. "She's just dead."

"Then somebody else musta killed her." Louie was thinking hard, now. He used a forefinger to slowly stroke a nonexistent mustache. "Maybe Eddie was assigned to pick up Misty's soul when a human killed her. He might have arrived a little early and seen Misty using the Blue Diamond. After somebody else killed her, he took her soul and the Blue Diamond, too."

Maybe Louie wasn't as stupid as I thought. He'd figured the situation pretty much as I had. "Okay, I like that fine. And I know that Eddie stole Eulalie Tortuga's soul because she rejected him."

"Could be," Louie said. "He didn't like it when she told him to get lost."

"But that still doesn't explain why Eddie is stealing the souls of guys who look like me." It seemed needlessly complicated to explain the spell Lord Slex had put on my face.

"He's doing that?"

"Unless there are two Blue Diamonds."

"You think?"

"No. Yes, Eddie is making zombies out of guys who look like me."

Louie continued stroking the space between his nose and his upper lip. "You never crossed Eddie, did you?" he asked.

"Not that I know of, but apparently he thinks I did, or would. He came after me and demanded I stay out of his way. To that point I didn't even know he existed. Even now I have no idea what he wanted me to do or not do."

Astraea was looking at me with interest. She hadn't heard this part of the story before.

"Do you know what Eddie wanted?" I asked.

Louie shook his head slowly, more confused than ignorant. "Eddie's a funny guy," was all he said.

"Do you know where I can find him?"

"Eddie? Naw. All us keres keep pretty much to ourselves: no meetings, no conventions, no dinners." He shook his head as if it were a sad old world and he knew it. "I hate renegades. When keres go bad, they stink on ice. They spoil things for everybody."

"You're right about that," Astraea said.

I tapped Astraea on the shoulder and she stood up. "Thanks for your help, Louie," I said.

Louie nodded as if he were thinking about something else. "You know about Merlin?" he asked.

"Yes," I said. "Lyda told me."

"You might try talking to him. He and Eddie were pretty tight for a while back in Prohibition days."

It seemed like a good idea except that I didn't know Merlin's real identity, or even if he was still alive. "Do you think Misty found out who Merlin was?" I asked.

"If she knew," Louie said, "she was the only one."

"You don't know who he was?"

"No. Never. Unless he was Brent Martin. That's who Merlin looked like. But I never saw him dance or sing or nothing like that. Sure you guys won't stay to see the end of 'Feathers'? Lotsa good dancing." Louie was almost pleading.

He was obviously a lonely guy and I hated to turn him down, but I had a lot to do. "No, thanks," I said.

"Perhaps some other time," Astraea said.

"Can you guys find your way out?" he asked, his hand already raised, fingers extended, ready to gesture the TV back to life.

"We'll be fine," Astraea said.

I conjured up a will o' the wisp and it led us out of Louie's hovel. We walked back through the fishing village with the wind off the ocean pushing us along.

"So you've seen Eddie twice now," Astraea remarked.

"Yes. The first time in Harold Silverwhite's lab. I don't know why he was there. If keres can't kill people, he wasn't there to kill me. And he didn't have the Blue Diamond yet, or he would have stolen my soul."

She nodded but remained calm. "Perhaps he was just trying to frighten you into cooperating."

"Perhaps. If that was his intention he did a piss poor job of it. Even if I wanted to cooperate I couldn't because I didn't know what he wanted me to do." I stopped and snapped my fingers. "I bet he didn't know either or he would have told me." I smiled, liking this new notion. "Any idea what a keres would want from a mortal such as myself?"

For just a moment she looked as confused as Louie. Being a goddess, she might have reasons for not telling that I had no way of guessing. "No," she said at last. "What will you do now?"

We walked through the tunnel and back out into the open. The chain link fence was before us, and beyond that my little Puck. "I'll drive you home and then go home myself. When I get there, I'll—well, I'll do what needs to be done. I can't put it off any longer. I just hope I live through it."

"You'll live."

"Is that official?"

"No. Just a wish."

CHAPTER THIRTY
A VERY SPECIAL INDIVIDUAL

We got our beautiful drive at last. If I'd had a rag top, I would have lowered it then. In many ways that late-night drive along Highway 1 was a classic Los Angeles experience involving a beautiful blonde, her hair blowing in the wind, sitting next to her handsome boyfriend, both looking out at the calm ocean, moonlight glinting off the scalloped edges of the waves. It was a perfect fantasy come true except that the beautiful blonde was a goddess with a predilection for virginity, and her handsome boyfriend was a cheap shamus. Not to mention that I couldn't lower the top on my car without a machine shop. Besides, I had a lot on my mind. Try as I would, I couldn't quite manage to feel wild and unfettered.

I took Astraea back to Enough Rope. We sat in the car for a moment before she went in. "I think I'll visit Lord Slex tomorrow," I said. "Maybe invite Vic Tortuga and Lyda Firebough, and the other lords, too. Want to come?"

"You know who killed Misty Morning?" Astraea asked.

"Let's say I have a suspicion."

"And why Eddie 'The Ender' Tips bothered to make those three other men into zombies? And why the attempt on your father?"

"Not to mention why Eddie threatened me. I have no idea," I admitted. "But I think we'll find all that out tomorrow, too.

"Very well," she said as she cracked the door on her side. "I will drive over to your apartment in the morning." And then she was gone, like a deer leaping from a patch of moonlight. No kiss again, but I was getting used to it now.

It was late when I got back to my apartment complex, the kind of lateness that doesn't come in clocks. I was still muddled by thoughts of Astraea and Misty's murder and so on, so I had to go back to my car to get Misty's log book out of my trunk. I carried it against my chest as I took the elevator to my floor and let myself into my apartment.

Later, wearing nothing but a terrycloth robe of uncertain age, design, and color, and formerly white cotton socks, I sat down at my desk with Misty's log. If Harold Silverwhite couldn't make anything of it, I don't know why I thought I could. Still, I felt obligated to try.

I admit that it was past my bedtime, but that fact alone shouldn't have accounted for the impenetrability of Misty's notes. I should have recognized words, symbols—something. But the twisted ink scribbles continued to make no more sense than snippets of barbed wire.

I stared at the stubborn pages for almost half an hour, flipping through them now and then, hoping to see some kind of pattern that Silverwhite may have missed. I was reminded unpleasantly of the homework I used to attempt for my Stilthins Mort classes. Then an idea came to me that made me smile. Fanning myself with the log book, I marched to the bathroom, and held the pages up to the mirror. I assumed that like Leonardo da Vinci, that other famous southpaw, Misty had written the log in mirror-writing. But no, even in reflection the writing remained chicken scratches. I closed the toilet cover and sat down with the log book in one hand.

I thought about Misty, the sort of person she was, her interests and enthusiasms, and decided that I hadn't known her long enough for those thoughts to mean anything. Even so, we'd talked in my car on the way to her apartment, and I'd snooped around some after discovering her body, and I had heard the opinions of the people closest to her. I had an opinion myself, and I was stuck with it even if it was wrong. I kept going back to the one clunker—that triple mirror in her laboratory.

If she wasn't using it to pluck her eyebrows or to put on her make-up—and I didn't for a moment believe that's what she was doing with it—what was the three-way mirror for? Such a setup allowed one to view one's face from the side, and to a limited extent from the back. Looking at one mirror in another, one saw progressively darker reflections going around a curve to infinity.

I rummaged around in the bathroom cabinet beneath the sink for a shaving kit I'd been given as a gift and never used. In it was a three-way mirror—a much smaller version of the one on Misty's desk. I took the mirror and the log back to my desk. I stood the mirror up on its three reflecting sides, held the log up to one reflecting surface, and let it reflect onto another.

"Hah!" I cried and grinned. Of course, under normal circumstances if you reflected something twice you ended up where you began. But Misty had obviously enchanted the writing so that in the second reflection the squiggles snapped into focus, as if someone who had been speaking a foreign language suddenly fell into English.

No wonder Silverwhite hadn't been able to decode the book. He was used to dealing with magic—pure and simple or pure and complicated, it was always pure. Dr. Hamish at PrestoCorp would certainly be hobbled by the same kind of thinking. The idea of enchanting writing in such a way that you needed only a set of mirrors to decode it would be something only a very special individual would think of—that would be Misty Morning. The only reason I'd been able to figure out the puzzle at last was because I'd had two clues: One was Misty's mention of Leonardo da Vinci, and the other was the triple mirror that didn't belong. Plus the fact that I couldn't depend on my knowledge of magic, so I had to try something else.

Though I now had the secret to reading Misty's log book, it was still slow going. I'd forgotten a lot in the stretch I'd been out of school, and this was not easy stuff to begin with. I dragged out some of my old textbooks and they helped. After banging my brain against Misty's notes for an hour or two, I was pretty sure that the knots were the one-way doorways I had been assuming they were. Misty herself didn't know whether she was working on a system for transportation or waste disposal, but she seemed pretty clear on the knots' one-way nature.

I learned some other stuff, too, all of it pretty minor compared to the business about the knots. By that time my mind was chasing its own tail. I locked the three-part mirror in my desk along with the log and left the rest of my books in stacks on top—sort of a decorating statement.

I went to bed thinking about what I had to do the next day. Call Harold for one thing. He had the right to know the solution to the problem I'd given him. That would be the easy job.

After much tossing, turning, and tangling of sheets, I eventually slept.

CHAPTER THIRTY-ONE
CURIOSITY

The telephone awakened me the next morning. At the other end was Harold Silverwhite. He'd beaten me to it. "Rise and shine, old chum," he said jovially.

I hate jovial in the morning. "*You* rise," I suggested nastily. "*You* shine."

"I'm sorry I've learned nothing that will improve your mood," he said. "My sources can find no connection between Misty Morning and Merv Lupinsky."

"I didn't really think there would be," I said in a more reasonable tone, "but I had to try. Thanks for your help."

"Delighted to do it, old chum. I'm only sorry that I wasn't able to help you with Ms. Morning's log book."

I said nothing while I decided which was kinder—to let him believe the problem remained unsolved, or to tell him the truth.

"I know you're out there, old chum," Silverwhite said. "I can hear you breathing."

Silverwhite was a big boy. He could take it. When I told him the truth he listened without interrupting. "My, my," he said when I was done. "I'll have to remember that."

"Another learning experience," I agreed. "Let's have lunch sometime."

"Isn't the phrase 'do lunch'?"

"Only in deepest darkest Hollywood."

"At any of several rates, we'll eat together," Silverwhite said. "Cheerio, old chum. Thanks for the lesson in ingenuity."

"Thank Misty."

After hanging up, I sat on the edge of my bed for another few minutes scratching my head and gathering my forces, then went to get the paper.

Both Trask and Philpot were on the front page just as Astraea had promised—head shots, not news photos. While doing research on Misty, the police found documents that indicated Lord Trask was in reality Ian Tahern, notorious con person. Someone had also tipped Morris Devore, the president of Stilthins Mort, that Lord Philpot and one of his students were having an illicit affair. Trask was in custody and Philpot had been suspended pending an investigation.

"Well, what do you know?" I said out loud. Apparently Astraea had been busy. And she had arranged things so that the police were involved, though nobody had called them, not exactly. I was impressed. I wouldn't be inviting Trask and Philpot to my tawdry little event that day after all.

Someone knocked on my door and I was suddenly aware that I was still sitting around in my "Grumpy" night shirt. "Just a minute," I cried while I threw on my bathrobe and quick-marched to the door.

"I am early," Astraea said when she saw me.

"No," I said, "I am late. Come on in."

This morning Astraea was dressed in a pink tailored suit and matching shoes. The outfit should have clashed with every-thing else in the world, but it didn't. I showed her the paper. She seemed pleased, but only enough to raise the ends of her mouth a little. Her teeth didn't even show.

"If I asked you how you did that would you just tell me that you're Justice?"

"Yes," she said, smiling a little wider now. "These two are merely irritants, not public enemies. Justice is measured. It comes differently to each."

Astraea waited in the living room while I cleaned up and then put on a nice gray suit that wouldn't have a problem standing next to the pink dream Astraea was wearing.

I left my bedroom and found Astraea standing at the window, one leg cocked to emphasize a hip, looking out at the city. It was a sexy pose, but she didn't seem to be aware of it—which may have been why it was sexy. As far as she was concerned, she was just looking out the window. I let her continue while I went to the kitchen and sat down at the table I used for an office where I searched through my files for Lord Slex's home address. When I had it, I called Vic Tortuga.

He answered the phone with his usual challenge. "What?" he demanded.

"It's Turner Cronyn, Mr. Tortuga. I'm about to wind up the case. If you want to be in on it, be at Lord Zorn Slex's house as soon as you can. It's south of Rancho Park just off Motor Avenue." I gave him the address.

"Who done it, shamus?" Tortuga asked.

"Be there or be square," I said, and hung up on his blustering.

I dialed again. "King?" I asked when the man at the other end answered.

"Who wants to know?"

"It's Turner Cronyn, King. How's the heartburn?"

"Oh, I never get sick from them Fink's dogs. Cast-iron stomach. You ever make head or tail of Misty's lab log?"

"Hah!" was all I replied. "But I'm about to throw a party at which the guest of honor will be Misty's murderer. Want to come?"

He chuckled as if I'd told a dirty joke. "Not if that's the only attraction," he said. "Who killed her ain't my business. I don't care and Dr. Hamish don't care neither."

"All right, then. Good luck to you."

"Wait a minute, Cronyn. Who done it?"

I chuckled back at him as I hung up. I waited a moment, half-expecting him to call me back. If he did, I would give him all consideration I would give a telemarketer. Sometimes it's fun to talk to a person when it doesn't matter what you say.

Lastly I called Lord Slex to warn him that he was about to have company. "Why here?" he asked. "Why now?"

"It's the end of the road for somebody," I explained. "I know who's been making zombies all over town, and I'm within inches of knowing who killed Misty Morning."

"Oh, really?" he remarked, disbelieving. "Who would that be?"

"The culprit should be clear soon enough," I said. "You and the others will be the first to know."

Lord Slex said nothing for a moment, but I imagined I could hear the rumble and bump of his thinking. "You're not the police. They don't have to accept your invitation."

"Of course not. But I think they'll be curious, don't you?"

"This is a private residence. I don't have to let anybody in— not even you."

"Aren't *you* curious, sir?"

Lord Slex was silent for another moment. "You take a lot on yourself," he said irritably.

"Not so much, really. As you may recall, I felt pretty bad about Misty's death."

Lord Slex grunted and hung up.

Astraea spoke to me without turning around. "Will he let us in?" she asked.

I tried to remember whether she could have known enough from my half of the conversation to ask that question. I couldn't do it. Maybe it didn't even matter. Being a goddess and all, listening to the far end of a phone conversation had to be peanuts for her. "I think he will," I said at last. "He's as curious as anybody else, if only to see if I screwed up the way I used to in school."

When I'd lifted my one and only physical clue from the pencil drawer in my desk and shoved it down into one of my vest pockets, I was ready to go.

We left Astraea's sedan chair, and I drove us down Fairfax, past the delicatessens, Ethiopian restaurants, and antiques stores, to Pico. At Fox Studios I turned left onto Motor, driving through Rancho Park, then deeply into the upper-class labyrinth that was Cheviot Hills. I had been to Lord Slex's house back when I was a student at Stilthins Mort, so I got lost only twice looking for it now.

Lord Slex lived on a street lined with camphor trees, each with its own enormous cloud of green leaves. From a low brick wall the lawn swept up a hill to a long surprisingly modern house done in the classic Spanish style, with white stucco walls, red pantiles on the roof, and lot of black ironwork. Vic Tortuga's car was parked on one side of a large area paved in the same type of bricks as the wall out in front. Astraea and I walked across the parking area and used a brass lion's head to knock on a door only slightly smaller than a ping-pong table.

Lord Slex opened the door and then blocked our way. He was dressed informally in gray slacks and a very pale blue sport shirt with a fanned deck of cards on the pocket. He wore brown loafers but no socks. His eyes, hung with puffy bags, glared out from the morose and tired face of a man who hadn't gotten much sleep lately.

Beyond him, Vic Tortuga and Lyda Firebough stood in the center of the entryway looking like strangers waiting for a train. Vic wore a vest covered in a print inspired by peacock feathers over a brick-colored shirt with the sleeves rolled to the elbows. Judging by their appearance, the heavy work boots he wore had not been involved in any activity more strenuous than walking across a room. Lyda wore a black sweater that matched her tights and buckled shoes. Her skirt was plaid and held together by a large decorative safety pin.

Tortuga lit up like a hundred-watt bulb when he saw us—or saw Astraea, anyway—and immediately pushed past Lord Slex to open the door wide. "Come in, come in," he invited as if it were his house and his party. Lyda gave me a soft but suggestive kiss on the cheek, which I suspected was more for Tortuga's benefit than mine.

Tortuga's face shriveled into a sour expression. He noticed Lyda watching him and blew her a big theatrical kiss, which she ignored.

The house was bright and modern and almost empty of

furniture. Chairs, which ran in hard angular lines, looked as comfortable as milk crates. Obviously, some decorator had sold Lord Slex on a theory. Light came in through sliding doors that would open onto a pool if anybody cared, and through big round skylights that looked as if they'd been punched in the roof by falling meteorites.

Tortuga stared at Astraea hungrily before briefly glancing in the general direction of Lord Slex, Lyda, and me. "This better be good," he said.

"I think you'll like it," I said. "Besides, you might as well stick around. The lecture is free."

Tortuga was about to say something even more clever when I took a packet of Spell-Be-Gone from my pocket and held it out to Lord Slex. "I'd like you to remove the spell you put on my face a few days ago."

"Come on, Cronyn," Tortuga said. "I can't believe you invited us here to watch Lord Slex remove a simple commercial spell."

"As a matter of fact, I did," I said. "But," I continued and held up a hand to stop him from making the obvious complaint, "I think you'll be more than entertained by what happens when he's done."

"And what would that be?" Tortuga asked.

I said nothing but held out the packet to Lord Slex again and shook it. He frowned, but took it from me with a single angry swipe of his hand, turned, and walked along a short hallway carpeted in white chenille to a white door, which he opened. We followed him into the room beyond, which was a large laboratory that reminded me of the one on the second floor of Misty Morning's apartment but was much neater. Bright afternoon sunlight came in through four enormous windows, each one made up of a dozen or so smaller panes. Not much went on in this room—not recently, anyway. It looked like a store display advertising laboratories.

Like a doctor about to do an examination, Lord Slex asked me to sit down on one of the stools lined up along the big stone table in the center of the room. As I sat down, a cold fear covered me like a blanket soaked in alcohol. What I was about to do had to be done, but that didn't mean I was happy about doing it.

CHAPTER THIRTY-TWO
OLD HOME WEEK

Lord Slex read the instructions on the back of the packet, mumbling the words to himself, then tore the packet open. He threw the dust from the packet over me while saying out loud the words he had mumbled earlier. Lyda gasped and Tortuga smiled with secret knowledge. Lord Slex twisted the packet and threw it into a metal wastebasket.

"How do I look?" I asked and smiled engagingly at the crowd. I knew how I looked: eyes a little smaller, a little less chin. For better or worse I was myself again.

"You look cute and wonderful," Tortuga remarked sarcastically. "But what's the point?"

"The point is that I'm expecting one more guest, and changing back to my original appearance is the only invitation he'll accept."

"Who—?" Lord Slex began and was interrupted by the sudden appearance of a man standing in a martial arts crouch in the center of the stone table. He was a strong-looking but compactly built man with dark ragged hair. He wore a red satin jacket that I'm pretty sure had the words HOUNDS OF HELL on the back. It was the same guy who'd attacked me at Silverwhite's house, the same guy who'd harassed Dad and knocked me cold at the airport.

With hot black eyes he glared at me out of his square ugly face. "Yeah. You look like the guy. Maybe you're the guy." He made fists and tightened his arms as if he were about to perform something acrobatic, but before he let loose I surprised him by introducing him.

"Ladies and gentlemen," I announced in a voice so calm I impressed myself, "I'd like you to meet and greet Eddie 'The Ender' Tips."

Still tight as a muscle with a charley-horse, Eddie looked around at the crowd. He didn't like all the people staring at him. His eyes went up and back between Astraea and Lyda.

"Hello, Eddie," Lyda said. Astraea merely watched him with disapproval. She could not be anything but beautiful, but her expression was grim, dangerous, and sharply pointed. I hadn't known her face could do that.

"Hi, Lyda," Eddie said. "Long time no see. Uh, you know all these people?"

"Small world, huh, Eddie?" Lyda said.

Eddie licked his lips. "I'll deal with you later," he said to me and threw his hands into the air as he had at the airport. But he didn't disappear this time, which seemed to surprise him. Then his eyebrows dropped, and he got a tricky expression on his face. "Let me go, Astraea," he said, "or there'll be trouble."

Astraea chuckled at that, as if Eddie had told a funny joke, but one she'd heard before. "I am Justice, Eddie. I will not let you get away."

"What am I to you?" Eddie asked as if he really didn't know.

Not quite so worried now about what Eddie might have in mind for me, I explained it to him. "You've been turning guys into zombies all over town," I said, "guys who look like me. You even tried to get my father. You would have gotten me, but you found me before you stole the Blue Diamond from Misty Morning, and you couldn't find me after you had it."

"So what?"

"That's the question, isn't it?" I suggested politely.

"Tell him, Eddie," Astraea said. "Or should I tell him? I have guessed most of it."

"Have a good time," Eddie said and folded his arms.

"Very well," she said and took up a classical pose, one hand raised as if holding a balance scale. "The Fates assigned you to pick up Misty Morning's soul after she was killed. You went to the scene of the crime, but you were a little early. Just early enough to see Ms. Morning try out her Blue Diamond. In the Blue Diamond you saw an opportunity to increase the chaos of the universe. The Fates knew what you had in mind, and they gave you just enough rope to hang yourself. Some time before your assignment to pick up Misty Morning's soul they had warned you that your attempt to create more chaos in the universe would be thwarted by a man who looked like Turner Cronyn."

"Who?"

"Him," Astraea said as she pointed at me.

"But," I said, "you didn't know how I would thwart you, of course. And because you are a keres and couldn't hurt me, the only thing you were able to do was bluster around making empty threats and hoping I would just go away. By the time you stole the Blue Diamond I didn't look like my usual handsome self, so you never found me—just a squad of guys who looked like me."

Eddie shook his head as he chuckled gloomily. "That's how the Fates are," he said. "They never tell you everything you need to know. They tell you what a guy looks like but not that he don't look like that no more."

"Bummer," I said.

Eddie agreed. "And you're right when you said I couldn't hurt you because I am a keres. Keres don't kill, which you obviously know because you hang around with Astraea so much. The whole Misty Morning incident was legal from my point of view—a human killed by a human, and therefore part of the regular order of the universe."

I nodded. "I'm convinced," I said. "But if you didn't kill Misty, who did?"

Eddie seemed to think, but I could tell he was enjoying the dramatic silence. He stretched it until it began to vibrate. "Him," he said at last pointing at Lord Slex. "Mr. Lover Boy."

Eyebrows went up all over the room.

Lord Slex made a short bitter laugh. "You can't possibly believe him," he said to nobody in particular.

"Under ordinary circumstances," I said, "I wouldn't. But it just so happens that other evidence points to you too."

Lord Slex went slack and pale. "Oh, please," he said, trying his best to pretend he thought I was bluffing.

"I'm being foolish, I know, but I'll tell you what I have just for the fun of it."

Lord Slex sank to one of the stools, looked over his shoulder at Eddie—who was showing a lot of teeth in his satisfied smile—and then back at me. "Go on," Lord Slex said as if I were about to give a report in his class.

"First, the killer had one of Misty's house keys, so he or she must have been somebody Misty knew. But that still gives us, say, a few dozen suspects."

"I didn't—" Vic Tortuga began. But when everybody turned to stare at him, he waved one hand to throw away whatever he had been about to say.

"Second," I went on, "a kid named Herb Hillyer had been following Misty because he had a crush on her. He saw the killer leaving in a Brent Martin disguise spell. Merlin, a magician who worked during Prohibition, always wore just such a disguise when he met with his people. As it happens, the car in the photo on your desk in your private office at Stilthins Mort was manufactured during Prohibition, too. A wizard, who was probably out of work during Prohibition, certainly could not afford such a car. But he wouldn't have had any trouble if he were bootlegging. I think the owner of that car was you, Lord Slex."

"Old home week," Eddie remarked, almost to himself.

"Nice seeing you again, Merlin," Lyda said angrily. "Looks like you'll get what's coming to you at last." She smiled at me. "May I help?"

"If you're good," I said. "But I suspect you'll have to wait in line."

Gathering his forces, Lord Slex drew himself up. He didn't even look in Lyda's direction. "I never wore a Brent Martin spell," he said. "And even if I did, that doesn't mean I—or even this person, this Merlin—killed Misty."

"Maybe not," I admitted. "But there's more."

"Perhaps what you still have is better than what you've give us so far," Lord Slex said.

"Much better." I let him have it right between the eyes. "I don't think you killed Misty because she found out that you were Merlin. I found no evidence to support that idea. I think you killed her because you were jealous. Herb Hillyer said that you were never the wizard Misty was. That was it, wasn't it?"

As I spoke, Lord Slex's face became hard. He moved his jaw up and back and licked his upper lip with his pointy pink tongue. He caught himself doing these things and stopped, but his face remained hard. "I see that you are still the idiot you were in school," he said.

"That's exactly why you hired me," I said.

"Oh, really? I admit that I am fascinated."

"You hired me to give yourself an alibi. If you were ever suspected of Misty's murder, you would be protected to some extent by the fact that you had hired a private detective to find the murderer. And then you went and hired *me*, hoping I'd be just as incompetent a detective as I was a magician."

"Apparently I was correct."

I smiled. "That's what you say now, but you were enough afraid I might surprise you that you hired Louie 'The Mouth' Stuckler to distract me."

"You found Louie?" Lyda asked, delighted.

"I did," I said. "He sends his regards."

"I could have saved myself a lot of trouble," Lord Slex said as if Lyda had not spoken, "if I'd killed Misty before I suggested the board hire you to protect her."

"True enough. But you're not a natural-born killer. You had to work up the nerve to whack her, no matter how jealous you were. Accidentally running into Louie gave you an idea how you might do it. You saw the moment before I went on duty as your last chance to make the whole plan work."

"Everything you say is mere theory," Lord Slex said, dismissing it all with a wave of his hand.

"All theory," I admitted, "but I have some physical evidence, too." From the pocket in my vest I took an empty magic packet twisted in the middle to give it a feminine waist. "I found this one," I said as I held it up, "in the wastebasket in Misty's lab. It contained the same kind of rat poison spell that killed Misty, maybe the very spell itself." I strode to the metal can at the end of the stone table and with two fingers pulled out the empty magic packet Lord Slex had used to change me back to my original appearance. I held the two packets out on the palm of my hand. "You see," I said. "Both have been twisted in the same way."

"I am Lord Zorn Slex, a board member of Stilthins Mort College. Even if I wanted to kill Misty, I would not need a commercial spell."

"When you walked into Spell-Mart you were looking for a commercial spell to help with an intimate itching problem. I wondered even then why you didn't just mix up something on your own. The day I met Misty for the first time I saw Eulalie Tortuga leaving your office. Like Herb Hillyer, she also was of the opinion that you were no longer the magician you had been. That was two votes against you, maybe three. Herb and Eulalie and I could have been wrong, but you can see how taken all together these little incidents would also make a person suspicious."

"Certainly I can see how they would have made someone like *you* suspicious," Lord Slex said, making the admission an insult. "Do you have any more of your hard evidence?" he asked and folded his arms. "I don't find that twisted paper very convincing, and I don't think the police will, either." He was one cool dude.

"I do," I said. "Eddie, did you see Lord Slex take Misty's log book?"

Eddie shrugged. "Sure," he said agreeably.

"Eddie," Astraea said. It was a warning.

Eddie glanced at her nervously. "If you mean that flat book Misty wrote things in, then yeah, I saw him take it. It was just laying around. After Misty was dead she didn't care."

"So you say," Lord Slex said. "Maybe he has it." Lord Slex nodded at Eddie.

"Sure," I said, "he might have it. The police didn't find it, which means that somebody had to take it. But the time between the moment I last saw Misty Morning alive, and the moment I found her body was very short. If Eddie doesn't have it, the only other person who could have taken it is the murderer."

Lord Slex begot a smile, but it was a poor weak thing.

"Actually," I said, calm as pudding, "*I* have it."

Lord Slex's smile went away like smoke on a windy day. Everybody else looked from him to me as if we were playing tennis.

"It has a black and white marbled cover," I said, "and a coffee stain spreading from the spine. It looks as if it's seen a lot of hard use, but I'm just guessing about that."

Lord Slex's face collapsed into a horrified expression. He ran to a wooden drawer in the side of the lab table and used a small key to open it. He anxiously pushed things around inside until he fished out a book very much like the one I'd described. He shook it in the air triumphantly.

In the time it took to blink once he became aware of the corner he'd painted himself into. Suddenly he pulled a packet from a pants pocket. In one swift motion he tore it open and flung the powder it contained at me. Before the dust settled, he was running for the door with the book in his hand. I attempted to run after him but discovered that I couldn't move.

CHAPTER THIRTY-THREE
JUSTICE HAPPENS

Vic Tortuga took a fast step toward Lord Slex, but Lyda Firebough put an arm across his chest to stop him, and though he glared at her he stayed stopped.

Meanwhile, Astraea pointed at Lord Slex. She didn't hurl a thunderbolt, but she did prevent him from opening the door—or maybe it was just stuck. He glanced around with the eyes of a trapped animal, looking for another exit. Lyda motioned at me with both hands and suddenly I was free. I approached Lord Slex, and he shrank back toward the door. Using a little kid's binding spell I tied him up. He clutched the log book against his chest, and squirmed like a caterpillar hanging by a silk thread, making incoherent but angry grunting and growling sounds while I gently lowered him to the floor with his back against the wall. I pulled the book from his hands and handed it to Astraea. He continued to struggle against the simple spell while he jabbered on about showing respect for age and experience.

"You're your own worst witness, Lord Slex," I said, interrupting him. "Before this I thought maybe all of us were just prejudiced against you, but, well, if you can't get out of that little bitty spell with nothing but your pinky finger it's obvious even to somebody like me that you're not the wizard you once were."

Lord Slex howled, and seemingly by force of will alone he broke through the binding spell. His eyes were wild and mad as he clumsily got to his feet and then rushed me with his gripping hands ready to tear flesh away from bone.

When Lord Slex passed one of the big multi-paned windows, it suddenly exploded inward as if a giant fist had punched it from the outside. The crash seemed to go on and on. We all ducked as glass and wood flew across the room to make a tattoo of loud thumps when the sharp pieces struck the opposite wall. Some of them impaled the wall like knives in a circus act. As suddenly as the crash began there was silence. The tinkle of a piece of glass settling only made the silence seem more absolute.

Years later, debris slid off me as I uncurled and looked around. The others were doing the same.

The only person not moving was Lord Slex. I walked carefully through the splinters of glass and wood until I got to him, then felt for the artery in his neck.

"I'm no doctor," I said, "but I'd say this man is dead."

I looked up at Astraea. "Freak accident?" I asked.

She was standing very still and her face showed no emotion. "I am Justice," she said.

She had told me that before, but its meaning had never struck me so hard as it did then. I didn't think she would hurt somebody who wasn't guilty, but then each of us was guilty of something, if only of stealing a candy bar when we were five or of reading under the covers by flashlight. She was a goddess, all right, but I didn't want to sleep with her—not at that moment, anyway. A woman who could kill a man with a window was worth fearing.

A spot of light appeared next to Lord Slex's body, and it quickly unfolded into Louie "The Mouth" Stuckler. He glanced around. "Wow," he remarked. "What happened here?"

When nobody seemed ready to tell him, Louie shrugged and went on. "They told me to pick up Lord Zorn Slex," he said. "Is that him?" He studied the body with a professional eye.

"That's him," I said, feeling as if somebody else was talking with my mouth.

"Hey, that's the same guy who hired me to follow Misty Morning," Louie said with surprise.

"What do you know?" I remarked, enjoying the fact that

things were going my way. "You told me he seemed to know you, yet you didn't know him," I said to Louie. "I think it's because the last time you spoke to him before that he was Merlin, and all dressed up in a Brent Martin spell. What do you think?"

"Could be," Louie allowed. "I've always liked Brent Martin," he went on, brightening up. "He's one of the few guys who can both sing *and* dance." He blinked at the crowd. "Hey, Lyda. How are they hanging?"

"I have nothing that hangs," she told him forcefully, but with good humor.

"Hah!" Vic Tortuga remarked. Lyda punched him hard in the shoulder, causing him to shy and then laugh.

"Whatever," Louie said. "Hey, Eddie. Long time no see."

"Yeah," Eddie said. "How have you been, Louie?" His desire to know was not strong.

"Okay, I guess. I'm here to pick up the guy on the floor. What about you?"

"I came for him," Eddie said, pointing at me.

Louie was confused. "But he ain't dead," he said.

"Bummer, huh?" Eddie said.

"Whatever you say, Eddie. I got work to do." Louie knelt and plunged his hand into Lord Slex's body as if it were no more substantial than air. After a moment of feeling around he pulled out something that consisted entirely of a silvery sheen, something that made a spider's web look as gross and rugged as the hairy cordage in the window of Enough Rope. Louie deposited the silvery thing in a small basket that hung from one shoulder. "See you in the funny papers," he said, and raised his hands above his head.

"Wait," Astraea said. "There will be more work for you."

"Yeah," Tortuga said. "Pretty soon we're going to run out of windows."

Nobody thought that was funny. After Louie put his arms down, he and Astraea looked at each other with a gaze you could drive traffic over. I think they were exchanging information, but what did I know? Eventually Louie pulled himself up to sit on the edge of the stone table. He looked up at Eddie and waved. Eddie ignored him.

"This is all very entertaining," Vic said, "but it makes no more sense than one of my early novels. I can see that Lord Slex killed Misty, and maybe even why, but I still don't understand what this has to do with Eddie and his need to create zombies."

"Perhaps I can explain," Astraea said. She set the log book onto Lord Slex's desk and rested the palm of one hand on it.

"I'm all ears, schutzie-putz," Vic said, and smiled at her warmly. Lyda scowled.

Astraea looked at me and I nodded. Astraea began:

"Eddie hated Lord Slex because he was able to date Eulalie Tortuga when he, Eddie, couldn't. As much as he hated Lord Slex, there was no point in Eddie's stealing his soul because he had no way to permanently dispose of it. But then the Fates sent Eddie to take away Misty's soul after Lord Slex killed her, and he learned about the Blue Diamond."

"Blue Diamond?" Vic asked.

I explained. Vic took it all in as if he heard that sort of explanation every day. "So why," he asked, "didn't Eddie make him a zombie after he could take Lord Slex's soul and use the Blue Diamond to make it stick?"

"Eddie was interested in revenge," I said, "but he was also clever. He had no idea what happened to the souls that went through the knot made by the Blue Diamond. Maybe they danced in the sunshine and ate ice cream all day. He wanted to give Lord Slex all the trouble he could. He figured that Lord Slex would be in more pain—first, if he lost Eulalie, and second, if he was prosecuted for Misty's murder."

"That prosecution part seemed to work out," Eddie said, enjoying the memory. "I guess if he was Merlin, he deserved it even more, huh?"

Vic was still trying to understand. "So," he said, "what it amounts to is this—Eddie took Eulalie's soul because she wouldn't date him?"

"Yeah," Eddie said. "The bitch."

Vic growled like an angry dog and pulled himself up onto the stone table, scattering glass and wood bits.

"Vic!" Lyda cried.

Vic paid her no mind, but leaped at Eddie, surprising him so much that Eddie did the first thing that came naturally—he morphed into an enormous black dog dripping flames. The growl he gave as he attacked Vic was something from the back of a prehistoric cave, something that made the little hairs stand up all over my body. Eddie fiercely tore at Vic's chest and with much less tenderness than Louie had shown, yanked free Vic's soul—leaving behind not so much as a scratch. I couldn't have coughed twice in the time it took.

While the soul struggled to get free of Eddie's fangs, Eddie took his human form again and pulled the Blue Diamond from his jacket pocket. He took the soul from his mouth and held it tightly in his fist while he raised the diamond aloft and said a few well-chosen words, causing a knot to open in the air before him. Before he could do anything else, I picked up a hunk of wood from the table and in the same motion flung it at the hand holding the Blue Diamond. The diamond flew out of his hand and shattered against the far wall, leaving a big spot of sparkling blue dust.

The soul struggled free and, like tinsel in a hurricane, flew across the small space to once again bury itself in Vic's body. Lyda went to Vic, gently brushed his face with her hands, and cried over him.

"You bring shame onto the gods and goddesses," Astraea said sadly.

"My job is to bring chaos into the universe, isn't it?" Eddie asked, breathing hard. "We can't all be goody-goody like you."

"Even so," she told him, "there are rules. You have broken them."

"Tell it to Moros," Eddie said.

"Even Moros knows his limits. You would do well to follow his example," Astraea said.

Eddie ran for the door, but as he stepped off the edge of the stone table it flipped into the air and fell onto him with a boom that shook the whole house, crushing him flat.

We were stunned all over again.

Louie recovered first. "I told you," he said, "when a keres goes bad, he stinks on ice." He approached the stone table and with surprising strength pushed it aside. Beneath, there was no blood and no distortion of the body—Eddie looked like a two-dimensional drawing of himself. Louie felt around for Eddie's soul, found it, and put it into his basket. I wondered how Eddie and Lord Slex felt about sharing that tiny space.

"Take Eddie's soul to Mount Olympus above Laurel Canyon," Astraea said. "Zeus and the others will want to deal with him."

"My pleasure," Louie said. He raised his arms over his head, then shrank to a point of light that soon faded.

CHAPTER THIRTY-FOUR
FREAK ACCIDENT

I strolled to Lord Slex's desk chair and settled down in it with Misty's log book on my tummy and my hands laced across the book. I hoped I was not being overly confident. Astraea moved to stand near me, her hands clasped behind her back. Vic sat up, though only with Lyda's help. His face was as empty of personality as a tub of butter. It did not even contain confusion. "You two better go," I said. "We don't want to upset the police."

Lyda nodded, said a quiet "Thanks," and got Vic to his feet. She had no trouble opening the laboratory door and helping Vic through it. A moment later Vic's car growled to life and maneuvered out of the carport. The engine noise faded in the distance.

"Now is it time to call the police?" I asked.

"Now," Astraea agreed.

A moment later I had Fotheringay on the phone. He promised to hurry right over.

I glanced around the room. It was quite a mess, and a little difficult to explain under ordinary circumstances, even given the use of magic. Wood and glass were everywhere. One body, now nearly two-dimensional, was sprawled on the floor next to the top of the stone table, which lay like a surplus playing card; another body lay in front of a window that had blown in as if from a violent explosion. I had a lot of explaining to do, but I would bet that not even the truth would satisfy the police—especially not the truth.

"Can I tell them you're Justice?" I asked.

"You may. They will not believe you."

"You could blast another window for them."

"I am Justice," she said. "I do not perform like a trained animal."

I considered that unhappily. Obviously, I couldn't make her perform, not even if I were the kind of guy who would try, which I wasn't. While I considered my options, I took Misty's log book out to my car and put it into the trunk.

When I got back, I found Astraea sitting in the chair I had vacated with her legs skillfully and artistically crossed. She watched me as I picked my way across the littered floor and stood near her leaning against the lab table. "You could have told me about Eddie," I said.

My accusation surprised her a little. "But I didn't know," she said.

"You're the granddaughter of the Fates," I reminded her. "Don't they tell you things?"

She nodded. "I see how you might misunderstand the role of the Fates," she said. "It is their job to spin, measure, and end the lives of all creatures. But the results of their labors are secret. They don't reveal how the lives of mortals, or even of the gods, are woven together. Zeus himself is kept ignorant."

"So I have a destiny and can't change it?"

"Ah," she said. "The debate between free will and predestination."

"And the answer is?" I asked like a game show host.

"Your life has elements of both."

"And the Fates come into it how?" My head was beginning to hurt.

This time she only smiled at me. But it was a sorry smile, a sad smile. I was a nice kid, but not very bright. She shook her head slowly.

I suppose I could have continued the conversation. It was kind of fun in a masochistic way. But the wail of an approaching siren sliced into the silence of the room. It stopped in front of Lord Slex's house and died. A moment later there was impatient pounding on the big front door. I went and let in the cops.

Fotheringay and Siltz followed me back to the laboratory along with some plainclothesmen carrying equipment. Astraea had the usual effect on the male of the species, and Fotheringay had to remind the lab guys twice why they were there. Siltz smiled at her like the creature he was. She nodded in his direction as if he'd only said hello.

"I can't wait to hear all about it," Fotheringay said. He tapped Siltz on the shoulder. "Take notes," he said.

I told them everything, just as it had happened, leaving out only three things: the presence of Vic and Lyda, the discovery of Misty's lab log, and anything to do with keres, including the fact that Astraea was Justice. Maybe that was four things. I explained that Eddie had been responsible for all the zombies in town, but made it out to be done by magic rather than by special talent. The sparkling blue smudge on the far wall was corroborative detail that lent verisimilitude to an otherwise bald and unconvincing narrative.

"So Eddie had a locator spell?" Fotheringay asked.

"It sure looks that way," I said. It was even the truth as far as it went.

"Sure would be handy if the cops had one," Siltz said.

I didn't like to agree with Siltz, but this time I had no choice.

"So," Siltz said, "you called these people together like Nick Charles to present your case. I feel kind of bad that you didn't think to invite the police."

"If I'd called you in and hadn't been able to close the deal, you'd have said I was wasting your time."

Siltz had a remark to make, of course, but we never heard it because Fotheringay interrupted. "Okay," he said, "I understand that these two dead guys on the floor were real bad men. I got that. What I don't understand is how they got to be dead."

"Freak accident?" I suggested.

Fotheringay nodded and worked his mouth. After studying the floor for a moment, he looked at Astraea. "What do you say, miss?"

"These things happen," she said.

Fotheringay still wasn't happy. "Which is to say," he said, "that neither of you knows—not for speaking purposes, anyway."

"Would you believe us if I said you were right?" I asked.

He looked around the room, at his men sweeping stuff into plastic bags in one corner, at Siltz shaking his head with cynical disapproval, then back at us. Whatever private theories he had he kept to himself. "All right," he said. "Just sit tight."

We sat tight.

A half hour or so later the police had squeezed all the clues they could from this turnip of a room, and Fotheringay suggested we all go downtown to make formal statements. Like any good citizens, Astraea and I agreed immediately.

CHAPTER THIRTY-FIVE
TWO PROPOSITIONS

They recorded our statements into a philosopher's stone so it didn't take long. Fotheringay gave me the impression that he and his department would not be trying very hard to clear up the deaths of Eddie and Lord Slex.

It was barely mid-afternoon when Astraea and I got back to my apartment. Astraea used my bathroom and when she came out, she looked so serious I thought she'd found a hair in my sink. She took one of my hands in both of hers and our eyes locked. Her hands were warm and dry, her purple eyes large and melting and full of intelligence. "We are great friends," she said.

"Yes," I said, wondering what she was getting at.

"You will be doing a lot of work."

"That's good. I—"

"I am Justice and you will bring criminals to me."

Her statement was a surprise. "I hadn't thought of us having a business arrangement."

"You object?"

"No, no. Just trying to get used to the idea."

She smiled, let go my hand, and went away to drive home in the flashy sedan chair she'd parked nearby hours before, leaving me standing in the middle of my living room with nothing to do and nowhere to go.

Then I remembered that I did have a chore to perform. Glad I hadn't yet removed my shoes, I sighed when I took the long ride back down in the elevator, then went to my car for the log book I'd taken from Lord Slex. I came back upstairs, and this time I did remove my shoes. I allowed myself a few moments of pleasure wiggling my toes against the carpet before I opened my desk drawer and took out the log book Nosmo King had given me.

I held one book in each hand, knowing they were filled with knowledge that might not be discovered again for years, if ever. But I'd already spent a long time considering what I was about to do, so I took them into the kitchen, made a little roof with them in the sink and set them on fire. It took three or four matches to get them going, but eventually I had a merry little blaze suitable for toasting marshmallows. I set up a small fan to blow the smoke away from the smoke detector and out the window.

Both books burned to ash in about ten minutes, leaving black scum that I had to scrub out with kitchen cleanser. The smell of chlorine mixed with the smell of burning paper. A good clean smell.

After that I took a lot of time making lunch and cleaning up the apartment, taking comfort in the quiet normalcy of the routine. Meanwhile, I thought about Astraea's statement. It seemed less like a proposal than a prediction or even an order. Any way I looked at it, it seemed agreeable.

* * * * * * *

The next morning when I went out for the paper I found a special delivery letter from Spell-Mart. Inside was the money they owed me and a nice thank-you note from the store manager. Well, well. Everything was coming up roses.

While puttering around in my second-best pair of jeans and my Philip Marlowe t-shirt I called my parents and told them it was all right for them to return to Los Angeles. Almost immediately after I hung up somebody knocked at my door. I didn't think it was the police. The knock had been polite rather than impatient.

Astraea was standing at my door, dressed all in denim. She

looked terrific, as usual. "Have you had breakfast yet?" she asked as she gave me a smile that lit up the room, even against all that morning sunshine.

I had, but I would have been stupid to admit it. "Uh, no," I said. "Let me get some shoes on."

We were about ready to go when somebody else knocked on my door. "Union Station," I grumbled wittily, and opened the door.

"Lyda," I exclaimed. "How did you find me?"

She was dressed in white hiphuggers and a fuzzy pink belly shirt. "I'm sort of a detective, too," she said. "Actually," she went on shyly, "I looked you up on the maJsys under 'Detectives.'" Eyes suddenly alight, she ran past me and hugged Astraea as if they were sisters. Well, that was fine. I didn't really want a hug of my own anyway.

"Breakfast?" I suggested.

I drove my harem down to Singer's deli, where we variously ordered eggs and pancakes and breakfast meat. I actually got a word in while we waited for the food to arrive.

"You took quite a chance yesterday," I said to Lyda, "unfreezing me after Lord Slex enchanted me with that spell."

"No chance at all," she said.

"And you without a license to do magic."

She shrugged at that. "Who's going to report me? Eddie and Lord Slex, the happiness boys?"

Astraea put down her orange juice. "What did you do with your copy of Misty's log book?" she asked before I had a chance to agree with Lyda.

"You really did have a copy?" Lyda asked. "I thought that was just a gag to get Lord Slex to show you his."

"How could I describe it if I didn't have one of my own?" I asked.

"You're right, of course," Lyda said. "But you were lucky Slex showed you his copy instead of accusing you of murdering Misty. You said yourself that only the murderer could have taken the log."

"It was a calculated risk," I said, though it had not been very calculated. "Lord Slex was most interested, one might say he was obsessed, with using Misty's notes to bolster his sagging reputation. He needed to know, and right now, that he still had possession of the log book. He probably assumed that he would be able to decode it eventually. That makes Lord Slex more than a little single-minded, but that's the way I figured it."

"You were lucky," Lyda commented again.

"Maybe," I said, sharing a glance with Astraea.

"So what did you do with the your copy of Misty's log book?" Astraea asked a second time.

"I destroyed it," I said. "And the original, too."

"Huh?" Lyda remarked. Even Astraea seemed surprised. "I didn't peg you for the 'things man was not meant to know' type."

"Thanks," I said. "I'm not. But there are some things that are more trouble than they're worth. I think Misty's knots qualify."

"Anyway," Lyda said, "you said you had a copy. That and the original is gone, but there may be other copies."

"It doesn't matter," I said, thinking of Dr. Hamish. "The log is in code."

"Were you able to decipher it?" Astraea asked.

"Some of it. Just barely. I'm not going to lose sleep over it."

"Me neither," Lyda said and turned to Astraea. "How do you like Cronyn better," she asked in a sly voice, "with or without the spell on him?"

"I can take him either way," Astraea said after studying me for a moment.

"That's a relief," I said.

"The photograph your mother showed me was not as handsome as you are in reality."

"You met his parents?" Lyda asked, charmed and delighted, almost giddy.

And they were off again, this time discussing my parents, of all things. I was pleased Astraea liked me for myself rather than for my good looks.

The food came, interrupting them. Eating cut down on the conversation, but as we nibbled we eventually began to talk again.

Astraea sipped her coffee. "I have been thinking," she said. "You could not have known who killed Misty until you saw Lord Slex twist the packet of Spell-Be Gone. Why did you gather us all together before you knew?"

"Good question," Lyda said and shook a fork at Astraea.

"I knew somebody in that crowd must have done it," I said. "All I needed was Eddie's eye-witness report, which I knew I could get as soon as I looked like myself again. With that and the packet, the answer was obvious."

"Obvious, hmm?" Astraea remarked. "If you knew looking like yourself would attract Eddie, why didn't you change your appearance back earlier?"

I settled my fork in a puddle of syrup. "Until I learned from Louie that Eddie could not possibly have killed Misty, he was my number one suspect. I wanted to collect more evidence before I confronted him." It sounded good, even to me.

"Nothing else?" Lyda asked as she looked at me out of the corner of her eye.

I shrugged and smiled and would have shuffled my feet if I hadn't been sitting down. "Well, confronting Eddie would be dangerous, of course. I guess I wanted to avoid being a zombie for as long as possible."

"I say there are enough zombies in the world, many who never met Eddie." Lyda saluted each of us with a forkful of pancake.

"Speaking of zombies," Astraea said, "Olympus is sending money to the families of the men from whom Eddie stole souls."

"You mean you really are Justice?" Lyda asked, wide-eyed.

"I am," Astraea said.

Lyda looked to me for confirmation. I made a tiny confidential nod, and Lyda studied Astraea again as if the truth were written on the front of her shirt. Lyda took a slow drink of coffee while she considered. Astraea and I gave her all the time she needed.

"And you're from Mars, I suppose," she said to me.

"Cestus Omega III," I said.

"Yeah." She seemed to make a decision, shrugged and licked her lips. "All right, then. Can't Olympus put the souls back?" Lyda asked.

"No, Lyda, I am sorry. Perhaps Misty Morning could have figured out how to get something out of a knot, but nobody else can, not even Zeus and the others."

I took a swig of coffee. It was getting cold. "Still speaking of zombies," I said, eager to change the subject, "how is Vic doing?"

Lyda set her hand on my arm and leaned toward me grinning. "This is good," she said. "This is very good. A couple of hours after we got home, he wanted to talk about Misty and the keres and the whole mystery. The good part is that he thinks it's all a story idea. He wants to turn it into a novel called *Dangerous Hardboiled Magicians*."

"Dad'll be happy to hear that," I said. "It'll make a better novel than a newspaper story, anyway."

"I approve," Astraea said as if her approval was necessary.

"How's Eulalie?" I asked.

"A little livelier," Lyda said, "but actually much the same." She laughed. "She and Vic have never gotten on so well."

"How is he getting along with you?" Astraea asked.

"We're great friends," Lyda said. "But he's entirely forgotten that we were lovers. So I guess we've kinda sorta broken up. Do you have any thoughts on who I might date next, Mr. Cronyn?"

For a moment I was stunned by the question. "I'm a detective, schutzie-putz," I said, trying to keep a grin off my face. "We'll find somebody."

Lyda laughed at that and patted me gently on the cheek.

Astraea grinned at both of us. "After all," she said, "there are all kinds of justice."

ABOUT THE AUTHOR

MEL GILDEN is the author of many children's books, some of which received rave reviews in such places as *School Library Journal* and *Booklist*. His multi-part stories for children appeared frequently in the *Los Angeles Times*. His popular novels and short stories for grown-ups have also received good reviews in the *Washington Post* and other publications. (See new publications under his name at the Kindle Store of Amazon.com, and his website at www.melgilden.com.)

Licensed properties include adaptations of feature films, and of TV shows such as *Star Trek, Beverly Hills 90210*, and *NASCAR Racers*. He has also written books based on video games, and has penned original stories based in the *Star Trek* universe. His short stories have appeared in many original and reprint anthologies.

He has written cartoons for TV, has developed new shows, and was assistant story editor for the DIC television production of *The Real Ghostbusters*. He consulted at Disney and Universal, helping develop theme park attractions. Gilden also spent five years as co-host of the science-fiction interview show, *Hour-25*, on KPFK radio in Los Angeles.

Gilden lectures to school and library groups, and has been known to teach fiction writing. He lives in Los Angeles, California, where the debris meets the sea, and still hopes to be an astronaut when he grows up.

www.ingramcontent.com/pod-product-compliance
Lightning Source LLC
Chambersburg PA
CBHW020759250626
47155CB00003B/1144